STEPPING STONE

Karin Kallmaker

Bella
BOOKS
2009

Bella Books, Inc.
P.O. Box 10543
Tallahassee, FL 32302

Printed in the United States of America on acid-free paper
First Edition

Editor: Katherine V. Forrest
Cover Designer: Linda Callaghan

ISBN 10: 1-59493-160-7
ISBN 13: 978-1-59493-160-4

Acknowledgments

Dedicated to Barbara Stanwyck, who made every kind of movie a treat to watch. Strong, professional and hard-working, she has crept into more than one book. Also, thank you Duffy for the haunting rendition of the song that titled this story.

This novel, and every novel, has greatly benefited from the artistry, tenacity and example of Katherine V. Forrest. Sorry, really, about the commas.

For my family, as always, and my readers.

There'd be no twenty-two without all of you.

Buzztastic # #

Looks like Hollywood's most eligible bachelor is having the birthday of a lifetime. We've got pics of girls girls girls enjoying the festivities, and the party has hardly started! They've gone wild for Hyde Butler! What's Selena Ryan doing here, you have to wonder. She plays for the other team. If H.B.'s the church, maybe S.R. is changing her religion?

We'll be posting pics all night and tomorrow a round-up of who was zooming who!

Chapter 1

There are three kinds of Hollywood parties—brawls, benefits and bright lights. As a rule, when an evening had all three, Selena Ryan attended them in that order. After a polite appearance at a brawl, she could be gone before the police were necessary, still stay awake during the speeches lauding everyone's favorite charity of the evening, and arrive at the strut-posture-and-pose after the A-list had sated the paparazzi.

She showed her invitation to the security guard at the foot of the long driveway, then shaded her eyes as she navigated her Prius between parked cars lining both shoulders of the private road. After she'd been sitting indoors all day, the burnt orange sunset made her eyes water. During her cautious negotiation she was passed by blue-vested valets hoofing it up the hill to the turnaround for the next sports car or Mercedes haphazardly abandoned by eager partygoers. Adding to the logjam were a number of limos disgorging A-listers, who immediately went inside, and D-listers, who gawked and lingered in the driveway.

She rolled to a halt behind the queue of cars, and a young man quickly tried to open her door. He tried again, obviously not used to finding the doors locked.

His cursory "Welcome, madam," was spoken through the window as she lowered it.

"I park my own car," she said firmly. When he didn't withdraw his extended hand she added, "Would you point me toward the reserved area?"

She'd exceeded his English, but a familiar stocky figure wielding a clipboard waved him away. "Evening, Ms. Ryan. If you'll wait just a minute, we'll have you into the rear garage access."

"Thank you, Mr. Garcia, sir, I appreciate it. How did that Perkins party end up last week?"

"I thought for sure there'd be paramedics, but the young man's grandmother shut it down at midnight by cutting off the bar."

"That'll do it every time." The car in front of her moved forward, and she turned into the narrow access once the helpful Garcia unhooked the chain and gestured her through. Anyone who went to enough A-list parties got to know the security detail. Garcia-Zimmer Security was at the top of her list when savvy, discreet services were needed. Kim hadn't even needed to call ahead—Selena Ryan's name on the guest list had cued him to allot her space in the rear.

As she got out of her Prius she was aware of the buzz of the night security lighting overhead. The shadows in the rear of the house were long, and by the time she had locked the car and made her way up the stairs to the garden level, moths had fluttered to the glowing glass. Moths had always mildly upset her, and she'd had more than enough English at UCLA to draw the obvious analogy between the moths and the starlets gathered in the bright lights poolside. Beyond them, the long curving line of beach to the south had not yet taken on its night colors, but within an hour there would be nothing but black velvet studded with jewels of light as far as the eye could see. Looking west from the pool level, the Pacific was deepening to indigo.

She opted for the long way around the pool, taking another flight of stairs to the main level of the house. She'd find her host, wish him a happy birthday, express her continued interest in adding his name to the cast of *Barcelona*, then mingle for exactly fifteen minutes before returning to her car.

From the vantage point above the pool she scanned the guests, not immediately sighting Hyde Butler. There was plenty of eye candy, though. More than one tanned and perfectly trim starlet had already decided that Hyde's birthday gift was an unobstructed view of her body. If the swimsuits were off before the sun was down, a brawl it would be, no question about it. Around the naked starlets was a circle of muscle-flexing males. The nudity didn't bother her, but the use of a supine woman's flat stomach to snort lines of coke did.

That this particular event on an abnormally humid Malibu evening was going to devolve into a brawl bothered her even more. Hyde Butler was a rising star noted for rugged good looks that sold magazines and tickets. Two anomalies had caught Selena's attention: Hyde was thirty-eight, a little old to be breaking into the movies; and surprise of surprises, he could act. He had the kind of face and ability that would bring him parts for the next forty years—but he had to survive the first three years in Hollywood. Everyone from old friends to his agent to whoever was producing his next action flick was backing the Hyde Butler horse, and anything Hyde wanted, Hyde would get. Younger heads had succumbed to the many temptations of newly initiated stardom, but she had hoped Hyde was old enough to have seen the tricks and treats for what they were.

She was aware of eyes watching her as her heels clicked across the still-warm Spanish tiles of the expansive covered patio. Some gazes slid past, not allotting any value to the plain black suit—even if it was Dior—or her simple tucked-behind-the-ears bob. Other gazes locked and followed, knowing who she was. She

3

avoided eye contact, taking in the clusters of vivacious men and woman in her peripheral vision and using her ears to separate voices into simple categories of *avoid* and *okay*. She chose the path with least to avoid.

Looking at the partygoers she wasn't so sure Hyde was as wise as she had hoped. She was here to encourage him to join *Barcelona*, but no star was big enough to be worth dealing with their addiction issues—not to her, at least. Other producers might roll with, or even encourage it, but she'd never found it easy, and after Jennifer it would be impossible. She hated to write Hyde off, though. They'd talked three or four times, and she hoped the rapport she'd felt hadn't just been his magnetism.

"Selena! Darling!"

Putting on her best party face, she turned to the voice, offered a cheek to Bertram Glassier—who was too smart and too old to stick around for a brawl—then to his wife, who was young, pretty and wore a rock the size of a golf ball on her third finger. She would want to stay, no doubt. "Bertie, we have to have lunch, seriously. The distribution contract expired and we have to update the terms."

He winked, which was always disarming. "I'll get us a table at Spago's by the end of the week—"

"Cut the crap." Selena smacked him playfully on the arm. "Chili dogs at The Pantry. How about Friday?"

He mimed a heart attack. "You always know how to seduce me, Lena."

The fourth Mrs. Glassier wound her arm around her husband. Selena wanted to tell her she was no threat, at least not in the bedroom sense. Bertie loved smart women, he just didn't marry them. "You need to remember your cholesterol, honey."

He gave her an indulgent smile and Selena another wink. "Friday."

"I'll bring carrots," Selena said over her shoulder. She smiled as she drifted away—two of her allotted fifteen minutes had already crossed something off her To Do list. If she found Hyde her time would be well spent.

Instead of Hyde, however, she was confronted by BeBe LaTour. "Selena, don't tell me you were going to run out without saying hello!"

"Okay," Selena answered. *I won't tell you*, she added to herself. She saw agents as necessary participants in the industry, just as producers were. Agents and producers typically saw each other as evil incarnate. Most agents, to her, were in fact looking out for their clients, but BeBe's track record of looking out for BeBe was the only successful thing about her. Selena was also willing to bet there was more than a mere personal stash of white powder in BeBe's cute little evening bag.

"I know you really want Hyde for your little movie, but the whole world is clamoring for him to blow up their bad guys first."

"There aren't any gunfights in *Barcelona*." She tucked a loose lock of hair behind her ear again.

"Yes, well, that's one of our hesitations about him doing it."

Selena gave it one last try. "He could be the next Henry Fonda, you know. An actor who can do a western, a love story, theater."

"Theater!" BeBe threw back her head and laughed, displaying her smooth-as-silk throat and perfectly sculpted cleavage in the process. "There's no money in theater, darling, you know that!"

"If you make Hyde enough money blowing up bad guys, maybe parts where he's not typecast could make him…I don't know…what's the word?" She paused, not bothering to hide her sarcasm. "Happy?"

BeBe gave her a sparkling what-a-bitch-you-are smile. "You are such a dreamer."

"I try," Selena said, moving away. To herself she muttered, "A dreamer with two Oscar nominations, you parasite."

She managed to make her way upstream from the bar, into the house proper. She kicked balloons out of her way as she crossed the vaulted foyer, picturing each of them as BeBe's head. Hollywood wasn't full of BeBe's, thank goodness, and a few of the cheek kisses and brief conversations along her path weren't difficult at all.

"I think he's in the library, showing off some new gadget," someone told her, and Selena decided a room called the library was likely on the second floor of this type of mansion. The stairs were draped with people holding drinks and crowd-watching. At the landing she navigated around a guitarist with milky skin and torture in his eyes, singing to a bevy of cute young women, most of whom, she guessed, believed he'd written *Blowin' in the Wind* all by his soulful self.

You're getting bitter about your age, sweetheart, she told herself in BeBe's singsong delivery. She'd felt old all day, not a good thing with the big Four-O two months in her future. How would she feel then? She wasn't an actress, but the cult of youth included all women in this town. Her usual avowal of striving to be as elegant as Lauren Bacall and as accomplished as Edith Head was interrupted by the puzzle of a hallway of closed doors.

She didn't relish the idea of opening doors to look for her host—guaranteed she wouldn't want to see whatever was behind some of them, not at this kind of party. Fortunately, a burst of laughter drew her to the second door on the right, and she found the library, complete with a fireplace and bookshelves that even contained books. The contents of the mansion had probably been bought along with the building, however, so the collected novels were no indication of Hyde's personality or proclivities. Neither were the Cubist reproductions that adorned the paneled walls, though they underscored his masculinity.

There were a half-dozen beautiful women in the room, lounging on the sofas and side chairs, but Selena didn't look at any of them. Her gaze went immediately to Hyde and stayed there.

Hyde Butler had a craggy, quintessentially American face, framed by sandy blond hair with a touch of world-weary grey. He was riveting on screen and unmistakable in any crowd. When the camera turned off, he didn't, at least not that Selena had seen. He had been married when he was much younger, while still selling heating and air conditioning systems in West Virginia, and though he was constantly interviewed in the trades, she had no sense of really knowing him as a person. Did he even know how to turn off that stomach-tightening, pulse-raising magnetism? She thought of her own sanctum where she could curse if she stubbed her toe, leave her clothes on the floor and nobody ever knew, cry out a frustration, or, more recently, just cry over her stupid, broken heart.

From his lounging position in the corner of a leather sofa, he turned his head as she approached the cluster of seating and locked gazes with her. The brown eyes with green highlights that had graced dozens of magazine covers in the last two years glinted with pleasure, and that look sent an undeniable tingle through her stomach. "Selena! Sweetie! Just who I wanted to see."

Taken aback, but amused by her own physical response to him, she answered, "Happy birthday, you adorable rascal." Though the open-necked polo shirt and Bermuda shorts were picture perfect American male style, she wasn't interested in anything under his clothes, as visceral as the sex appeal was. What was above his neck was vastly more intriguing.

He rose, saying, "Out with the lot of you, you sorry gits. I want to have it off with Selena."

There was grumbling from the assorted starlets as they exited, giving Selena curious looks. They were no doubt running their database, and coming up with the right last name. The word "lesbian" on the MySpace page in their brains was at odds with Hyde's playful, effusive hug. They wanted to dislike her for monopolizing Hyde, but on the other hand, Selena was an even more likely ticket to a part than he was. The lingering glances were for both of them.

She returned Hyde's hug, and tried to gauge if he was high. The feigned British accent was decent, but not like him, as he was proud of his southern drawl and didn't mask it except when required by a role. After he let go of her he kicked the library door closed and returned to sprawl elegantly on one of the sofas. "Help me, Obi-Wan Kenobi. You're mah only hope."

She chose a deeply cushioned chair opposite him, settling

comfortably, legs crossed. In a skirt and heels she wasn't about to sprawl. "What can I do for you?"

"Work a Jedi mind trick on BeBe. She is dead set against me doing *Barcelona* but I loved the script. Charming bad guy, dead at the end."

"I think her issue is with your compensation. We're not going to make millions in the worldwide DVD market."

He sat up slightly, not the least bit high that she could see. "BeBe has done well for me so far."

"Look, Hyde." Selena chose her words carefully. "BeBe and I are natural enemies in this process, but I'm not going to be an effective sub-agent against her. That's not going to get you what you want, and it won't get me what I want."

"What do you want?" He was back to lolling, but there was nothing casual about the question.

"To make a good picture, and show the world that Hyde Butler is not a pretty face capable of only one kind of role. That makes me look like an insightful genius. I believe—and the director believes—you can play Elgin to perfection. Instead of six months out of your life, I'm asking for six weeks, tops. It films here in L.A. at the Carlisle, and two weeks on location in Spain. This is a little picture, as they say."

His drawl peeked out in his voice, and Selena hoped it meant he was relaxing. "But could be a good one, the kind that gets me the blockbuster parts that are more than dawg-run-point-shoot."

"I want you to have a long career," Selena added, surprising herself.

"What you're really asking is that I trust you over my agent."

"I guess so, yes."

"Why should I?"

"I'm not in it for the money." It was an answer she often gave to the same question during negotiations. Once again, to her surprise, she added, "And I'm not in it for your body, for something to stick up my nose or blowing my own horn in the trades at the expense of yours."

"In other words, you really don't belong in Hollahwood." He sat up again, and turned to look at her directly.

God in heaven, that face, she thought. A dozen other male stars flitted through her head and she couldn't think of one who had those chiseled features combined with eyes that glowed with emotion. Right now it was uncertainty, and a touch of suspicion. He's an actor, she reminded herself, and it's possible none of what's in his eyes is real.

She said, "I've been told that more than once. But Hollywood is where I can find actors idle for a month or two out of their schedules and squeeze my little pictures into their lives." She leaned back on the sofa, loosening her jacket.

"Why don't you take that thing off and have a drink?"

His lifted eyebrow and the flirtatious angle to his denim-clad leg brought a low chuckle from her before saying, "Mr. Butler, are you trying to seduce me?"

"Clever woman." He rolled to his sandaled feet. "I was serious about the drink if you want one."

She slid out of her jacket as she watched him open a cabinet to reveal a small bar. The room was getting stuffy and the rose silk blouse was going to go limp before she made it to the next party. "I'm serious about the movie—just a club soda."

"Twelve step?"

She noticed that he only poured a club soda for himself as well. "No, but it's going to be a long night. What about you?"

"Solidarity. I've got a little brother who got all the vices. I promised him I'd make it every day he did. I like a whiskey as much as he does, it just doesn't affect me the same way."

"If he got the vices, did you get the virtues?"

He gave her the highball glass full of ice and sparkling soda before resuming his former half-supine position on the sofa opposite that allowed him to gracefully balance his own glass on his chest. "Depends on what you consider virtues."

"Justice, prudence, hope, charity, restraint, courage, faith…"

"Then, no, I didn't get all the virtues. There are a few things

I have no restraint whatsoever about. Selena, honey, can we just cut to the chase?"

It was her preference, most of the time. "It *is* going to be a long night, so just tell me what's on your mind."

"I want to trust you. I want to trust that if I take a chance on this little film, you're not going to let me look like a fool who overreached in a character role."

She nodded her understanding. "I've hired the best director I can, Eddie Lynch."

Hyde nodded. "He won an Indie Spirit Award, right? For *Royal Candide*."

Selena nodded. "Eddie and I—no one affiliated with Ryan Productions—has any interest in doing a project that the talent later finds an embarrassment. I make you look bad, I don't get chances with the next Hyde Butler to cross my path. I make sure my stars and crew are proud of our work." She paused to take a cooling sip from the glass and to break the intensity in her voice. "I don't suffer prima donnas, but I promise you access to me, direct access, if you have concerns. For what anyone's word is worth in this town, I give you my word."

"Just like you gave your word to Jennifer Lamont?"

The glass almost slipped out of her hand. She caught herself, knew she couldn't help the angry flush that rose from her shoulders and swept up her neck. She made her jaw unclench by sheer force of will. "Surely you've been in this town long enough to know that gossip has its own life. It rarely represents the truth."

"I have. But the papers agree you locked her out of a picture, and broke the contract. The union protest was mysteriously silenced."

It had cost her a bundle and been worth every penny. Hyde—and the gossip machine—had no idea what else she'd paid. "Do the papers agree that I have never commented on the matter?"

"They do."

"That fact is not changing today. I have no comment to make. If that's a deal breaker, so be it." Relax your posture, she told herself. Take a deep breath. Shake it off or you'll get a headache.

10

"The papers agree that you and Lamont were a couple."

She shrugged and reached for her jacket. "If that's a deal breaker, too, so be it."

"Why should it be? Not like you and I are ever going to end up in the sack and be bitter about it by morning. I've never met her, either."

"Then what's your concern, Hyde? What aspect of my ability to honor a contract I make with you, and honor my word, troubles you?" She took a long draught of the cold soda before folding her jacket over her arm.

"The gossip blogs say that she signed on to a multi-picture agreement with the understanding she had project approval, and your lawyer told her it was play when you said, like it or not. After she balked and dumped you, you had the film editor excise half her performance from the last picture."

Unable to keep the sharp edge from her tone, she said, "You left out bribe all zillion members of the Academy to boycott her at the Oscars."

His shrug was almost lazy but Selena abruptly focused on the muscles along his neck—he was as tense as she was. Bucking his agent to take on a project was one thing, but to take on something that was risky to his public persona, something that could either be brilliant or make him look like a fool and a hack, was another.

He wants to be a Henry Fonda, she realized. If I screw this up for him, I ruin that dream. Her voice softened. "One thing I have learned is that you can't say or do anything when nobody else has any vested interest in the truth. So I choose silence whenever I can." She smiled and rose to her feet. "The older I get the more time I need for make-up, so I don't need reasons to avoid looking at myself in the mirror."

His lopsided smile was a heart-melter. "Do what celebrities do—hire someone for the make-up and you never have to see what you've become."

He followed her to the door and they paused. She didn't need to warn him that a dozen camera phones were likely pointed at it, waiting for them to emerge.

"Well, thank you, Selena. Thank you for talking to me instead of telling me not to worry my pretty little head about such things, of *course* nothing I could do could *possibly* turn out bad, I'm just too *talented* for that."

He had BeBe's nuance down pat. With a steady look, she said, "To that idea I have only one word to say: *Ishtar*. I promise you, Hyde, I will not let you make the worst film of your life in the prime of your career."

He nodded. Drawl back in full force, he said, "I'm pretty sure which dog hunts here, Selena honey."

She could listen to him say her name all day. "You are such a charming southern boy."

He laughed politely, and opened the door. The insta-gossip-uploads would have pics of them sharing a laugh, unmussed, unremarkable except that any picture of Hyde smiling was hot property in the blogosphere.

She walked away, head up and doggedly keeping her lips from showing a bitter twist. She was so invested in tamping down her rage at the mention of Jennifer Lamont, that she was backing her car toward the gate before she fully realized she was actually in it. Calm down, she warned herself. Don't let her win anymore, just let it—

She yelped and slammed on the brakes at a loud thud and cry at the passenger door. She saw a flash of a pale face, masses of golden hair, the torn neckline of a little black dress. The woman began pounding on the window.

"Please, please, I need help. I just want a lift. I need to get out of here. Please, please…"

Selena paused with her hand on the door lock. Her safety instructors had drilled her over and over on this scenario. Deets would slap her silly if she opened the door. She had enough money and her own company insured her plenty, and that made her a kidnapping risk.

She lowered the passenger window just a little. "What's wrong?"

The woman pressed her face to the opening. "Please, just a lift. He…he—I have to get away. I don't want any trouble, but I have to get away. I didn't know he was like that. Please, just help me."

"Who?" Again, her hand hesitated on the button to unlock the door. Then she came to her senses. If she honked three times, short, Garcia would come running. "I'll get help."

"No! Just get me out of here. I don't want anyone to see me like this."

She raised her cell phone. "I'll call the police."

"No! You can't—I, he, he gave me something. I don't want to get tested by the cops."

All plausible reasons, which was why the scenario was a favorite with kidnappers. But who would do something that audacious behind the lines of the security people? A kidnapping would have been better launched in the road just outside the gate. Trusting her judgment, but still prepared to honk the horn for help, she shifted the car into park, checked the mirrors for anyone else lurking, then opened her door and put one foot out so she could stand up and talk to the woman over the hood. "Who are you talking about?"

"Him. Mr. Big Star. Look what he did to my dress! And what he did to me was…I would have said yes. But he didn't want yes."

"Are you taking about Hyde?" She flushed with anger for the second time that night. Her voice cold, she said, "What exactly did Hyde do?"

"He was—I should have known better than to come to a party like this! My mother warned me, but I thought I could protect myself. He caught me off-guard." She pushed back her hair making her face finally fully visible.

"Who are you?" The woman looked familiar now, but not live—Selena had probably seen that face on an audition feed of photographs, scanning through actors sent over for a recent casting call that read, "Female, age twenty to twenty-five, crowd shot, speaks."

13

"Well, I go by Vivienne Weston. Can we just go? I don't want to make trouble for him."

Weston had taken the time to clearly enunciate her name before resuming her quavering, uncertain delivery. The leg supporting Selena's weight trembled as a bolt of pure rage swept through her. Her own voice was shaky as she asked, "When did this happen?"

"Just now. He…I got away and I just need your help for a few minutes. A ride to a bus stop or hotel where I can get a cab."

Slowly, jaw clenched, she said, "But Vivienne, in solidarity, we should confront him. Just tell me what he did."

The penny still hadn't dropped for Weston. Tears standing in her eyes, she assumed an ashamed, grieved, shy look that almost worked. "Do I have to spell it out?"

"As a matter of fact, you do. I want to know exactly what lies you are going to spread about Hyde so I can give him the grounds to sue you for malicious slander."

She had the pleasure of watching Vivienne nearly jump out of her skin when she hit the horn three times. The little bitch didn't care whose reputation she ruined. She was just like Jennifer, just another—

Garcia's voice rang out. "Is there a problem, Ms. Ryan?"

"Yes, there is. Ms. Weston here is alleging sexual assault against Mr. Butler. She claims it just happened, and I know, with my own eyes, that Mr. Butler has been surrounded by guests or in my company for quite some time. What I don't know is if she was just hoping to get into the gossip mill or hoping to make me feel so sorry for her that I gave her a part."

Weston's bravado failed her. "I didn't say he'd raped me."

"No, actually, you didn't, you just said drugs and sex against your will. Playing innocent and I-didn't-really-mean-anything-by-it won't work with me because I'm not a court of law. I don't have to give you a chance to explain your side and consider being merciful." Her inner warning bells were telling her to shut up, but she rushed on. "I get to squash you like the termite you are. You've ruined your party dress for nothing."

14

Weston was clearly astonished that her ploy hadn't worked. She also clearly didn't think it could have any downside. "But— oh come on. I know lots of girls who did the same thing, and they all got jobs out of it, so why are you being difficult? It was just a joke."

"I don't have a sense of humor. People like you have ruined it. By nine a.m. you won't have an agent. If you're still living anywhere in the area by noon, you won't have a SAG card."

"You can't do that, you bitch!"

"Yes, I can." Selena actually had no idea if she had that kind of pull with the actors' union. Probably not, but Weston was a stupid, dangerous little girl. "What you tried to do to Hyde Butler I can, and will, do to you."

Garcia had moved around to Weston's side of the car. Two more members of his detail were standing at the rear of the car, blocking the most likely paths of escape. "You're leaving, and with an escort, miss. If you don't come willingly, I will call the police and you'll leave with them."

"Fuck off!"

Can't anyone in this town buy a vocabulary? Selena abruptly felt weak, so she settled back into the driver's seat. When she put the car into reverse everyone cleared out of her way.

Her usual pleasure at the vista from the heights of the Malibu hills was lost in a flurry of ranted expletives. She vented until she ran dry, then tried to let the distant twinkling lights of the Ferris wheel on the Santa Monica pier wash away some of her anger. Making movies was about fantasy and magic—it was supposed to be *fun*. But it brought out the worst in so many people, their evil, manipulative, selfish worst, and mostly those people didn't care who they hurt. They thought all that mattered was what ended up in front of the public. She wanted to feel sorry for them, because they believed they were only as good as their last box office. The insecurity of most performers was mammoth. Trouble was, they didn't stop at themselves. They thought the world ran on box office numbers and billing rank. Someone like her could tell them there was so much more to it than that, but they wouldn't listen. They'd go right on digging a hole they would never climb out of. Then they would want someone like her to rescue them.

When she'd calmed enough to speak evenly, she left a message for Kim, first to tell her to follow-up on breakfast Friday with Bertram Glassier, then detailing the Weston incident. Kim would put her on the No Work list. Every production company had one for their own reasons. *Blackmailer* was such an ugly word, but that's what their list would say next to that woman's name. There was little point in a euphemism. It was all such a distraction from making movies, trying to sort the Westons out of the process.

Feeling somewhat calmer, she turned east, and hoped unrealistically for decent traffic. Her on-board navigator picked a route for her based on traffic flow feeds. Slowly making headway, she spent the next thirty-five minutes listening to messages from Kim and Alan and answering back to their voicemail. Finally tapping off the Bluetooth speaker, she heaved a sigh of relief as she cleared the 405 and traffic picked up through Beverly Hills. Climbing above the basin once again, she switched off the navigator because she knew the way to the Spelman's home. The quiet in the car was welcome.

She passed inspection at the community gate and again parked, but this time there were no obvious valets, just the unobtrusive presence of security personnel. The lane was thick with trees on both sides and wooded areas separated the houses. Too old to be what passed for mansions these days, that was still the right word to her. Complete with columns and second floor balconies, they were brilliantly white against the wooded hills behind them, stately and calm. Ahead of her, a well-known power couple—both lawyers—had parked and were strolling to the main door like any ordinary couple would on the way to a friend's party.

She let herself relax. Ellen and Alex Spelman were hosting a gathering of compatible people for congenial conversation and wonderful dining. Over dessert they would tell their friends how much they cared about—Selena pulled the large Ziploc out of the box on the passenger floorboard. Kim had written *Spelman* and the date and time in Sharpie. The invite was visible through the plastic. Oh yes, over dessert Ellen and Alex would tell them about the West Africa Girls' Empowerment Movement.

Also in the Ziploc was a jeweler's box where Kim had stowed a glittery necklace and matching bracelet and earrings to dress up Selena's business-day attire. There had been no time to change. She loosened the collar of her blouse so the necklace showed, slipped the bracelet on her wrist, swapped out the earrings and stuffed her cell phone and keys into the last thing in the Ziploc, a suede evening clutch. There would be no photographers here, so she left on her simple day heels. She would have a complete head-to-toe change for the last party, but for this one, at least, she got to be comfortable.

She was glad she had made some effort, because as usual she had forgotten that Ellen Spelman's décor surpassed the skill of most decorators. Her hostess hadn't adopted a Mediterranean motif that smothered visitors with elegant trappings, rather, simple whitewashed and papered walls with family photos, small rugs over sandstone tiles and windows open to the evening breeze made her feel like she was visiting someplace where people lived happily. As a child, her father had driven them past houses like this and promised that someday they'd be that kind of family.

Dinner, served at a long, scrubbed wood table decorated down the middle with coils of grapes still on the vine, was elegant, tasty and simple, with a crepe orange dessert and pinot grigio noble that vastly improved her mood. While she couldn't exactly say she was among friends, these were not people of whom she had reason to be wary. She was the only film industry person there, just as the lawyers were the only ones from their profession. There was no reason to talk business or flex rival muscles. Interesting, congenial conversation that avoided politics and religion, touched on art and theater, the economy, stories of travel, amusing anecdotes...it was soothing, and reminded her that there was a great, big world outside Hollywood, filled with nice people, all of whom had their own stresses, concerns and lives.

Just for the pleasure of the few hours' diversion she would have written the Spelmans a large check, but their story of the struggling missionaries who were learning how to evade the black marketeers and war lords who took anything of value was truly moving. With clandestinely delivered seeds and instructions, girls were being given a chance to grow a small garden, which led to barter and food. How she could not afford to fund a thousand packets of seeds?

As she was leaving, Ellen Spelman gave her a hearty kiss on the cheek. "You've lost weight again, Lena, and it doesn't look good off you."

"If I ate here every night that would change." She squeezed Ellen's hand affectionately. Their mutual work on a fundraiser for the Getty Museum had cemented a friendly, if not close, rapport.

"How is it going—*Madrid*? That's not right, is it?" Ellen's height had always given her a regal air she could use to freeze almost anyone in mid-step, but when she smiled she became anyone's favorite grandmother.

"*Barcelona* is the name of the movie. And it goes well. I hope to have a dynamite cast listing." She briefly mentioned the two other projects under the management of her two associates. "So Todd will be in Hong Kong for some time yet."

"I loved hosting that investor's party for *Royal Candide*. And we all did well from it, too."

"The same could be true for this one—if I think so, you'll be the first to know."

"Splendid." She kissed Selena on the cheek again. "Give us all another reason to go to the Oscars."

With Ellen's cheer lifting her spirits, it wasn't so hard to find the energy for the drive to West Hollywood. The traffic had calmed considerably, though it still snarled in the logical places for a warm Friday night, so she avoided the malls and clusters of sports bars and theaters.

Just outside WeHo she pulled into Betty's Diner. It was truly

18

a neighborhood place where no one expected to meet up with anyone famous, though on occasion it happened. She grabbed the dress bag that Kim had hung in the back seat of the Prius, and headed into the bathroom, which she knew was Spartan, but clean.

The owner, familiar with Selena's quick changes, didn't seem to be working, and Selena caught an odd look from the young woman carrying plates to her customers. No matter. She made a beeline to the restroom, unzipped the bag to find a silky, frilly electric blue cocktail dress, a quiet Donna Karan number no member of the paparazzi would comment on, for good or bad. The jewelry she had already put on matched—Kim had reliable taste in such things—and all that was left were suede pumps to complement the evening clutch. After refresher touches to her make-up and a quick comb through her hair she felt assured she would make no one's best or worst dressed list.

She pulled the waist of the dress tight by pinching several inches at the back. Ellen was right. She would go back on the protein shakes, as Kim had suggested last week. She'd put on a few pounds at the beginning of her two years with Jennifer. Happiness did that, apparently. Those pounds were gone, and she didn't like the expression on her face when she thought about Jennifer. She traced a crease around the corner of her mouth. It didn't look like a laugh line. That one belonged to Jennifer, all right.

On her way out of the diner she paused long enough at the counter to ask the obviously startled waitress for an iced tea to go. Given the way she fumbled snapping the cover on the tea, she hadn't been doing the job for long. Selena idly hoped the regulars would be back the next time she had a hankering for late night waffles. She paid for the tea, left the change and hurried back to the car.

There was no need to deal with valets for this party. She had a parking pass at the nearby Design Center—being a big donor had its benefits. It wasn't a far walk to The Joint, a two-story warehouse-style dance and hangout that had become popular for rock album release parties. As expected, the sidewalk was roped clear in front of the entrance, and both paparazzi and stargazers crowded against the ropes to see if anyone of interest arrived.

An older woman arriving alone, and that late, was never interesting, and Selena smiled to herself as only a few flashes went off. She paused to answer a familiar reporter's open-ended question about how she was feeling about her next project. She gave a standard pat answer and went inside to the overheated cacophony of the party.

The smell inside the club hit her first. The lingering pleasant memory of Ellen Spelman's dining room, redolent with basil and orange, was instantly blotted out. With the poor ventilation, the mix was too many bodies in too little space combined with too much cologne, all seething in a base of alcohol. Sometimes the smell was intoxicating, just right, and sometimes it was nauseating. Tonight it was in the middle, but heading toward nauseating as the air grew increasingly sticky.

She waved off the first cocktail waitress who spotted her without a glass in her hand. It was part stubbornness and part practicality. Drinks dripped, and her dress was silk. Also, a watered down club soda on a night like this was $20, including the tip. She had just written a check for a hundred club sodas and wouldn't miss the money, but it stuck in her craw to pay so much for so little. There was a difference between generosity and stupidity, and she hadn't amassed the money she had by not being careful how it was spent. During her growing-up years, her own producer father's income had been boom and bust, and she remembered the lean times, vividly. She probably never would take money for granted. It was also a handy way to end a conversation, claiming the need to go and find a drink.

The food tables were no temptation. A photo with a drink in one's hand was one thing, but there was hardly a day when an unflattering photo of a celebrity with a fork halfway to her mouth or in mid-chew didn't get posted online with speculations about her weight gain. Camera phones all over the room were pointed at the buffet and she wanted no part of it.

The music was too loud to use voices to guide her through the club, but Levi Hodges was likely in a rear upper floor conversation zone, guarded by his entourage. The narrow stairs were lined with photographers from vetted news sources, all snapping away. Again, a woman of no intrinsic face-value fame, unaccompanied, was of little interest. She made her way around the knot of people at the top of the stairs, cutting through the hopefuls to the front of the informal queue. All were trying to make eye contact and get a few words with any member of the band, though most would be looking to connect with Levi, just as she was.

She gave her name to one of the gatekeepers and waited. There was no reason to bluster or push through. Film and rock didn't crossover that much, and she wasn't sure she'd recognize the name of every mover and shaker in the music industry either. Levi had been given her name by his agent and she was expected.

She watched him cock his head to hear what was whispered, then he glanced at where she was patiently waiting. A moment later, he left his particular group and reached out to shake her hand as she joined him inside the circle of chairs and love seats. Flashes went off. They air kissed cheeks while the strobes kept popping.

"Over here," he signaled. "Sorry I couldn't get away this afternoon to see you. We head for Spain tomorrow for our first gig."

"I understand," she assured him. She joined him on one of the loveseats as it was rapidly vacated by a couple of groupies. "Your agent said you're free to thumbs up or down my idea."

"Yeah, Greg said if I was go, you'd make a decent deal. But I'm not a soundtrack kind of composer." Comfortable in a snug tee promoting the new tour, faded namesake jeans and worn leather boots, he stretched out his long, lanky legs.

"I have a composer for the soundtrack. What I need is an inspiration." She leaned closer as the music changed to something even louder. "*Barcelona* is about a charming con man after his biggest score. While the movie is his story, and how he's trying to con both his latest girlfriend and his wife into thinking he's going to give them both what they want, as well as running his con, it's also about Barcelona. One legend says the city was originally founded by Hercules. It's very, very old. It's also the capital city of the Catalonian government, and he's trying to con people who are raising money to create a nation independent of Spain. But it's also a new city, with a rebirth of artists and musicians— skateboarders love it. There is nothing like it on this continent."

His eyes told her he was following, but she had only a few more seconds to grab him. "I need a Bruce Springsteen."

One eyebrow lifted. His lopsided smile reminded her of Hyde Butler's. She couldn't recall an evening when she'd encountered quite so much male charm. His attractive, low voice took on a note of laughter. "That's very flattering, but I don't think anyone compares me to The Boss."

"Your first tour gig is in Barcelona. I'm looking for a song with a statement about survival, because our hero is like the city—still standing in spite of history. Worn down, still proud, clinging to a sense of humor, surprising, being reborn, not entirely safe, a culture within a culture. It's an unusual, wonderful place, Barcelona."

"So how does that make me like Springsteen?"

"His song 'Philadelphia' set the tone for the whole movie. The movie had a wonderful score by the kind of composer I just can't afford, but the one I have is solid and gifted. We need something to anchor his work. Find us a rhythm, a sound of a younger beat, beyond the surface. A feeling about the city to a foreigner, some words, then hear what he's working on and see if it leads to a song."

He rubbed long fingers over his stubbled jaw. "Kind of thing that would play over the end credits?"

"Or the opening credits, like 'Philadelphia' did. That's the director's call."

She watched him shake back his long blond hair as he thought it over. His band's last two albums had gone platinum, with room

22

to spare. Their concerts sold out on the day the tickets went on sale. He wanted for nothing, and had no reason to take on something else. Except, perhaps, the same reason Hyde Butler had—he was more than his current gigs allowed him to be.

"Tell you what. When we're there, if something happens, it happens. I'll let you know."

"That's all I hoped for," she said. Well, a commitment would have been ideal, but the way his agent had left her to sink or swim on her own pitch had made her realistic about her chances. She wanted a firm foothold into the 18-25 demographic that made up his fan base, and her intuition said he would put a spin on the sound that would elevate her composer's work.

There were more photographs as they parted, and she heard Levi telling a reporter that they might be working together on a film. No doubt tomorrow Levi would be the lead role or some such, reported faithfully in the blogosphere and then picked up by the print trades. By the time they cast the movie a street buzz could be flying, the kind that kept her future market looking for the release date.

And everybody wondered what a producer did. She skipped back down the center stairs and decided her evening had been well-spent enough to deserve a real drink after all. A glance across the sea of heads revealed a few faces she recognized. At the bottom of the stairs she glanced around for a waiter, then turned toward the bar.

In spite of the noise, her ears saved her. She heard *that* voice. The one she never wanted to hear again and had spent far too many hours hoping she would. Without hesitation she spun in place and headed for the door. Please, she prayed, let no one take a picture of Selena Ryan hightailing her ass out of a club the moment she realized Jennifer Lamont, her ex and supposedly wronged former talent, was in the place.

Her smile felt brittle, as if her face was going to splinter any moment. She sketched a flirtatious wave toward a cluster of faces, as if she saw someone she knew, was waylaid for several seconds to kiss cheeks with a woman she recognized only as a best supporting actress nominee from years past, and was safely out the door. She did not want to go back and find out if Jennifer was with someone new, and wasn't the least bit curious whether she'd switched back to women again. She counted her steady steps all the way to the car, working backward through her To Do list, through the day, through all the conversations, decisions, what she'd eaten for lunch. Detail by detail, she buried her anger under layers of work until Jennifer Lamont didn't exist anymore. She had never loved her, never trusted her, and had never felt all four inches of Jennifer Lamont's stiletto heels buried in her back.

After a numb return drive to Beverly Hills, she punched in her personal code at her gate, and drove forward once the old wrought iron had parted. Like many of its neighbors, the high fence had a high-tech security system along the top and at each access. As the gate clanged shut behind her she felt the need to be Selena Ryan slip away. Now she got to be tired and hungry. She'd gotten home without crying and without ranting herself so wide awake she wouldn't sleep for hours.

Her headlights swept over the first story of the house and she gave it her entire attention. The old-style Spanish showplace had been built by a 1920s studio executive, but was small by today's standards. Its real beauty was an acre of grounds crusted with orange trees. Her production offices used seven of the eight bedrooms, and the common areas met many needs for entertaining and small media events. The centerpiece great room had been built for film screenings and she still used it for that, albeit with completely modernized equipment. She loved where she lived and where she worked, and that it was paid for. No one could ever take it away from her and she should count her blessings.

She circled around to the back, pulling the car into the garage. She left it unlocked so Kim could easily retrieve the clothing bag, netbook and paperwork in the morning. She gathered up her personal belongings, making sure she had her Blackberry. God, she was tired, and now she felt it.

The pool was inviting in the moonlight, but she wasn't tempted. She walked its perimeter to the pool house where she gratefully unlocked the door and stepped into the cool interior. As the door locked behind her she let everything she was carrying slip from her hands to the wicker chair just inside the door. In a few steps she had kicked off the suede pumps and peeled the dress off as well. In the morning she'd take it back to Kim for cleaning and eventual return to her "bedroom" in the main house. It was a room she never slept in.

Instead, she had the pool house, and it was all hers. Expanded to three times its original size, the low ceiling, open transoms and patio flagstones combined to keep it cool in the summer. A press of a button heated the floor, which made it quickly cozy if temperatures turned cold on days she was home. Careful attention to the space had let her add all the amenities she might need. What she loved best about it was that no one else, not even a cleaning service, came inside on a regular basis. It was her space, and when she was in it the only access to her was her phone; not one member of her staff would ever disturb her for any reason. Once her phone was off, she was off the grid, even if only for a few hours a night.

Nobody knew that sometimes she left her clothes on the floor, and didn't do the dishes for days. Nobody to comment on the overstuffed divan where coffee stains, a clutter of pencils and bound scripts, and the indented cushions made it clear where one person did a lot of reading. The last person aside from her to be inside had been a plumber, and before that, Jennifer. There was no one to gossip that Selena Ryan sang in the shower and swore when she did her morning yoga routine. Nobody to report that maybe her favorite coffee wasn't holistically organic fair trade, and that she had a penchant for Snickers bars. Right now, there was no one to see her hands shaking and the sheer effort it was still taking not to relive every bitter moment with Jennifer, especially the one when she'd known it was hopeless. She'd given Jennifer all that she could, and in the end, it wasn't enough. Because by then Jennifer wanted something else. Jennifer would always want something else, and more of it.

She quickly showered, shampooing out the smell of the club. Her hair might be a dull brown, but at least it gave her no trouble. A cursory slather of moisturizer on her face was all she could manage before she pulled back the soft, light blue covers and climbed into bed. She switched on the foot warmer and pulled a body pillow close, molding it to her arms and hips. Drowsiness washed over her as the sheets warmed to her body. Eyes closed, she put everything out of her mind. Right now her job was to sleep so she could tackle another day tomorrow.

Warm. Home. A last fumble with the alarm clock to make sure it was on. Everything in its place. Safe. Nothing, she felt nothing. Nothing missing, nothing wanted…

Buzztastic # #

We were right, boys and girls! Just last night we said that handsome dude Hyde Butler and shocker rocker Levi Hodges were being stalked by indie girl about town Selena Ryan. Pics below! She bagged them both. Production is very hush-hush. Maybe Brokeback Ballad? We wish we had a pic of Serene Selena and ex Jennifer Lamont at the same party last night! Sapphic reconciliation? Can we watch?

Meanwhile, H.B. had quite the birthday party. After the 90210 9-1-1 the beautiful people fled the scene. Check out this cutie, carrying off a bottle of A+ agave as her souvenir. From what we heard, we should check the delivery rooms in nine months. Will there be baby Hydes all in a row?

Chapter 2

Selena slapped the alarm off and drowsily tried to remember if that was the first time or the second. She didn't want to open her eyes yet, but taking an extra half-hour to wake up could spike the day's calendar, especially when there were production updates due from someone on the other side of the planet. She tried to treat Kim and Alan better than that. She didn't expect them to treat her better than she treated them. As she dragged herself out of bed she chose a favorite curse word for the day. If she swore now, she wouldn't slip later.

The refrigerator yielded up some orange juice. While she sipped she liberated a ripe avocado from the mesh basket on the windowsill. She scooped out the contents, mashed in a little lime juice, salt and pepper and smushed the result on a half of an asiago bagel—her favorite breakfast, by far.

With a couple of bites in her stomach she started her yoga

routine, annoyed by the series of creaks and pops that increasingly accompanied every position. She did this every day—why didn't it get easier?

Because you're not getting any younger, she told herself. You don't eat right most of the time, you don't eat enough, you don't get sufficient sleep and you have too much stress.

Stretching her arms over her head, she answered herself that she'd cut down on her travel by opening the firm to two more producers, and each day she was home she had a healthy breakfast at least.

After a quick shower to rinse away bed head, she turned on her phone and looked first for texts from Alan or Kim. Kim's said, "Allswell." Alan's said, "HOUSEONFIRE."

She sighed. Tapping over to her calendar she saw that the first time someone beyond staff would be on the premises was ninety minutes off, so she slid into comfortable jeans and a casual polo. She'd find appropriate meeting attire in her bedroom in the main house.

"What's up?" She poured herself a cup of coffee—one of the latest interns really made great coffee—and took note of the lines around Alan's eyes. Whatever it was, it was serious, but she hadn't expected differently.

"Todd needs you to call him ahead of the production check-in, because Michael is going to hit the roof."

They walked side-by-side toward her office. She had long since adapted to checking her step so as not to outpace him. At four-foot-six, Alan was by far the shortest member of her staff, and also the most organized. While Kim's desk was a flurry of chaos that somehow became beautiful order when she snapped her fingers, nothing on Alan's was ever out of place, and he rarely wasted words.

"The location temple in Hong Kong went religious on us. They decided they don't want to make a gay film."

She almost stumbled. "Say that again, but so it makes sense."

"The executive producer—that would be lovable you—is gay, the writer's gay, ergo it's a gay film. Against their principles."

All the swear words she'd uttered during yoga wanted to bubble out again, but she caught them back. "How did they determine our sexuality?"

"They do have Google in Hong Kong."

They shared a long glance as she worked down the list of eventualities he no doubt already had considered. Director Michael would be furious with producer Todd for losing the location, but Todd wasn't to blame for something so stupid. She wasn't apologizing to anyone for being gay, but she did not want any notoriety around the monks' decision—it was their temple and the production was a guest in a foreign country. Todd was probably looking for feasible alternatives now.

"He said he'd have two more options by the time you called." Alan glanced at his trusty iPhone. "That's the fire. Everything else is merely smoldering."

She thanked him, waved at Kim to join her as she went into her office. She immediately noticed the rich, heady scent of a lavish bouquet of roses.

"The flowers are from Hyde Butler."

And what beautiful flowers they were. Three dozen white roses, and one rose of vibrant pink, looked glorious on the corner of her desk. "Was there a card?"

Kim leaned against the doorjamb, her solidity always a welcome sight. As chic and modern as Alan was classic and buttoned-up, she was a series of colorful curves today in tailored jeans, a raspberry print top and cute teal flats, a combination Kim carried off with aplomb. With all that flair, people might not be surprised she was in the film industry. They definitely were surprised that the soothing, coaxing voice on the phone belonged to a mid-forties mom with a daughter in her last year of high school.

Kim gestured at her desk. "It'll make your day."

She plucked it out of the envelope and took in the words no doubt dictated to the florist. *Let's get into bed together.*

She couldn't help it—she whooped for joy. "This makes my whole *week*!"

"The bloggers are sure you're starring Levi Hodges, too, and maybe the two boys are going to go gay for this one."

"Oh please," Selena scoffed. "I guess it's good that they're clueless."

"His agent has already called three times. BeBe's not happy, baby."

"I'm sure she isn't. I need art concepts on the façade of the Carlisle Theater ASAP for the first set of investor's packets. Oh, and put Ellen Spelman on the potential investor list."

With a quiet clink of bangle bracelets and the subtle click of the beads at the ends of her cornrows, Kim retired to her office with a happy skip. Dozens of people, from casting directors, art designers to gaffers were waiting to find out when they began work. First thing was the contract from her lawyer to Hyde's. BeBe could be a real pain in that process, so it was time to make nice.

After listening to a diatribe about her underhanded tactics and how Hyde's schedule was too tight to allow for this project, she focused BeBe on the supposed sticking points. The real issue was compensation, and they both knew it.

"Yes, there will be penalty provisions if we make Hyde late for any of his other projects. But that's not going to happen. Every single element of production that involves him will run around his availability. I only need to know when he can do the location shoot in Spain. That's estimated at twelve days. Here in Los Angeles, it's probably fourteen days over four weeks, at the most."

"Your little film is going to exhaust him. His only availability is either before his next Miramax—that's a Miramax full distribution summer next year release, sweetie—or right after, and right now he's recovering from the hell they put the poor man through in Jamaica."

Hyde certainly had looked wasted to nothing last night, Selena thought sourly. "I'd prefer before the Miramax deal, and

31

we can be ready. Why don't you give me the dates where he's committed and we will work around them?"

"What's the point—there's no way you're going to meet his minimum."

"I think if you talk to Hyde about it, he'd be willing to take a far lower up front. This is less time and prep than a big pic for him, and I'm willing to do an honest deal on the cable and DVD licensing shares, which will jump if we get into some awards finals." She didn't come right out and say *Academy Awards* but BeBe knew the possibility existed, and the resulting guarantee of sales it would create. Add to the mix the reality that her star's action pictures were not paths to Oscars. BeBe also knew, even though she might consider honesty a character flaw, that Selena was telling the truth about making and keeping an honest deal.

"This is all just putting a stake right through my heart. I only want what's best for my client, that's all I ever want."

"Let's see if we can't make him happy, then." Selena counted to ten as BeBe wailed on for a bit longer about poor Hyde, then they agreed to review a draft within two days and she sent BeBe on her way to make life more dramatic for someone else.

"Change now, or you won't have time after the production check-in call," Kim said from the doorway. She'd pulled on a brown suede jacket that fit her better than the proverbial glove.

"Who is coming in again?"

"New reps from that start-up distributor in South America, followed by a video call with the audience research people in New Jersey. They'd love our business."

She nodded. "After that I want to talk to Mirah Zendoza so she can start casting out the rest of the parts. Then let's calendar the timing for the Spain shoot and get Eddie Lynch thinking about a start date in five weeks, which is Hyde's first opening. It'll be a crunch getting ready in time—there's no time to lose on casting." Eddie Lynch was experienced, but not with foreign locations, which bogged down all too easily in local difficulties like sudden requests for additional permit payments, and guilds turning up mid-shoot to require hiring from their ranks. He thought he had a lead on a good local associate director, though, which would help them avoid expensive and time-eating delays.

She bolted from her office and took the rear stairs to her bedroom, avoiding most of the staff. Their friendly greetings were a welcome part of her day, but there was no time for them.

Fifteen minutes later, she turned in front of the ornate bedroom mirror to make sure the back of her tailored shirtdress fell smoothly over her backside. For a moment her gaze strayed to the reflection of the formal room behind her. The woman in the dress fit that room: carefully elegant, emotionally reserved, expensively understated, well-appointed, but not a showstopper. She was more comfortable with the dress than the room, but it worked as a stage for reporters who were doing "personal" profiles and photo shoots. She couldn't imagine bringing a lover to the sterile cleanliness. The muted taupes and golds, high pile carpet and thick draperies wouldn't go with sheets on the floor in a heap, piles of pillows strewn across the window seat, or mess from shared popcorn, let alone the telltale signs of living in the room, like DVDs to watch, stacks of scripts to read, even a water glass to drink from during the night.

For longer than she liked, her mind replayed the memory of waking up to enjoy the sight of Jennifer wrapped in a sheet, her body dappled with the sparkle and flicker of sunrise reflected off the swimming pool so it bounced on the bedroom ceiling. She nearly smiled, then pushed it all away. She'd loved Jennifer, but Jennifer's emotions were tissue thin about everything but making movies. The tissue had shredded and she'd put that lush hair and vibrant smile to work on someone else. Snorting coke had been part of the bonding with her next conquest. Somehow, in something less than a heartbeat, they'd gone from lovers to enemies, though even after more than a year to think about it, Selena couldn't identify exactly when that had happened. There had been no gradual shut down, no sense of slipping away from each other. When Jennifer had needed her help the most, she'd given it—maybe that was when Jennifer had decided to hate her. Maybe she figured if she hated Selena she didn't have to feel beholden for favors, some of which had been expensive in coin and pride.

Selena Ryan, in the full regalia of a successful Hollywood independent film producer, met with distributors' reps, caught up on authorizing payments, interviewed a possible catering and comforts vendor for the Carlisle location shoot in L.A.'s old theater district, talked to her tax planner, had a hastily arranged and lengthy telephone meeting with the *Barcelona* casting director, and talked one more time with Todd in Hong Kong before she had to leave for drinks with sales reps for a DVD rental store chain. Fortunately, it was her only evening engagement, so she found herself finished with all pressing work while the sun was still up.

All in all, it had been an exhilarating day with a new project begun, and a new location shoot for the temple in Hong Kong secured with greater ease than anyone predicted. Michael didn't chew Todd's head off either, and had even teased her about being notoriously gay, worldwide.

Thanks to the good graces of one of Kim's interns, her gym bag had fresh clothes. She parked near the WeHo diner and went into change into sweats and a tank top. After she dropped off her work clothes back at the car she cinched ankle weights into place and took off for a long, hilly walk in the local neighborhoods, grateful to blow out cobwebs.

She circled one of her favorite enclaves, stopping several times to admire the view. If she didn't think about why the setting sun spread orange across the sky it was pretty. Thoughts of air pollution turned the colors garish, so she pretended it was a movie shot. Life was simply better in the movies. It was why she loved them. However, every day she reminded herself she made movies, but she didn't live in one. In a movie you could say something catty and waft away on laughter, no permanent harm done. That kind of sleight-of-mind she left to all the Vivienne Westons and Jennifer Lamonts—even the Hyde Butlers. In real life, the person you'd wounded was waiting in the very next scene for an apology or to deliver payback.

At the bottom of the last hill her stomach growled right on time. The diner was brisk with customers, but a shallow booth tucked just around the corner from the counter was still empty. It was her preferred place to sit, her back to most of the diner.

There was no sign of the owner. Maybe the irascible Betty, unmistakable because of her signature beehive and smoker's raspy voice, was on vacation. The new waitress from the other night was there, as well as a slender Latina at the counter she knew by sight. The newbie got to her first, scribbled the order of English muffin, no butter, grilled chicken and vegetable-of-the-day onto a crumpled tablet. The new waitress had no name tag, and Selena smiled to herself thinking of one of her favorite screenwriters who would come up with a pithy name for the walk-on. Delilah never stopped at *Waitress 1* and *Waitress 2*, descriptions that casting directors hardly found inspiring. The wry Latina would be *Arched Brow* and the newbie... She hesitated, studying the woman. Thirty, maybe, unmemorable except for a bad haircut and narrow hips that made her shoulders look broad. In profile the tight wrap of the apron underscored a flat tummy, but the unflattering uniform made her arms seem too long for her frame. Delilah might opt for *Scrawny*.

A moment too late she realized that the waitress had become aware of her steady appraisal. She crossed the diner to ask, voice neutral but shaded oh-so-subtly with annoyance, "Did you want something?"

"No, just staring into space." Selena knew how to fight down a blush, and she was successful now.

"Your dinner will be right up," Scrawny said, before turning neatly on her non-slip soles to return to her other customers.

Trying to recover from having been caught staring, Selena surreptitiously unwound the ankle weights and set them on the seat next to her. Her Blackberry vibrated on the table, but a quick glance revealed the message as spam. She set it down, feeling a little odd that after such a busy day no one needed her for anything. She could unwind over her comfort food, then head home to read scripts, feet up on the sofa. Add a glass of red wine and perhaps a Goldberg Variation or two.

She realized that Scrawny was approaching with two plates balanced along one arm, and two of the diner's ubiquitous caddies of condiments in her free hand. She paused long enough to deliver one plate and caddy to another table before continuing toward Selena.

It happened so quickly that Selena had no time to react. The waitress's non-slip sole stubbed on the floor, refused to slide and the plate of food and caddy continued forward, right out of the woman's grasp. Selena was still at the point of saying to herself, "There's relish, mayonnaise and chicken in my lap," when the waitress finished falling.

Selena amended her shocked list: She now had relish, mayonnaise, chicken, and a waitress, face down, in her lap.

The waitress said, "Damn it, I'm sorry," as she finished her fall by rolling back off Selena, ending up on her butt right next to Selena's feet.

A part of Selena formed the words, "Are you okay?" But that part didn't get to her mouth first. Instead, she said, "I hate mayonnaise."

"I'm not loving it right now either." The waitress clambered to her feet while fishing napkins out of her serving apron. She mopped at the mottle of mayo and relish on her face, but did nothing for what was in her curly blond hair.

Selena nearly smiled in sympathy, but it froze before it began when the waitress added, "So that's the proper way to do a prat fall. My acting coach will be *so* pleased."

Damnation—another actress.

Arched Brow arrived with towels. "Oh, you poor thing! You're a mess!" She applied herself to helping Selena pick the food and goo out of her lap while directing the other woman to clean up in the bathroom.

"I think I'll just go," Selena said. No amount of mopping was going to take care of the sensation of butter-like oil seeping into her underwear.

"Let me get you your dinner to go—on us, of course. Gail

36

has never dropped anything before. Just one of those flukes."

Scrawny—Gail—reappeared, her hair wet in places. "I am so sorry. I don't know what happened. Can I get you anything?"

"No, this was quite enough." She knew she sounded upset, but she *was* upset.

Even as she stalked out she knew she didn't need to add being rude to the situation, and it was paranoia that presumed the waitress had done it deliberately to get an introduction. The two women followed her to the door, still offering help and a replacement dinner. She said, over her shoulder, "It was an accident. Another night, maybe," and escaped into the not nearly dark enough WeHo night.

She ranted herself into a thoroughly sour mood, including speculation on the cost of cleaning the driver's seat, which would henceforth always smell of pickles. Great, every time she got in the car she'd want a burger. She sat in the car for a few minutes, feeling greasy, then glanced at her Blackberry when it vibrated again. She'd had no messages except the spam, and now a half-dozen loaded, some with time stamps several hours old. Technology sucked sometimes, she groused. None were labeled urgent, so she started with a message from Kim with the subject line, "You're famous sort of," and containing only a web link, which she clicked and followed.

Variety.com was scooping the entertainment world by announcing the probable signing of both megastar Hyde Butler *and* rock superstar Levi Hodges to the latest Selena Ryan indie project. It included photos of her with both men.

Cursing at length, she could blame only herself. She was used to photographs with the famous, but two such famous men in one night had caught the eye of the gossip mill. While the publicity was exactly what she wanted for *Barcelona*, she hadn't realized that photos of her would be the link the columnists would use to tie the two men to the same project. It was the biggest accumulation of pictures of her since her relationship with Jennifer Lamont had hit the blogosphere.

No doubt aspiring actress Scrawny Gail kept up with the

latest news, and had seized the day. Selena wondered how this Gail woman would feel knowing she wasn't the first actress to fall, spill, stumble or drop the proverbial hanky in front of Selena Ryan. The lack of originality alone was vexing, though no one had tried chicken and mayo before. Looking as if she'd just soiled herself in public was intolerable. She snapped off her Blackberry with an annoyed snort, resisted the impulse to throw it, and headed for home.

It didn't help that she wanted a burger every mile of the drive.

Buzztastic # #

Baby bump—oops! That popular nun who's dropping in for laughs every Tuesday night has been looking a lot like a penguin lately, and word has it the producers are hopping mad that the star in question didn't think viewers would notice. Do we hear frostbite in the penguin's future?

Meanwhile, we've got all the latest pictures of that beloved soap star's final days. Surrounded by family at the end, two of the four exes and even the infamous bad boy son—remember him? We're all so sad. Click here for the funeral close-ups!

Our eye has been caught by glamour gal Vivienne Weston. The pool is on for who she'll date next and how long till she gets her big break. The number crunchers are figuring out if there's a relationship between how long and how many cup sizes. We already know that answer: Yes!

Chapter 3

Bad enough taking the bus home at ten o'clock at night, but it was an hour when everyone was tired and hungry, and Gail Welles knew she smelled like a hamburger, with a twist of chicken. Usually, she was merely the aroma of grease.

Waitressing didn't pay well, but it paid enough and steadily. Betty's Diner had been a good move from the chain coffee shop she'd worked at before, because the free food made all the difference. On her lap sat tomorrow's lunch of salad and fresh fruit, plus a smashed piece of peach pie and some already grilled chicken breast. It would all go into the tiny refrigerator in her itty-bitty kitchen. Tomorrow morning's cattle call was way too early after a night at the diner, but the last two miniscule acting jobs she'd gotten had both come from that kind of audition set-up. She was getting shots at two bit parts on sitcoms, and maybe a half-dozen commercials. The ads were harder to prep for, but when she got home she'd run through the lines she'd been given—not many—a couple more times, then sleep on it.

But first, she fantasized about a much-needed hot shower. Her shower might be hardly big enough to turn around in, but the water was piping hot and she didn't have to share it with anyone. She walked briskly toward her building, passing numerous panhandlers and an increasing number of working girls. The Lorelei Arms had been bought from a madam—or so the story went when discussing such things in the laundromat across the street—by investors from a church group. The formerly by-the-hour rooms had been converted to apartments with the addition of the so-called kitchen. She went up the sturdy, recently washed steps, reminding herself that it was exactly what a starving actress from Iowa could afford. At least she had Aunt Charlie's generous gift of high quality sheets and pillows, and a soft as a feather mattress topper, to make sleeping a joy. Her equally generous Christmas gift of a two-cups-at-a-time coffee brewer made mornings bearable.

Hair finally scented once again with her favorite vanilla-lavender shampoo, she wrapped herself in her robe and sat down at the little table which served as her desk. The lines for the sitcoms and ads were very sparse, and her ego wasn't pleased with the tenor of the casting instructions: Average blonde for Secretary 3. *You're perfect*, her agent had gushed.

Working at the diner virtually seven nights a week had extended her careful savings to allow this third year of trying to break into television or movies. She'd arrived on her twenty-ninth birthday, realistic but still hopeful that the accolades back home for community theater had been truthful. But if she didn't get something substantial by fall, she would have to think about going home to Iowa and disappointing Aunt Charlie, who still believed that all Gail needed was that One Lucky Break.

Too bad she hadn't fallen into the lap of someone famous. Why couldn't her victim have been Lindsay Lohan or Mark Wahlberg? It would have made the tabloids—maybe even gotten her a quip from Kathy Griffin. No, she had to pick some stuck-up businesswoman. She brushed her teeth and told herself to be very careful what she wished for. It was Errol Flynn or someone like him who'd said that the problem wasn't what people said about you, but what they whispered.

None of that mattered as she gratefully sank into her comfortable bed. Or when she switched off the alarm too few hours later. The timer on the wonder-coffee machine had worked, and she could smell the caffeine. A half-hour later she backed her car out of the narrow slot. The bus was cheaper transport than the paid parking near the diner, but the casting call was at a Culver City studio with free street parking just a few blocks away.

She had just successfully wedged into a space when someone called, "Is that you, Gail?"

"Hi, Regine." She turned to the welcome sight of Regine's pretty smile. Like Gail, she wore no make-up beyond a good foundation, but her lush Afro was controlled by a black bandeau. Gail's thin curls needed no such restraint.

Regine nodded in the direction to Gail's left and a glance revealed another actress they both knew, dressed in a trim designer suit and made up to the nines. She ignored them though Gail knew she had to see them staring. "If she was nice I'd tell her she's blowing it with that get-up."

Gail glanced down at her simple khaki Dockers and utilitarian v-neck T-shirt. Blank canvas was the whole point of how most of the actresses dressed for things like this—an appearance that looked too fixed might make a casting director think it couldn't be changed. The other actress was maybe aiming for only glamour parts, while Gail would be happy with a dishwashing liquid commercial where the product was made up prettier than she was. "Let's console ourselves thinking that we're naturally beautiful, while she has to work at it."

Regine rolled her eyes. "If you say so. Hey, I've got invites to a party in the hills on Friday."

"I've got work."

"Maybe for just a few hours? It starts early—five. It's a foodie thing with an open bar."

Free gourmet food sounded heavenly. "Let me see if I can work it out."

After giving their names at the guard post, they were quickly separated. Regine went in the direction of the "quirky black girl" roles while Gail headed for "average blonde."

Her first stop was a new sitcom where she might be the next door neighbor's occasionally visiting cousin. She watched several other girls emerge from the room looking crestfallen. When it was her turn she was confronted by three sleepy faces, still hanging heads over their coffee. There wasn't even a placard with the name of the show, which usually featured the star who would anchor it. Great, she didn't know anything more that she could use to customize the part.

"Name?" The woman on the left didn't look up.

"Gail Welles."

"Got it. So, Valerie, how long will you be in town?"

It took Gail a moment to realize she was being fed her line. She botched her response, then took it from the top, dropping into a sex kitten coo. "That depends on how long you'd like me to be."

"Sorry, not what we're looking for."

A few seconds later, Gail was on the other side of the door, still wanting to snarl, "What? Not *average* enough?" None of them had even looked at her. They wouldn't find anyone interesting until midmorning, after two more cups of coffee. She might be a nobody, but that didn't meant her time was theirs to waste.

The voice of practicality—which she disliked most of the time—reminded here that they had the jobs, so yes her time was theirs to waste.

She moved further down the corridor to the next call on her list, for a commercial. Waiting with at least a dozen other actresses, it was nearly an hour before she went in.

At least these people were looking at her. They had her walk forward, backward, lean against the wall, then stand in front of a bright stage light while they discussed her hair, eyes, stomach,

43

height and skin hue as if she weren't there. While they talked, she studied the text of her lines, written neatly on a grease board. She had not a clue what the product was, but she loved it, apparently. Finally, they explained that the commercial was for a growing chain of coffeehouses.

She relaxed slightly. "So would you like me to look like I'm healthy and having my coffee treat, or at the end of my tether and getting my coffee fix?"

One of the women smiled, slightly. "Go with the treat concept."

She gave it her best bubbly delivery. "In my busy on-the-go day, I look forward to the ten minutes I can forget about everything and enjoy just being me." She prattled through the rest of it, thinking it might as well have been copy for a tuna sandwich or spa.

The woman who'd spoken earlier was frowning. "Try it the other way."

Gail gave herself a slight shake, then took it from the top with her tone slightly flatter, and a weary set to her shoulders. When she was done she looked for any sign of success.

"It was interesting what you did with it..." She glanced at the two other people at the table. For all Gail knew, they were mannequins. "But I don't see it working."

She said thank you and left.

It was going to be a long, long day.

Regine confirmed the equally stressful results of her morning as they swapped bits of the lunches they'd packed. "Room 312—that's a coffee place, then?"

"Yeah. I tried a sort of organic-I-deserve-it and a junkie-gotta-have-it, and neither of them flew."

"Maybe they need ethnic? 'Girl, you got to get yourself some of this!' What do you think?"

"I would say too showy, but what do I know? Give it your best shot."

Two more commercials later, she waited for her chance at the second sitcom. This time there was a placard for the series, and she recognized a popular comic who specialized in jokes about his redneckedfather and hippy mother. The part was the daughter of a long lost friend from the commune where the mother had grown up. She gathered much would be made of the star's wife's jealousy of the potentially Free Love believing visitor. With the context of the show now in mind, she went through the lines in her head, and then, in response to the prompts, delivered them with a confusing blend of sensual innocence.

"Thanks, but no thanks," was essentially the response she got and she was heartened to hear one voice say, "That was one of the best so far, you know." Her immediate hopes that maybe they would call her back were dashed by the bored response, "She had all the comedic timing of bubonic plague."

Great, she was being judged by people who thought their own wit was cutting edge. She didn't know how she would find the energy for one more commercial. It was past three, and she was due at the diner in two hours, and her inability to sell dog food or whatever it was would feel like another nail in her acting coffin.

She really wanted to blow off the last call of the day and have a good cry, but if she did and her agent found out, it could jeopardize how many shots she was given in the future. She made herself go, just barely managing to say, "Gail Welles, W-E-L-L-E-S," instead of "Average Blonde 477."

Herbal shampoo, oh goodie. They let her smell it, which was a good thing, because if she hadn't she'd have recoiled during her lines. The scent was strongly peppermint and something akin to fennel. Not exactly a smell she wanted in her hair. The outside of the bottle proclaimed it was "Energy for your hair and YOU."

They gave her the lines on a sheet of paper and she scanned them quickly. Generally, it was exactly what she expected by way of copy. She felt too tired to summon up a bubbly demeanor and wondered if she drank some of the shampoo would it give her the vitality the copy promised, not to mention the sensuous sex appeal every woman wanted to attract the right man. If the smell hadn't turned her off, the idea of using it for man-bait would have.

She started off okay. "I can always use more energy, and not just to survive the busy day. Herbal Attractions is the way I stay attractive and focused after the workday is over." It was such tripe that she couldn't help putting a little Marilyn Monroe oomph on it. "With Herbal Attractions' clinically tested blend of the finest, mmm, very freshest extracts, my hair still—" She giggled. "Still turns heads when I go out with the girls. Who knows what will happen?"

There was no stopping her now. One shoulder pitched forward as she swayed her hips seductively, she added with a wink, "Men notice a woman with confidence, and Herbal Attractions helps me look and smell my best."

She inhaled the aroma from the bottle, without flinching, and held her breath as if she was getting the most from a drag of marijuana. "It makes every shower filled to the brim with fresh, powerful scents of nature."

To hell with it, she thought, surveying her audience of four. They all looked like deer in her headlights. She went completely off script. "Sometimes I shampoo two or three times a day, for more, oh, and more, oo, and *more* powerful sensations that make me, oh oh oh, explode with—oh....." She gasped, clutched her head and let out an orgasmic squeal with matching stomach to shoulder crunches. "Deeee-light. Oh baby!"

The room was silent when she was done. One man and the two women just looked stunned and offended. The second man put his head down on the table and laughed helplessly.

Well, at least someone got it, she thought. "I don't think I'm what you're looking for," she announced, and she exited the room in time to hear one of the women exclaim, "Certainly not!"

She walked half the length of the corridor, passing a row of weary but curious eyes belonging to equally starving actresses who wondered if her high color meant she had gotten the part. Gail had no idea what they would make of her laughing, gasping collapse against the wall. She had never been going to get that part, so it had felt good to perform without a care what the onlookers had thought.

Regine was nowhere in sight as she made her way to her car. The glamorous life of Hollywood, she told herself as she drove back to the Lorelei Arms, full of rejection, a uniform that didn't fit right and another night of dumping food in customers' laps ahead of her.

No day started well when Selena was awakened by a ringing phone. Few people had the number, and her staff would rather die than use it. She answered it groggily, expecting it to be her brother, a travel writer who called from all over the world with no awareness of anyone else's local time. Instead it was a low, too familiar voice.

"I always did love waking you up."

Selena bolted upright, and struggled to keep her tone casually level. "What do you want, Jennifer?"

"Direct as usual."

"How else should I be?"

"I was hoping for maybe a how-have-you-been or a long-time-no-talk."

"What do you want, Jennifer?" She stopped herself from demanding that Jennifer recall even one instance where she had woken up before Selena had.

"I just—you make it hard, you know. I thought maybe we could talk."

"That's what we're doing."

"Face-to-face. Maybe I could come over to keep it private."

Kim would kill her, and then Alan would dance on her corpse if she let Jennifer "come over." She wanted to live through the day. "You should just tell me what you want and get it over with. I can do without all the coy suspense."

Jennifer's tone sharpened. "I just wanted to... We didn't part on good terms."

True. Being told to take her smug, judgmental ass to the Mormons in front of a bunch of rehab staffers hadn't been the best of partings. "Fine, we're pals again. I have to go."

"Can we have lunch? Coffee?"

She took a deep breath as she smoothed her index finger over the vein fluttering in her temple. "No. Just tell me what you want."

"To see you."

Selena decided then and there that today's swear word would be *bullshit*. "Call Kim and she will make you an appointment. That's the best you're going to get from me."

"I swear, Lena, you sound frightened of me."

"No, just bored."

"Fine, then, I'll call Kimberly. But if she blows me off, I'm going to call you back."

The line went dead and Selena took a few seconds to text Kim, "JLamont five mins or less." Kim would fit Jennifer into a slot that would be squished from both sides. If Selena was lucky, Jennifer would get no more than three minutes to ask for whatever it was she wanted. There was only one certainty: the object of Jennifer's desire was not Selena. And Selena didn't want it to be, either.

It wasn't helpful that all through her yoga her swear word for the day echoed over that denial: *Bullshit*.

A very busy week served to give Selena a sense of equilibrium. In the back of her mind she knew that Friday, 1:30, she would see Jennifer again. She had hardened her heart, read her Al-Anon guidelines again, forced herself to relive the indescribable hurt of having her actions to get Jennifer out of a tight jam—all of which had dealt blows to her pride and self-esteem—thrown back in her face. But for her, Jennifer would have had a coke possession charge on her gossip dossier. But for her, Jennifer would have missed the opening shoot day of her next project, costing her tens of thousands of dollars in penalties. Instead of county time, Jennifer had signed into a rehab facility because Selena had dropped everything and chartered a helicopter to Desert Backwater, California with a defense lawyer right behind her.

A question about probable cause for search of her purse and

a promise to seek treatment and Jennifer had walked away. At no point had she ever twelve-stepped even a hollow apology Selena's way.

Jennifer's rehab stint had cemented her growing celebrity—welcome to Hollywood. She'd even done talk shows about her addiction issues, to applause and sympathy. Nobody gives a standing ovation to the person who never touched the hard stuff to begin with, in spite of the fact that it was as accessible as candy at Hollywood parties. Why was regaining sobriety an act of heroism far more lauded than abstention? Damn it, she knew it was hard to get sober because her father had never even tried, but Jennifer had milked it all the way to the Tonight Show. Selena sourly pulled on a second dress, trying to find something that screamed, "You were such a fool to let me go."

What she really needed was five dozen roses and "Thank you for last night" on an easily visible card, signed by a twenty-something hottie. That silly creature Weston would probably do it in an instant. It was galling to see the woman's name starting to pop up in the blogs. She'd be in *Variety*'s print edition before long.

Kim kept Jennifer waiting in the great room for exactly two minutes past the half-hour. Selena heard them approaching her door, Kim's voice lacking its customary warmth while Jennifer oozed familiarity with questions about Kim's daughter's life in prep school. Crisply gestured to a seat, Jennifer relaxed into the leather, crossing her million dollar legs, which Selena refused to look at. That meant looking at the million dollar face and into those dusky bronze eyes, courtesy of magenta contact lenses.

Kim tapped her pen on her notebook, said, "Bitterman is already here," and stalked out.

"Was it something I said?" Jennifer shook her hair back, likely knowing full well that the sunlight from the high windows was extremely becoming. The full mane of hair only had two extensions that Selena knew of, and she knew that her own unaugmented, unhighlighted, uncurled brown didn't even get out of the haute couture gate. Most of the time she was proud of that fact. She was hoping eventually to have the simplicity of Isabella Rossellini.

"What was it you wanted?" Selena ignored the trickle of hope that maybe this, nearly a year later, was the apology. That Jennifer would say, "I dumped you because I needed him. I told him some secrets about you to make sure he knew I was over you. Now that I've dumped him I admit he's the one who gossiped to the tabloids. I hurt you on purpose, and I take full responsibility for my actions and my addiction, and maybe we can..."

"To say that I am sorry we had that fight. I've felt bad ever since, and, well, never got the chance to tell you what was going on."

"You were in a trumped up rehab group session, and I was the guest of honor, without my knowledge. You humiliated me without a thought for purposes of your own, and made it sound as if I was only there to get money you owed me, and you knew that was a lie."

She tipped her head thoughtfully to one side. "Why were you there?"

"To see how you were, of course. Once upon a time, in a fairy tale, I cared about you."

"I was fine." She seemed genuinely puzzled. "I wanted to talk to you, but you got so...angry."

The scene flashed through Selena's mind. "All you did was deride me in front of your fellow addicts."

"Darling!" She threw back her head and laughed. "You never could tell when I was acting."

You're acting now, Selena thought. Jennifer wanted something. That was all this little scene was about. "Exactly what was the act?"

"I was playing my addict part. I was never addicted to anything. I just wanted Cary to think I was suitable for his purposes. Didn't you ever notice he prefers talent with substance issues? He thinks that makes them controllable. And I am just now starting to pull in the back end revenues from the movie—the DVD far outstripped the box office, which is what we thought all along.

It's the summer's hottest selling release."

A pulse was pounding in Selena's temple. "Are you trying to tell me that was all an act? Then why did I have to sweet talk that sheriff into letting you go?"

"Really, that's what I wanted to say sorry about the most. The stuff belonged to Cary and he never meant me to get busted with it. You got us both out of a jam."

"And he told the tabloids to go dig up my father's history anyway?"

She shrugged. "He's an addict. You have to think like one to understand."

"No, thank you." Selena stood up, feeling dizzy. Jennifer was a fake. It was in her DNA to lie, and actors were gifted liars. Professional liars. She could work with them because of the contract that would force everyone to deliver. But she was never dating one again. Ever. "You've apologized for—I'm not sure what. Fine. We're done."

Jennifer reluctantly got to her feet as Kim appeared in the doorway, tapping her notebook. "I didn't realize you thought all this time I was an addict. I understand you missed all the cues that I was moving on to Cary, but... Wow. You thought I was acting like your dad, and dished out the Tough Love. Now I get it."

"Jennifer, do me a favor, if I can ask one thing."

She slung her Vuitton bag over her shoulder, looking elegant and cool, if a person could ignore the poisonous tentacles. "What, sweetie?"

"Stop trying to get me. It's not a winning strategy."

"If you say so." She waved as she followed Kim while Selena translated the words to mean that Jennifer would do as she pleased, like always.

Selena pulled her small spray bottle of odor killer from her desk drawer. She kept it for the rare visitor she would allow to smoke. Now she used it to vanquish the scent of Jennifer Lamont, wishing there were something equally effective for her brain. She visualized her stupid, foolish, childish hopes as Janet Leigh and

51

stuck them in a Bates Motel shower. She let knife-slashing music skirl through her mind, but Jennifer's Cheshire cat smile still lingered.

So. Jennifer had never been an addict? It was all an act? Therefore nothing to apologize for? Had there ever been love? On her side, there had been, of that she was certain. She knew how to love. She had given all she could to The Relationship. She hadn't held back and… She viciously threw the spray bottle back in the drawer. And nothing. Done, over, finished, fade to black. The End.

Swear word for the day clenched behind her teeth, she met with the next appointment, agreed that she was all for packaging DVDs in more environmentally friendly containers as long as they discouraged shoplifting and piracy, then managed to get through a series of calls about mind-numbing minutiae that were nevertheless of *extreme* and *immediate* importance to those involved.

She had a headache that would not go away, and finally dragged herself out of the office to her car, looking forward to a cocktail party followed by a benefit dinner with the same joy she'd feel for a root canal followed by a colonoscopy.

"I'm sorry I can't stay longer," Gail told Regine. "You were great to get us this invite, but Friday night is the biggest tip night of the week. I managed to get an extra hour, though, before I have to go in."

Regine led the way up the steep staircase from where the bus had dropped them at the final stop on the Mulholland Highway. The hill was riddled with private winding driveways and switchback turns. At least the staircase was the direct route. "I get it. You don't have to keep apologizing."

"Sorry." Gail paused to fan herself, hoping she wouldn't look too wilted by the time they made it to the top. "I'm guess I'm still telling myself so I'll remember to leave."

"We're nearly there. I can hear the party from here."

It was the promise of some lively entertainment and free

food and drinks that had convinced Gail to find time for the party. They'd parked Gail's car at the nearest park-and-ride lot to save tipping the valets. Besides, it wasn't the kind of party a person arrived at in a twelve-year old Corolla. Regine had heard about it from a friend of a friend who said that several casting directors and industry notables would be there, even though it wasn't an industry party. Thankfully, their names were on the list and they breezed in after mutually consulting each other on their appearance.

With a tart, slushy—perfectly lovely—margarita in one hand, Gail made polite conversation with as many groups as she could, but no one was really showing her any actual interest. She was a bit too plain and too flat-chested. Always had been, always would be, and she just didn't get the second glances, not when Regine was a smokin' hot babe with booty. If anyone gave her a conversational chance, though, she could hold her own. She read as much of the film news as she could, kept up on current events, read the Oprah books. She made sure to have several skewers of grilled salmon to keep the margarita from taking over, and it was over the quality of the salmon that she finally got a conversational nibble.

"I think it's quite nice, though it could use a little bit of zing. Acidity, I mean. Like lemon or lime." She took another bite and gave her attention to the man who had stopped to ask her if she thought they were any good.

"There are comment cards on the food over there. You should fill one out." He gestured with a shrimp. "You sound like a foodie."

"Not really. When I'm not acting I work in a diner." She peered in the direction he'd indicated. "Comment cards?"

"It's a food program of some kind. Testing potential talent."

"Oh, sounds fun!" She turned back to him with a smile. He was maybe five years older than she was, making him late thirties or so, and she felt a vague ping on her gaydar. It was hard to tell in Hollywood as most of the men were metrosexually turned-out, right down to their beautifully manicured nails. "Are you a foodie?"

"No, I just like to eat. Okay, this will sound awkward." He bit another shrimp in half, and after an appreciative pause, said, "You look familiar. Honest. Not a pick up line."

Gail frowned. "Now that you say something…" She shook her head. "I can't place it though."

She was thinking back over the last few weeks—the twinge to her memory felt recent—when he suddenly grinned.

"Got it. You auditioned for Herbal Attractions."

Gail felt the heat of a blush rush to her cheeks. "Oh… You saw that." He was the man who had laughed. The audition room had made everyone seem washed out, but now she could see traces of Latino heritage. She was certain those brown eyes were quite effective at getting what he wanted too.

"I did—best thing I saw all day. Is acting getting in the way of waiting tables yet?"

"I haven't had to choose between the two yet, no." She matched his droll expression.

"Hold this." He unceremoniously handed her his drink and plate, and began searching his pockets. She juggled his drink with her own, resulting in a slosh of margarita on her bare arm. At least none of it got on her shoes. They were designer knockoffs, but they were the best designer knockoffs she could afford.

The rest of his shrimp—where had he found that much and was there any left, she wondered—was headed for the edge of the plate, so she tried tipping it the other way. Great, now she had martini to go with the margarita. "I'm going to spill your drink."

"Sorry." He took the glass back and offered her a card.

She passed back his food and tried not to notice that he'd just dribbled martini on his tie. Trevor Barden, Associate, MLT Productions. She wasn't quite sure what to say. "Nice."

"We've got an audition for a sitcom—can't tell you which one, though. It's a replacement character because one in place is being written out, hush-hush. Probably appear in every third episode. Are you out?"

She blinked at him.

"Out—your agent knows you're gay, et cetera?"

"Oh. Yes, yes, I'm not really the romantic lead type so it was a no-brainer." Clearly, she had more than pinged *his* radar. Was it the hair?

"You'd need to add three cup sizes to be paired with Brad Pitt."

"Really? Is that why Playboy isn't returning my calls, ya think?" She gave him an angelic look.

"You strike me as a realist." He went back to munching his shrimp. "No steamy boudoir, but you'd make quite a butt kicker. And after that ad lib you did on the shampoo, I think you've got comedy chops which would be a different kind of boudoir scene. So come to the audition…"

She came to her senses. "Welles. Gail Welles."

"I know where there's more shrimp, Gail Welles. Follow me."

She scurried after him as he skirted potted palms and the pool. They came around a sharp corner to a smaller buffet table. Her eyes lit up at the mounds of peeled, chilled shrimp and more grilled salmon skewers, plus some roasted vegetables drizzled with a caramel balsamic vinegar on wedges of chapatti. Her stomach growled. She wondered how much she could get in her purse and wished she'd brought a plastic bag. "Trevor's not your real name, is it?"

"No, but if I'd kept Thaddeus everyone would have known I was gay."

She laughed and tried not to look like a starving actress as she filled her plate. Fresh pineapple, seared in spears…the glands under her jaw twanged with anticipation of the first sour-sweet bite. "It's really nice of you to offer me an audition."

"There aren't enough of us in front of cameras. Ellen's great. Rosie bulldozed down doors, but when you look around, we're really scarce in the spotlight, when we both know Hollywood wouldn't function without the gay boys for style and the dykes to build shit."

She laughed again, but his rejoinder was lost when she spotted the end of the table. "Chocolate dipped strawberries!"

It turned out Trevor liked chocolate, and she lingered with him longer than she should have. After he got caught up in conversation with other people, she and Regine discreetly worked together to make serious inroads into the food.

She had to take off her heels to get back down the hillside stairs quickly and safely. She couldn't afford the ruination of her stockings, so she peeled them off as well, hoping no one would see her. The whole way down she alternated between a study of the cement stairs and the W of the Hollywood sign she could just make out through the trees. The W stood for *Welles*, Aunt Charlie had always said. *Wishes*, maybe, or *Wonder*, she thought. Mostly when she looked at it lately she was *Wistful*, because she wasn't sure she was going to make it in this town. Trevor's offer of an audition was by far her best break, and she was going to give it everything she had.

The scolding from Betty, back from her vacation, was worth it. Gail was quickly forgiven as she slung plates of food at customers as fast as they came out of the kitchen. In some unbidden place she knew she was a decent waitress, but she wasn't ready to own that. It was hard work and an honest living but it wasn't her fall back. If acting didn't work out, she would try to deploy her communications degree into something related to the arts. She'd probably make more as a waitress, especially if she got get into one of the posh restaurants, but she counted being happy as part of the reason for living. Those who can't act learned to administer or fund raise or market—anything to be within a whiff of the grease paint.

"Grilled chicken, mixed vegetables, no mashed potatoes. Anything else?" She looked up from her notepad, not surprised by the single-woman-dining-alone order. Sometimes after a virtuous meal, the customer would want a hot fudge sundae. This one didn't look the type, though.

"I'd like it on the plate, not me, this time."

Gail did a double take, and recognized her most humiliating

moment of diner work to date. She felt a hot flush burn up her neck. "Oh, I am so sorry about that," she managed. "This one's on me."

"Forget about it."

"I insist." Gail walked away before the woman could add anything more. Why should she forget about it? The customer obviously hadn't. She scrawled "VIP" across the top of the ticket, which was their code for someone's family or good friend as the recipient. When she returned to pick up the meal, the chicken was plump and juicy, and the mixed vegetables looked like a fresh batch. She added a wedge of lemon, a pat of wrapped margarine, and picked up a condiment caddy, careful to make it her only delivery.

"Here we are," she prattled. "Chicken, vegetables, and all the relish and mayonnaise you probably don't want, but this time on the table."

There may have been a glimmer of a smile in the hooded dark eyes. "Much appreciated."

"I get it right, sometimes." The woman was attractive when she relaxed and smiled, Gail thought. The little twinge she felt reminded her that she hadn't had a date of any seriousness since moving to L.A. "I'll be right back with the iced tea."

She whisked back quickly with a tall glass and a basket of sweeteners. Her customer promptly added the contents of a yellow packet to it, stirred, and said a quiet, "Thank you."

"If you want anything, I'm Gail."

A nod was all she got, which was all she wanted, she told herself. She wrote "comp" on the ticket and gave it to Betty at the cash register and went about her business. The other night waitress, Angel, had called in sick, so it was a busy night. She checked back often, but the woman wanted nothing more, finally accepted that Gail wasn't going to give her a bill, and left a five on the table when she departed. It was generous, and maybe she was forgiven after all.

All in all, though, Gail had to acknowledge that the woman's lifestyle was not the kind of success she wanted. The designer suit was gorgeous, but it didn't make up for the loneliness, in Gail's book. She was always on her own, in spite of having a smile that indicated she knew how to enjoy life. The shoes could have paid her weekly rent, but the set of the shoulders spoke of a stressful day, one of many, and no seeming hope that it would change any time soon. The hair was a carelessly sophisticated cut she envied, though, and she watched the woman jaywalk the street with a confident step that Gail thought she'd try to remember. Everything about her exuded Woman of Substance, and it wasn't just the clothes. Elbows slightly out, not pushy, not cowed, and her stride almost at its full. Add the weary shoulders and she was the picture of lonely success at whatever profession. Art dealer? High-end finance?

Customers wanted refills and checks, so she gave up thinking about her own currently nonexistent professional career. She did have an audition, saints be praised, and for a little while the plates didn't seem so heavy.

Buzztastic # #

What's better than a bunch of celebrity chefs trying to jump to TV? We pity anyone who didn't get invited to the Foodies Showcase Next Star party. Was that Paris Hilton stuffing her face? Hardly. In fact, not a real celeb in sight to snap as they filled up on the free food. There should have been Fitness 21 Club membership coupons for all those grazing gordos.

Guessing game time! Two hotties together in one movie, but who's the dark horse babe in this summer's hottest DVD release who might also be joining the sure-fire blockbuster? Our guess revealed later tonight!

Meanwhile, we've got more pregnant nun pics. Plus click here for the latest list of The Viv-about-town's dates, complete with pictures! That girl is everywhere. We're going on the record: by the end of summer she'll be in somebody's movie, judging from the rug burn.

Chapter 4

Gail's hopes were high when she reported to MLT Productions a few days later. The offices, in a ubiquitous Century City building, were for a number of sitcoms, but she was surprised, intimidated and elated to deduce her possible gig was for a prime time network's eight p.m. Tuesday night lead-in. She was pretty sure she wouldn't be meeting up with the two stars of the *Will and Wendy Wise Show* at this kind of screening, but if they were there she could only pray not to make a fool of herself. Besides, the power over her career didn't rest in other actors, ultimately. It was the producers and agents who made 99% of all the decisions. Only later, when she was a Little Name Star would the good graces of Big Name Stars matter. Someday maybe she would have such worries.

"Can I help you?" The tone was skeptical, and the receptionist looked as if she was quite certain Gail was in the wrong place.

She was impeccably dressed in a chic layered linen suit with a blouse that framed perfectly molded bosoms.

"Trevor Barden is expecting me. Gail Welles." She did her best to assume an air of pity for the young woman's lack of good fortune at not knowing the work of Gail Welles.

After the receptionist disappeared behind the nearest door, Gail couldn't help but look down at her own chest. She didn't even have the equipment to get a receptionist's job. Her agent had suggested she take out a loan if it worried her. It was probably for the best that she had no way to borrow money for a boob fix as it kept her from having any kind of serious internal debate about whether she ought to buy a pair of C cups if she could. The parting glance in her mirror at home had reminded her that her first free dollars really ought to go for a better hair cut. Madeline, her agent, had told her again and again it was all about the package.

The Package of Gail Welles had been rejected so many times she really ought to get her priorities in order. She wondered if she actually pumped up her boobs, coiffed her hair and picked out a nice set of tinted contact lenses if her love of acting would survive. It seemed a bit like killing Tinker Bell. But the people who'd chant, "I do believe in the craft of acting, I do, I do," were all watching reality shows these days.

Gail, you're a dreamer, she told herself. *You'd think in a town based on dreams you'd fit right in*. While she was at the self-pity game, she reminded herself that sitcoms were under siege, most failed in the third year, and with her luck she'd be hired and get a reputation for being the kiss of death.

The receptionist returned, now looking mildly surprised— but still singularly unimpressed—that Gail did in fact have an appointment. "Have a seat. Mr. Barden will be right out."

Gail had scarcely sat down when the main door opened. She couldn't yet see who it was, but the receptionist transformed in a heartbeat. She offered the woman water, coffee—oops! Not a woman, a man, very short, but from the back his thick hair and diminutive height had fooled Gail. He refused all the solicitous offers, simply said, "Drake's expecting me," and settled himself in a chair not far from Gail's. The receptionist sweetly intoned, "Alan's here, Drake," before again offering water, coffee, etc.

He promptly opened his iPhone and was tapping away when Trevor emerged.

"Gail, wonderful to see—Alan! What brings you out of that heaven you work in?"

Gail had risen to her feet, but stepped back, not wanting to push herself into their conversation.

"Drake has an assistant I might be able to borrow for a shoot, and this was on my way home."

Trevor seemed to take that as sufficient, because he turned to make introductions. "Gail's up for a role—good comedic timing I'm surprised nobody has grabbed yet," he finished.

Alan nodded politely as they shook hands, and Gail felt as if his eyes had taken a snapshot and filed her away. She felt like a gangly giantess next to him, and hoped her awkwardness didn't show. She realized only a dolt would say nothing when she'd just been introduced to a producer or assistant producer, but all she could come up with was, "Trevor is being very generous."

After a glance at Trevor, Alan asked her, "Where in the Midwest are you from?"

How had he known? Oh, he's joking…*idiot, don't blush*. "Iowa, of course. It hasn't rubbed off."

"And we don't want it to," Trevor said. He gave Alan a congenial wave, and led Gail down the corridor.

Gail hoped she hadn't embarrassed him with her lack of repartee. "Thank you, really."

"Alan's a decent sort. I'm putting you in here—the script's on the table, and you have ten minutes or so. I can tell you, just because I like to play it honest, we did have someone this morning who is a strong contender. Don't be afraid to take a chance and put some meat on it, because that's what it will take."

"I appreciate knowing that," Gail assured him, even though her knees had started to shake. Great, one mistake from her and it would go to someone else. Well, that was always true, wasn't it? She did appreciate his honesty—she had to focus and that was what this was all about. If she couldn't it was time to tuck her tail between her legs and go home.

The little room was cold, so she stayed on her feet while she glanced through her part. It was indeed the sitcom and now she was connecting her audition to the rumor mill's suggestion that the nun character on the show was getting pushed out. She was sure whatever the bloggers were saying was 90% untrue. Regardless, here she was, a script in her hand.

She anticipated that the other lines would be fed to her in more or less flat delivery and she would have to engage the readers, perk them up, to show she could light up an ensemble. Still, the lines were predictably ordinary, designed to needle the male lead while the female lead found them funny.

"I don't know, Will," she read aloud, trying to find the right inflection for Cora, her character. "There's no way Wendy can ever have too many shoes."

She closed her eyes and thought of Maude, Rhoda, Jackay, Sue Anne, all those sidekick characters in sitcoms played by talented and vivacious actresses. Maybe she'd be lucky enough to channel Bea Arthur or Betty White or Gilda Radner or even Lily Tomlin—as if. She wasn't sure how many people she had inside her, but today would be a good day to find even *one*.

When Trevor came back for her she felt calm. She was thinking about how her character Cora would face these people and this test. From the bit she had, they wanted a strong personality who wouldn't show up so often that she threw the stars out of their characters. Cora was mouthy, independent, maybe even might be revealed as a lesbian—and perhaps that was why Trevor had also been intrigued by her. Cora might be attracted to Wendy, or maybe just a free-thinker who took delight in needling the male of the species. Well, if Cora was gay, Gail didn't want a stereotype. But there was a fine line...and she thought she could walk it.

Just as they reached the interview room door, Trevor said, "I won't introduce you until afterward so you don't have to worry about recalling names. These people are very hard to read, so presume you have knocked their socks off when you're done."

"Thanks," Gail said. "For everything. I really appreciate it."

"Do me proud." He gave her a bracing smile, opened the door and let her precede him into the room.

There were four people at the table already, and Trevor joined them with a gesture at a dark-haired, jeans-clad young woman sitting on one of the two bar-height stools. The reader gave her a welcoming smile, and Gail casually set her handbag down next to the empty stool before sliding onto the seat. She set her script on the music stand that was adjusted to the right height and hooked one heel of her pump on the rung, hoping to be the picture of confidence and ease. Her heartbeat was too high and she sternly ordered herself to calm down. She could *not* afford to have a shaky voice.

The reader, using a clipboard for her script, took it from the top. "Will: How can you possibly need more shoes. Wendy: It's a special event."

Gail gave the reader an arch look. "I don't know, Will. There's no way Wendy can ever have too many shoes." She hoped that her emphasis conveyed that she and Wendy were two different kinds of women.

The reader, no longer using dialogue tags now that they were underway, wasn't as flat as Gail had feared, and she was delighted when, in response to one of Cora's lines, the reader genuinely laughed, as did Trevor.

"Honestly, Will," she intoned with the slightest hint of New England, "I would think a man with such a beautiful wife would want his buddies fully aware that he's one lucky guy. You married well, right?"

As Wendy, the reader intoned, "You're taking too long to answer that, honey."

"Five seconds....eight, nine, ten..." Gail counted.

On cue, she and the reader crossed their arms and gave the imaginary Will a steely-eyed glare over the lack of response.

Trevor rose, saying, "That was great. I think I like that touch of Kate Hepburn at her schoolmarm best."

He performed introductions and Gail hoped she would remember the names if she ran into some of them at parties. They seemed happy enough, and she remembered Trevor's advice to presume she had done well. They did warm to her smile and the handshakes were firm.

Trevor escorted her out, and as the door closed she plainly heard one person say, "This is going to be tough."

After that, getting to her car and homeward bound was a blur. She *had* done well. She probably wouldn't get it, but she had at least proven to herself that she could absorb a part and get the basics across in a silly little scene after not much prep. She was an actress, not a waitress, and maybe she would still have to go home.

But for the rest of the afternoon, and through most of the dinner rush, she walked two feet off the ground.

Though it had taken the better part of a week, Selena had finally lost most of the kicked-in-the-teeth feeling from her three minutes in Jennifer's presence. The first morning afterward she had woken up in tears, just as she had for weeks after their breakup. Telling herself to suck it up had had only marginal success.

Alan studiously ignored all personal drama, not so Kim. Halfway through Monday morning, she'd given her a brown-eyed grow-up-girl glare. "You thought you lost her to drugs. That's actually a tragic reason and one other people get, you know? But now you found out you lost her because dumping you made her life easier. So you got dumped by a dumbass for dumbass reasons, join the club. Have a truffle, and here's your morning To Do list."

Selena had actually laughed, grateful for the no-nonsense summary. Yes, Jennifer wasn't an addict user, she was just a user. There was no amelioration of Jennifer's character flaws due to substance abuse, she was just a bitch. End of story.

Well, her mind knew it. Her heart was still wincing.

Her list of things to do now that it was Wednesday was much like Monday's. She needed to ride herd on the Hong Kong project expenses, which had taken an alarming turn based on the last updates. *Barcelona*'s production staff order was waiting her signature, but first she had the second draft of Hyde Butler's contract to review. She scanned the list for something pleasant. A name jumped out at her and she picked up the phone with a smile.

"Dollface, thanks for calling back." Trevor sounded his usual upbeat self, which was what Selena had hoped. "Just a name for the Rainbow List."

Selena tapped her mouse to close the gossip blog promising hot film news that had turned out to be already days old. Another click brought up her informal list of LGBT folks in the industry. Only a few people were trusted enough to give her a name, and she likewise had that right with them. It had been Trevor who suggested that they all came across queers who deserved but weren't getting work, and it would be sweet to have some names to always put on a list for consideration. "Who did you find?"

"Young woman named Welles, Gail Welles." He spelled it for her. "I just found out we have to cast our other contender for a sitcom because she's already under play-or-pay, so we got a bonus for taking her off another project's hands. Otherwise, we probably would have gone with Welles. You're going to think I'm crazy, but honest, she reminds me of Katherine Hepburn—she's not what anyone would call attractive, but she's got handsome out her fingertips, and timing like a dream. Very comic, in the smart way. I kept thinking about *Bringing Up Baby*—she could do zany, and I bet, wound up just right and after a few years of real work, she could flay someone at twenty paces, like *Adam's Rib*."

"Hepburn?" Selena couldn't help the skeptical tone.

"I know, it's crazy. I would never make that comparison lightly, and frankly, you're the only person I'd make it to because I know you won't make me eat my words in public if I'm wrong."

"You're right. I'd never make you eat your words. In public." Though she was still skeptical, it wouldn't hurt to audition someone with Trevor's recommendation, of course. "We've got a meaty part in *Barcelona* for an offbeat girlfriend. I've blown my budget on Hyde Butler, so I need an unknown, hopefully one on the verge of a breakthrough. What's her agent's name?"

She wrote down the information Trevor passed on and was about to hang up when Trevor added, "Alan met her last week, by the way. You might ask about his reaction to the visual. Her headshot makes her look like a high femme—it's an appallingly bad representation."

"Okay, I'll ask. Thanks, Trevor. Did you ever have reason to call that fellow I saw at the theater?"

"Not yet, but when something opens I will. It's even harder to get out gay men in front of the cameras."

She hung up, feeling loads better for the call. She liked their lavender list, and that Trevor expected nothing from giving her the name and owed nothing for the information she gave as well. She opened the Butler contract, read the first condition and reached for her highlighter. BeBe had ignored her first request for a change, but she wasn't going to let that spoil her mood.

Kim left her in peace until she gave back the changes, and Selena finally went in search of some coffee, even though Kim offered to bring her some. It was good to be out from behind the desk for a bit. She chatted idly with one of the interns but lost the distraction when Alan arrived, coughed and looked pointedly at his watch. The intern scurried in the direction of his desk.

"Sorry, boss," Serena said, smiling. "I was gabbing with him."

"I like to keep them scared."

She watched him meticulously pour coffee and add precisely one level teaspoon of sugar. "Trevor Barden said he introduced you to an actress."

"Last week, when I stopped to see Drake about the loaner."

"What did you think, visually? I already know he thinks she has ability."

"Tall—seriously. Probably five-ten. She thinks it, it shows. Funny, I do remember every shift in her expression, and it's not like she's...pretty. She has a Face."

"And she stuck with you."

"Yes, I'd recognize her. I was amused that I could see her thinking that she'd just been introduced to someone important—little ol' me—and she had to say something memorable. If she can put herself into a character and show that to a camera she'd have a good range. Are you thinking of her for girlfriend Georgette in *Barcelona*?"

"I'll have them audition her. There's a couple of small parts, too." She shrugged, topped off her coffee and went back to her desk for the information on Trevor's girl. Kim put her on the list and handed back the lawyer's quick comments on the Hyde Butler contract. If she got through this review, she promised herself a dip in the pool later to celebrate.

"I understand, Trevor. You're not making it up, right? I nearly got it?" Gail hoped she kept the disappointment out of her voice.

Trevor did sound absolutely sincere. "You'd have had it if our other candidate wasn't already in-house, so to speak. Look, I've put in a word for you in a couple of places. I don't know what might happen, but don't give up. If you do land something, let me know, too."

"I will. I can't thank you enough."

"Get a haircut—that'll be thanks in plenty."

Gail fought back her hurt feelings. She knew he was telling the truth. "Okay, I will." She didn't mention that she'd be giving up food. Trevor didn't want to bed her or charge her a personal image consulting fee, so she'd be a fool not to heed his advice.

Slumped at the little table and fighting tears, she turned his business card over and over in her hands. When her cell phone rang, she jumped, then answered, expecting Aunt Charlie, who had promised to call this morning. Instead, her agent's voice greeted her.

"I've got a hot lead on a part—you've been requested. It's an indie film." Madeline sucked in her breath as if she was about to faint under the magnificence of the project. "Auditions are invite only. You can*not* miss it. You can*not* reschedule it. You *must* go."

Gail said she understood the importance of it—no lie there—and scribbled down the time and then the address of the Carlisle Theater. "Will I get a script in advance?"

"No—it's cold. It's a simple screening. If you get a call back for a rehearsed reading, then *that* would be serious. Of course if you landed this you'll have trouble taking that sitcom spot—"

"I didn't get it. The assistant producer just called me."

"How *rude*. He should have called me—oh, he's on the line. Toodles—you're perfect for this part. Go get it!"

Madeline hung up, leaving Gail mystified at how she was supposed to be perfect for a part Madeline knew nothing about. Typical Hollywood pep talk.

She looked at her notes. Monday morning, four days to kill until then. Since this part came hard on the heels of her audition for the sitcom, she wondered if she also owed thanks to Trevor Barden for this chance as well.

When the phone chirped again, she was pleased to hear Aunt Charlie's quavering twang. They'd always been close, but after her parents died in an automobile accident, Gail had spent her last year of high school living with her. She still had a room in the little house to go back to, though Aunt Charlie had moved last year to the senior residence.

"I've got a second audition in a week," Gail told her.

"I knew it! The cards said your planets were lined up with the karma."

"Maybe you're right." Gail moved to her bed so she could stretch out for a cozy chat as she told her aunt about the party.

"Sure he's not sweet on you?" Aunt Charlie said after she had listened to every detail Gail could think to share.

"No, he's gay, I told you. It's not like he cares about me, per se. He cares about the possibility I represent and he must see a hundred possibilities like me a day. He's got no real vested interest in whether I succeed, so that makes him officially a nice guy I met and for once in my life, being gay actually worked very much in my favor."

"You've certainly worked hard enough to deserve a chance. An independent film? What does that mean?"

"That the production company isn't automatically tied to a studio. They own their end product, then give it to a studio's distribution arm to put in theaters."

"I see—" Aunt Charlie coughed, though Gail could tell she was trying to smother it.

"You haven't started smoking again, have you?"

"No, dear, but ever since I quit I just can't shake this thing. I suppose it's fifty years of tar trying to work its way out."

"When do you see your doctor next?"

"No such thing as *my* doctor anymore. But I see that skin guy about that spot he burned off last month. It looks fine to me."

"Make sure you go." Gail wished she had the money to go home for even a short visit. Her last trip had been a Christmas present from Aunt Charlie, and the next one would likely be her birthday gift, but that wasn't until September. Her aunt tended to believe she was indestructible, having outlived all of her siblings, but Gail had noticed the steady decline in her energy and resilience. "Promise?"

"I promise. Nadine will fuss me if I don't, too."

"Good." Gail wasn't all that impressed with Nadine's abilities as a daughter, but then she knew as well as anybody that Aunt Charlie epitomized stubbornness. "How's the grandbaby?"

"Nadine says it's the last one for her—the terrible twos will do that. It's time for them to stop, anyway. Three kids, and she's forty next year. She agreed."

"Nature may have other plans."

Aunt Charlie laughed. "She wants Paul to get fixed. Had quite the fight about it, apparently."

Gail listened to the rest of the family gossip, covering cousins and nieces and nephews she really didn't know well. Half were Pentecostals that Aunt Charlie didn't care much for either, especially after they had tried to make her feel guilty for caravaning to the state capital with her bridge friends from the senior center to celebrate the court ruling in favor of gay marriage.

Later, getting dressed for work, Gail looked at the picture of her aunt magneted to the refrigerator door. She and her three troublemaking friends—all wearing vibrant PFLAG tees—were being heartily embraced by a bevy of gorgeous gay men, all bedecked in rainbow leis. When I'm that old, Gail thought, I want to be that cool.

But more than that, she wanted to make something of herself while Aunt Charlie was here to see it. The financial sacrifices alone called for her sincere effort, but even more, the unconditional love was a debt of the soul she had hardly earned, and had yet to even begin to repay.

Buzztastic # #

It's official—excommunication complete! The nun is out and what's worse for her is industry insiders were saying trained monkeys could replace her. Is that why one of her "very dear friends" got the nod?

Looks like maybe that Ryan Productions hunky indie project is off—no sign of The Butler's signature on anything and The Hodges is in Europe doing sold out shows. So why was Sapphic Selena partying with both of them? When we know, you'll know!

Don't forget! You read it here just this morning that the glamour girl on everybody's arm this summer has been cast in the latest horror flick by Master Crypt. She's the First Dead Girl and we've heard it's a shower scene. No surprise there, given her assets. Pics on the next page. Great to see her hard work paid off.

Chapter 5

The Carlisle Theater was not one of L.A.'s oldest or grandest theaters, and when the handle of the stage door came off in her hand, Selena knew why the rent had been so cheap. The structure dated from the 1930s, when the love affair with lavish Spanish architecture had vied with an equal adoration of art deco. In the case of the Carlisle, the Spanish influence had won, and it passed, inside and out, for a rundown theater in Barcelona. Her wonderfully picky art director had pointed out the externals where English and Spanglish both ruined the authenticity. By the time filming began, it would all be fixed.

Hammering on the door with the knob finally brought someone to open it. She picked her way through the bare-bones dressing room area on the lower level and up the narrow stairs to the wings. She could already hear the intonation of an audition underway, so she veered toward the seats, keeping out of the stage lights.

In spite of the dim lights over the seating, Selena recognized Mirah Zendoza's chunky outline, complete with white blouse and dark leggings. An abundance of glossy black hair and a flair for flamboyant jewelry and scarves usually made her a visual treat, and today was no exception with its collision of nautical prints in tie-dye hues.

She settled into what she hoped was a secure seat, though she had a feeling that the thinning red velvet was disintegrating into the back of her suit.

Mirah joined her, referring to a clipboard. "We've got most of the major speaking parts narrowed to two or three callbacks—sent back a lot of dreck. I'm not happy with that new Sinclair Agency. They didn't follow any of our specs, especially the emphasis on appearance of Spanish heritage. It's not my job to throw cold water on all those scrubbed young faces who should have never been sent in the first place."

"You have my permission to tell Sinclair you'll drop them if they don't get up to speed." Selena knew Mirah would have done it anyway. As a casting director, she suffered no fools—but then who in this business did? "You said you had something for me to review?"

"The two supporting roles I have really good feelings about. I have head shots and just wanted to know if you had strong feelings about the visual before I call them back for rehearsed readings."

Selena studied the glossies of the three young men as Mirah passed them over to her. They were similar enough, though one was too young for her taste, given the ruthless streak the character would eventually reveal. "Are you sure about this one?"

"Enough to want a scripted reading. He's older than he looks, and has an intriguing voice."

"Okay. Have you scheduled the next round?"

"Thursday. Here's the women."

After glancing at all three, Serena observed, "There was someone Kim arranged for. Did she make the cut?"

"Welles." Mirah tapped the middle photo. "Just saw her this morning. She was impressive."

Serena grimaced at the airbrushed, over-teased hair and excessive false eyelashes. "Honest?"

"She looks *nothing* like that. Scrape off three layers of goop. I know her agent—it's a typical result of the woman's advice on how to look. I gave Welles direction, then Pat fed her lines and I was looking at the ditzy little witch Georgette who was still in love with the guy. And she made me laugh."

"Cool. So I'll see them all on Thursday?" She studied the photograph of Gail Welles, trying to see past make-up that was all wrong. Her eyes were memorable, a striking opaque shade of green, almost jade. She wondered if the color, too, was the advice of her agent.

"I'll get their scripts delivered today." Mirah glanced at the stage as she rose, eyeing the next young hopeful, who was running through a few lines in hopes of a minor part. "I'll list out the small and bit parts and get it to Kim."

"Butler is supposed to sign his contract no later than Thursday. Where are we with the wife?"

Mirah named two actresses who were available, both of whom were strong enough, though she wasn't sure about their ability to face off with Hyde.

Before she could even speak, Mirah said, "Yeah, I know. Both a B and we've got an A-list star."

"Well, we can go more on the up front pay, and once it's confirmed that Hyde is the star, we'll have a lot more interest from some real star quality. No avoiding paying more then."

Mirah rose, clipboard clasped to her chest. "That's what I thought."

"Thanks. You are, as usual, a dream to work with."

"Likewise," she drawled, as she made her way back to the row where she'd been when Selena had arrived.

Back in the car, Selena took advantage of a half-hour's idle time to review a status update from Hong Kong, glad of her car's array of plug-ins and chargers when her netbook and phone both chirped battery warnings. Installing a solar charger for her electronics plugs had been worth every dime. As she attached the phone it rang and she tapped her headset.

"I screwed up," Kim said immediately. Her usually laid back tone was taut with anxiety. "You confirmed being available to glad hand for the big Getty donors. That's at five, for cocktails, in the private dining room, forty-fourth floor of the Fidelity building. Maxim Marshall himself is your host. I know you want to be there."

"Oh heck—I remember agreeing. Yes, I have to show. His five hundred thousand dollars bought that." It wasn't on her daily list of appointments, meaning Kim had forgotten to enter it.

"Margaret Rothschild just called to make sure you'd be there. I'm *so* sorry. If she hadn't called—"

"It's okay. I'm not dressed, though."

"There was an angel looking out for me, that's for sure. As for clothes, you've got time to stop in at Parchez. Tina has already pulled out some choices."

"Fantastic." As she turned her car in the direction of the Hollywood Freeway, Serena updated her on the discussion with Mirah. Kim assured her the script packets were ready to go as soon as she got the names.

Traffic hadn't geared up to its worst yet, and Serena made it to the fashion district just south of downtown in a decent amount of time. Ellen Spelman had originally recommended the shop to her, and the owner was a contract seamstress for two big name designers. For known clients like Selena, she was okayed to fit and sell dresses and jackets on their behalf, and Selena preferred the little storefront to the glitz of the posh Rodeo Drive stores. Within fifteen minutes of her arrival she had chosen a sheath in her signature blue and been stitched into it, and accepted the recommendation of Italian-made sandals with heels just high enough to draw a wince. Tina even had a loaner of a vintage choker and bracelet she could have Kim return tomorrow.

Only minutes later, at the Fidelity Building, she was greeted warmly by Maxim Marshall himself. Even if she hadn't passed muster it wouldn't have shown in his face. Captains of industry were usually far too mannered, and their relationship was purely one of mutual interest in the welfare of the museum. His insurance company was a major supporter, and his willingness to host the soiree in the opulent corporate dining room had brought out the other major donors. Next month, they would all be getting a new appeal for building funds. But first, cocktails and chat.

She was shaking hands with the owner of one of the local teams, hoping desperately she didn't have to recall which sport it was they played, when she plainly heard that throaty, beguiling voice say, "Maxim, you are looking more handsome than ever."

She didn't freeze up. She didn't squeeze the owner's hand to bits. She even managed to laugh at whatever it was he said.

It was only sixty seconds, at the most, before Jennifer said, "Lena, I had no idea you'd be here."

Selena didn't believe her. She absolutely did not believe the vivacious smile, the coy tip to the head, the warm hug. She believed Jennifer's eyes.

She was prey.

Gail's impetuous exit out the front door of the Lorelei Arms nearly knocked over a messenger who stood there scribbling on a note.

"Sorry."

The young man gave her a weary look. "Hey—can you set this inside? I can't leave it out here."

"Sure." Gail unlocked the front door, prepared to put the envelope on the communal table where they all dumped packages, but then she saw the return address. She blinked. "Hey, this is for me."

She signed his paper and, in spite of being late, tore the envelope open. And screamed.

The messenger turned back, alarmed. "Jeez, lady, what gives?"

"It's a *script*." A script, a real live script, okay not a whole script, just part, one scene at most, a big scene though, and it was

77

in a Ryan Productions independent film binding and it had her name written across the top and even when she shook it, it didn't evaporate.

It was a script.

"Whatever. I can say I knew you when."

She flashed him a smile and got one in return. "Welles. Gail Welles, don't forget."

She was late, again, and Betty wasn't nearly so forgiving, though being shown a real live script did ease her scolding somewhat. Gail threw herself into the work, knowing the job was one she couldn't risk, but there was a party going on in her stomach—every time she thought about the script, her tummy butterflies did the samba. Reading it on the bus had been surreal. She was in fact studying lines in what would someday be a movie.

The evening trade finally waned, but a large party of skateboarders arrived for milkshakes and sundaes, so she didn't notice the woman on whom she'd dumped the plate of food until she was sliding into the empty booth at the end of the counter.

Gail approached, but was waved off with a distant smile and, "I'm waiting for someone. Could you check back?"

She agreed and continued serving ice cream concoctions to the skateboarders. They were rowdy but polite, and tried to leave tips, though sometimes it was in an accumulation of nickels and pennies. It wasn't until one of them said, "Is that who I think it is?" that she realized the woman's expected company had arrived.

To her shock, she recognized Jennifer Lamont, dressed to the nines, sliding into the out-of-the-way booth. Dear lord, she hoped the seat was clean.

She arrived with water glasses in time to hear Lamont say, "This is a little public, don't you think?"

"We'll keep it short," the other woman said. "Coffee?"

"Sure."

Gail walked away with an order for two coffees. Lamont was gorgeous—she looked as good up close as she did on the big screen. Gail knew she could get a full *Miss Congeniality* makeover and never come close to Lamont's kind of sex appeal and oomph. Her regular customer, though, was pale and pinched, with no smile in sight. When Lamont's unmistakable laugh flowed across the diner, the other woman wasn't laughing with her.

As she went back with the coffees she realized that a customer in another booth was trying to take a surreptitious photo with her phone. Gail tried her best to get in the way, but she supposed Lamont was used to it. It was all quite fascinating. She wished she were a fly on the wall, in the worst way.

"You weren't going to take no for an answer, and I didn't want to make a scene." Serena kept a grip on her volume level, aware that the waitress had been listening to every word.

"There's no need for us to avoid each other, is there?" Jennifer put her hands in the middle of the table.

Selena wasn't taking up the offer to touch—the hug at the cocktail party had been bad enough. That she had to consciously not respond to the gesture annoyed her further. "And no reason to seek each other out either."

"Lena, darling, it's just that I can tell you're angry with me, and I don't want you to be."

"I'm sure you don't."

"Can you at least try?"

"Okay." Selena crossed her arms. "I'll try if you'll answer one question." Jennifer's raised eyebrows were agreement enough. "Why are you making contact now, after a year?"

She won't give me an honest answer, Selena thought. It's not in her to just admit what she wants. She has to finagle it out of me, because I am just part of the game of her life.

"I saw your name and thought it was time. I really am sorry about all the misunderstanding."

The waitress delivered their coffee, and Selena poured in far too much cream so she could drink some as quickly as possible and leave.

"Okay, I've heard your apology." Against her will, Selena felt some of her anger fade. Just some, but part of her knew that it was a good barrier to the other, unmistakable feelings that coiled in her darker places. She should have found someone else to sleep with by now, or the allure wouldn't be so powerful, maybe. "Did you really give a pile of money to the Getty or were you someone's guest?"

"Pile of money. I can afford that sort of thing, and it's good for my visibility, especially with the new marketing campaign rolling out for the DVD—billboards with my picture again."

"I'm so pleased for you." Selena took one more swallow of the coffee and got to her feet. "Time for me to head home. It's been a long day."

Jennifer was obviously trying to think of a way to get her to linger, but then she shrugged. "Until we meet again."

It sounded like a threat. Selena settled her handbag on her shoulder before she asked, "Where exactly did you see my name?"

Jennifer was startled by the question, perhaps, because without hesitation she answered, "You were hanging on Hyde Butler's arm, handsome devil that he is."

"Oh." She put a five on the table and walked away, her brain turning the comment over and over.

She was all of three steps from the diner door when she realized exactly what it was that Jennifer wanted.

"Turn around. Give me the full three-sixty." Regine ruffled the curls on Gail's brow. "You got your money's worth. It's a really good cut."

"Honest? This is after I've washed and styled it myself. It looks okay?" Gail consulted the full-length mirror on the back of her door again. It still didn't look like her, but she could tell it was a big improvement. Her hair had been thinned and shaped and now appeared to effortlessly fall across her forehead in light waves. Two extra shades of color had been layered in, eliminating what the stylist had called, "Blahsville."

"It looks really good. You wanted sophisticated, you got it." When Gail's stomach growled, Regine laughed. "I brought peanuts."

"To quote Aunt Charlie, you are such a nice girl. No higher praise." She helped herself to a palmful of the nuts. She would make it to work where she'd be able to grab a piece of toast at least. It really sucked that she was wearing three nights' worth of tips on her head, but it had to be done. She wanted to look like a professional tomorrow morning. "Thanks so much for doing lines with me."

"I want to be able to be your hanger-on groupie." Regine followed Gail to the little table where she examined the script. "*Barcelona*? I know I read something about that recently."

"The producer recruited Hyde Butler for the lead and Levi Hodges is supposed to be doing music. I Googled it yesterday."

"Wow—you *have* to get this."

"Believe me, I know."

"Are we going to share this copy?"

"I've got my lines mostly in my head now," Gail said. "I memorized them instead of eating the last three days."

"Cool." Regine got comfortable in the chair, adopting the same semi-bored attitude that most readers had. "Is there a particular part you wanted to work on?"

"I marked it. Basically, it's Georgette's big speech in this scene. But let's take it from the top so I can get into the rhythm of it."

"You got it." Regine crossed her ankles and launched into the first line.

For the next two hours, Gail paced, pored over the blocking, worried that she'd be ready to move when no set would be provided and then her delivery would be stymied by having to stand still. But if they provided a minimal set—in this case a kitchen—she'd be expected to show how she'd make Georgette chop vegetables and flex that knife so that Elgin and the audience grew nervous, wondering just who she might have stabbed in the past, or might stab in the future. It had been intimidating, too, to think that if she got so lucky as to get this part she might be speaking her lines opposite Hyde Butler.

"I really don't know what your *wife* has to do with this, Elgin.

It's not like your *wife* cares about anything but money. I love you. I can't stand to think of you being beholden to that *bitch*."

Regine burst out laughing as Gail timed each emphasis with a down stroke of the knife. She hoped the sound editor would give it a juicy crunch.

"I give you love, honey. I don't ask for anything back. But your *wife* calls and you go running. What's she doing in Barcelona, anyway? I thought she didn't know where you were? She's like a *tumor*. A big sucking growth." Chop and grind with the knife. "And you know what you do with tumors—I'll get it."

She tried a jerky, slightly hyper dash to a make-believe phone. Breathily, she said, "I'm sorry, Mr. Crawford's not in right now. Can I take a mess—I'll tell him right away, Mrs. Crawford. Of course. Right away." She dropped the pretend receiver into its pretend cradle, her lips pursed as she turned to Regine. "That was your *wife*." She meticulously cleaned the knife on the dish towel tucked at her waist.

Regine read, "Elgin beckons from the chair. Georgette goes to him, leaving the knife on the counter."

Gail wasn't sure if she should make Georgette's parting with the knife reluctant—the scene seemed to call for it. If she read it right, Elgin was going to end up with a knife in him, but she couldn't tell from the piece of the script she had if it was actually Georgette's. Which would be the point for the audience, she supposed.

"What do you think?" Gail plopped on the bed and gave Regine her full attention.

"They chose a good scene—you'll either have what they're looking for or you won't. In that last bit, it's clear she's been increasingly pissed off as the minutes go by, but don't overpunch the emphasis. It's funnier if the wife/knife thing sneaks up."

Gail nodded. "I think you're right. Thanks for doing this."

"We have to get a real agent, you know? This is a big chance and Madeline could have arranged for a videotape so you could study it."

"Madeline presumes we all have those resources."

82

"Not if we're her clients—that's a Catch-22."

"So what did you think of Georgette?"

"I got that she's not a bad person, but she's no angel either. She's wound tight and while she's thinking about using the knife, I don't think she will."

"Well, that's what I wanted to convey. Can we go through the opening again? I want to be extra confident with those first lines."

Regine was a good sport and by the time Gail was sitting on the bus, bound for the diner, most of the butterflies in her stomach had been replaced by hunger pangs. She had always been good at learning lines, remembering blocking, hitting her marks—the mechanics of acting. But so far, other than biased community theater audiences and her college drama teacher's enthusiasm, she had yet to be assured she could do more than that.

She wasn't at that place with Georgette where she separated from herself and lived inside Georgette's skin. But she could be. She wanted to be. She didn't care so much about applause and acclaim, she just wanted to work and feel that mysterious, wonderful energy as often as possible. She watched the weary landscape go by outside the grimy window, wishing it didn't match her day-to-day life. She would not let the tedium of the work outshine the magic of it.

"Kim, hang on. No—wait. Hang on—" Selena really didn't like having to go through the pounding the knob on the stage door routine again. Finally, someone let her in. To Kim, she said, "Would you please send the broker for this theater a firm request to fix the damn door?"

"I will. I'm sorry this morning got derailed, but—"

"It's not your fault. Shove something explosive up the caterer's backside and tell him that the director will get the remote control for it if they don't start seeing vegan items on the buffet. There's tofu in Hong Kong, one would think. It's bull that you and I are having to deal with this from the other side of the world."

"I know, I know. I just wanted to clear with you possibly

dumping them. I hate to threaten it if we can't follow through. If they're nasty I can also threaten to let them talk to Alan again. Believe me, after the last call, they don't want to talk to Alan about this."

"Make sure you have a back-up before you load up the explosives." She was about to stomp up the stairs when she realized she had to cool off. "I'm sorry."

"I know," Kim said immediately. "A picture of you and Jennifer all over Twitter was not the best way to wake up."

"I figured after nothing showed up the next day we'd managed to get away with it." She reined herself in. Kim knew all this. "If anyone else needs a royal chewing on, just send them to me, though. I'm all geared up for it."

She clicked off and tried to calm herself on the way up the stairs to the stage level. She hadn't told Kim that she thought Jennifer was angling for a part on this movie because Kim would never believe Jennifer hadn't been the one to get the photo out there. Maybe she had—though it wasn't the best photo in the world. It was obviously Jennifer, not in her most flattering pose, while she was pretty fuzzy and obscured by the well-focused shot of the waitress's backside. Just the sort of "caught in the act" photo that the blogosphere loved. She was late, and they were waiting on her. She hated keeping other people waiting. They had jobs, so did she. She hoped they all knew her well enough that they didn't see it as some kind of power play.

Mirah was waiting in the wings for her. "We're ready to go, but nobody's antsy. Do you want some water?"

She gave Selena the unopened bottle with a look that said it wasn't really a question. The air outside was thick and unpleasant already, with the kind of smog that seemed to stick to her skin. She drank dutifully, and meant it when she said, "Thanks. I really did need that."

She followed Mirah out onto the stage, waved at the smattering of applause. "Sorry, everybody."

With no further ado, Mirah called out the name of one of the male hopefuls. Selena settled next to the screenwriter, Delilah

Connor, as the house lights were dimmed.

"About time you got your lazy ass here," Delilah said under her breath.

"Love you right back." Selena listened as the actor answered a few questions about his background. The set was minimal—a table for a desk. The few props that he would need, a folding chair he was supposed to move, but wouldn't ever sit in. Mirah, in spite of time pressure, liked to make everyone comfortable, so she had one man and one woman to read the lines so that there was more clarity who was speaking without having to always give the tag. The scene would flow so much easier and be a better evaluation.

Midway, Selena just wasn't loving the guy. She glanced at Delilah and was reassured to see a tiny frown. Candidate two, however, James Sherman, brought something more, particularly a disarming smile. But behind it was the sharp impression that the charming curl of the lip would become a snarl if crossed. That was definitely more like it. He was also flat-out pretty, which could be a great contrast with Hyde's rugged hypermasculine features. Selena had the sudden thought of adding a rakish scar to the model-perfect face and liked that even more. Delilah was nodding.

They conferred after the third candidate had come and gone, and Sherman quickly become the front runner to be called back for a full reading with all the principals. One major decision made today. Mirah went into the wings to tell Sherman the happy news and send the other two on their way while Selena finished the bottle of water. She didn't let herself think about Jennifer, though she expected another call from her soon. News of Hyde Butler's signed contract for *Barcelona* would break this afternoon.

After a break and a little bit of restaging to make the table into a kitchen counter and add a prop knife and stalks of celery, the three supporting female parts started to arrive, all on time. Unfortunately, the first two were obviously not good fits, evident almost from the start. One Selena thought would wash out to nothing in any scene with Hyde—even her voice was nondescript.

She wondered what Mirah had seen in her. The second flubbed her lines a couple of times, then steadied. Selena liked the voice, and visually she was stronger, but it wasn't what she'd hoped. Trevor's protégé, the Welles woman, was last. Though Trevor hadn't been wrong yet, she didn't hold out much hope.

She did a double take when she got a good look at her. Trevor had been right—her head shot was horrible. It didn't look like her at all. The actress on stage was more confidently sophisticated than that, and had a quiet patience as she listened to Mirah's minimal direction. The photo made her look bubbly and vivacious, but from this distance Selena wasn't getting any of that kind of energy. She was somewhat bony, not the physique of the typical starlet at all, but when she smiled at something Mirah said, there was a pop of energy that kept Selena's eyes on her.

At least she was tall—that mattered with Hyde. Selena sighed, expecting she'd be back in a few days to look at more choices. Welles was attractive in an unusual way, and Alan was right, she had a Face. But Hyde Butler would mow right over her.

The first few lines went well, though, and the way Welles changed her demeanor and stance in character was a good start. Still, she didn't have much in the way of presence, though with each line it did grow.

She wasn't sure when she stopped thinking of Welles as Candidate Three and instead saw her as Georgette. Maybe when she punctuated a scathing comeback with a loud bite into some celery, then adroitly swallowed it so it didn't interfere with her continued delivery. Or when the knife was planted, point down, into the table and quivered there as she went to answer the phone. For those few minutes, there was no resemblance to the actress who'd nodded and spoken clearly but quietly, and Georgette, who spoke so sickly-sweet to her lover's estranged, troublesome wife.

She found herself smiling and nodding. Two minutes ago she wouldn't have thought Welles had a chance of exuding enough personality to convince an audience she could keep a man like Hyde Butler interested. She wasn't in the dictionary under

Beauty, but oddly enough, might be found under *Alluring*. It was hard to stop watching her.

Delilah whispered, "She's a winner."

"Yeah—total unknown, too. I'd like to see both the male and female supporting candidates tested against Butler. We'll do that wherever is convenient for him."

When the scene was over, Mirah asked Welles to join the other hopefuls back in the wings, and she met Selena in the theater aisle. "Gail Welles—absolutely. That was a fine piece of work. She blew the stage direction on the knife, but I actually liked what she did with it."

Delilah was nodding. "It's all timing, but I agree. With the right lighting, her knife is a great red herring later."

Mirah went to the wings to tell the candidates the good and bad news, and Selena was certainly pleased that her low expectations had been proven wrong.

She was about to take her leave when Delilah said, "I'm not sure I should tell you this, but I had the most friendly phone call from your ex."

Selena stiffened. "Oh really?"

"We're best friends, didn't you know? I'm guessing it's about the wife's part."

Delilah's quicker on the uptake than I am if she got that after one call, Selena thought. "And?"

"How would you feel about that? I saw the photo of the two of you that's going around today."

Selena thought if she started telling Delilah how she felt about it, she wouldn't stop. "We had some old business to go over. You can see her handling it?"

"Lamont is more than eye candy, though eye candy is her strong suit. I think you'd agree it's not a stretch part for her."

Conniving, lying, manipulative, Black Widow… "No, it's not a stretch."

Mirah joined them. "Well, that's done. Welles was a nice surprise. After this picture, I'm casting a screwball comedy and she could work out in a couple of places."

Selena nodded.

"For what the screenwriter's opinion is worth, which I know is not much," Delilah said in her best diplomatic tone, "she seemed perfect to me. How would you feel about her opposite Jennifer Lamont as the wife?"

Mirah gave Selena a direct look. Selena shrugged.

"I had a call from Lamont's agent this weekend," Mirah admitted. "She wants the part. Only if Butler signs, I'm guessing."

"He's signing at lunch."

"Then we'd have her. Frankly…she's a good foil for Butler."

Another glance at Selena, who offered again, "We just had some old business to discuss over coffee. There's no emotional entanglement, so I want to hear your opinions."

Delilah, who was sometimes too darned good at what she did, persisted. "Well, what do we think of Lamont in the two scenes with Welles as Georgette?"

Mirah grinned. "Okay—that works even better. They'd be spitting jealousy almost on a purely chemical basis. You've got glamour meets brains. Those scenes ought to sing."

Selena, wishing her intellect didn't agree with them and her heart would shut up, carefully said, "I don't want the gossip mill about the two of us and the past to outshine the picture. The past isn't relevant. I can see how it might work, but let's say I'm recusing myself on this one. If she gets the part, she earned it from you two. I don't want anyone saying otherwise about any actor related to a Ryan film."

She didn't say what she really wanted to, that Jennifer could use someone else's back this time.

Both women nodded. Mirah said, "Fair enough. I'll get back to her agent. If we're setting up tests with Butler for Sherman and Welles, then we might as well bring in Lamont then and make a very quick decision."

Selena nodded and a few minutes later was headed to the backstage door. She didn't want Jennifer on this picture, and she didn't want to spend any time with her. But she was the first person to tell everyone else that their personal issues with anyone had nothing to do with making a good movie. She was hoist on her own petard, whatever the hell a petard was. Damn and damn, she owned the company. Couldn't she just have a temper tantrum for once and get her way?

She was nearly to her car before she realized she hadn't taken in any of her surroundings, and Deets, the security guru, would smack her for it. Still, there was no one around and she got inside safely. She glanced to check all was clear, waited for a bus, then pulled out.

By the time she reached the corner the bus was stopped there, disgorging passengers. As she waited for it to move on, she realized she was staring at an ad for the DVD release of Jennifer's last picture. There was her ex, larger-than-life, gazing lovingly at her co-star. Bloody hell, that thing would be all over town. Right then Selena would have paid people to Sharpie moustaches over Jennifer's full, red lips.

The bus pulled away and she realized that the actress— Welles—was sitting on the bench. Not just sitting, she was crying. She nearly stopped to ask if she was okay, though the woman had no reason to know her. But Welles mopped at her face and a smile broke through. A dozen feet away, tinted window glass separating them, Selena still found it difficult to tear her gaze away.

She finally turned the corner and her phone rang. The display confirmed it was Jennifer. To hell with actors, she thought. To hell with the unmistakable feeling south of her stomach when she saw Jennifer's name. Her finger hovered over *Talk* and wouldn't move over to *Ignore*. Thankfully, after one more ring, the call went to voicemail.

Buzztastic # #

After that cozy hope-nobody-sees-us photo of Jennifer Lamont and her ex, do we wonder if Jennifer is swinging back? Bi-bi-baby? As usual, nobody at Ryan wants to confirm it's their boss in the pic, but S.R. is the only sapphist in J.L.'s past that we know about so far. Anyone have pics otherwise? We'd love to see them! Maybe it's all business.

Big rumors that our favorite hunk Hyde Butler has signed with Ryan for a picture after all. Maybe coffee was a casting call for Lamont? Anyone out there recognize the eatery?

Meanwhile, we've got explosive new photos from Mr. Late Night's latest paramour. He's found every frumpy producer-wannabe in the business! Nice to know even chubby girls can get ahead the good old-fashioned way of sleeping with the boss.

Chapter 6

"Be sure you dress appropriately." Madeline was talking to Gail in a slow, patient tone, as if Gail were two. "Ryan Productions never pulls people in just to put pressure on someone else, so it's possible you're a serious contender."

Gail dabbed at her blotchy make-up. The last hour had been unreal and the call to her agent was adding to the sick feeling in her stomach. She wished Madeline didn't sound so uncertain about her chances. "The casting director was very clear that they're not trotting me out to get someone else to hurry up and sign on, and that if I hadn't yet brought my A game, I had to if I wanted the part."

"So keep running your lines and if you need an outfit, I can arrange an advance."

As if Gail would take Madeline's advice on how to prep. She had been given two more scenes to memorize for the next screening, but she didn't want to get stale. Madeline hadn't shown much expertise on anything but the most basic of her duties as an agent. Annoyed that the offer of an advance hadn't come last week when she could have used even a hundred bucks, she said, "I can't really afford debt. I'd rather not."

"But you *do* have something to wear that says you're serious, right?"

"Yes," she said, though she wasn't actually sure. She had been planning to stick with her one pair of designer label jeans with worn-to-the-point-of-chic cowboy boots and plain button-up white blouse. Regine had a suede jacket that would be too big at the bust, but would get her in the room and then she'd take it off. She was the scruffy girlfriend Georgette, after all. Let whoever was playing the pampered wife do the haute couture thing. After talking to the other hopefuls in the wings while they had waited, it had been clear that another agent might have gotten her more auditions and given her better guidance than Madeline had, so she also didn't want to owe Madeline more than she already did, contractually or morally. "I'll be fine."

After she got Madeline off the line, she thoroughly scrubbed her face free of the careful make-up she'd applied per the advice of several makeover shows. Not having waterproof mascara had been a mistake. Good thing the part hadn't asked for tears. Bawling like a baby afterward had left her a huge mess.

Sitting on the bus bench, it had all become overwhelming. She had tried to call Aunt Charlie to tell her she'd made it to the next level and would meet a movie star even her bridge friends had heard of, but her throat had closed up. The three years of wondering if she was actually worth anything might be over. So she'd sat on the bench and cried like a nervous schoolgirl finally asked out to a prom.

It hadn't helped that in the midst of her tears she'd seen one of the people involved in the film come out of the theater. From the stage, with the house lights down, she hadn't been able to make out clearly the scattering of people watching the auditions. Still, the woman's emergence from the same side alley Gail had used, the tailored suit, elegant bearing and bulging satchel all added up to one of the producers. Gail had tried to avert her face while the woman got in her car and drove away.

Remembering the moment, it played back in her mind in super-digital high definition. She dashed away the tears and tried to look as if she was at a park watching puppies play, not a smelly bus bench. The car approached, slowing as a bus paused at the stop.

"Don't look," she said to herself. But she did, a quick glance, immediately grateful that the other woman was fixated on the back of the bus. So she took a good, long look, and the smell of chicken and mayonnaise washed over her, mixing with diesel fumes. She could see the relish and oil pooling out in the woman's lap and for a moment she had thought she might be sick.

She wasn't going to tell Madeline that one of the people making decisions about her future had recently been wearing a plate of food, courtesy of Gail's clumsy feet. When the woman recognized Gail, that could be the end of all her hopes, and her face plant into the woman's lap was all she could think about.

Whoever had said that Luck was a Bitch-Goddess was right, though. Of all the people to have done that to, she had to pick a producer that Luck then put back in her path. It was even possible that the woman was Selena Ryan herself. It made sense. Ryan Productions was small, but they made films with clout. If the Hollywood bloggers were right, and Hyde Butler was involved, then Ryan herself might be the producer.

Mascara finally out of her eyes, she used her phone's Internet connection to find a picture of Ryan. The display wasn't very clear, but she easily recognized the covert photo of Jennifer Lamont at the diner. She was never going to tell anyone that was her butt, big as a planet, in the foreground. Twitterland was sure the other woman was Ryan. So yep, she'd dumped food on one of the female movers and shakers in Hollywood. One of the *lesbian* movers and shakers. She may have killed her own career before she even had one.

She thumbed through a lot of the outright gossip about the

two women, who apparently had been an item, something that had been below Gail's radar. Some tweets were saying there was a motel next to the restaurant, not true, and Ryan had been tonsil swiping Lamont when they'd left, also not true.

Her stomach, which had been pumping out butterflies of excitement for the last two days, was queasy with simple terror. She could earn the part and lose it over chicken and mayonnaise.

Selena waited until Alan had sent an intern on an errand of delivering make-nice gifts to a director she was courting for a future project before handing him two scripts she'd screened last night. "One for you, one for Kim. Doesn't matter to me which of you takes which."

Alan neatly penciled his initials on the top one and Kim's the second before looking expectantly at her again. "And?"

"Nice work on the catering brouhaha in Hong Kong."

"Kim stepped in and smoothed all the feathers. I'm sorry to say I was past trying to be reasonable."

"I'm sorry I missed it." She was, too. When Alan got angry his tie would go askew, and it was the most mussed she ever saw him. "I'm happy your good-cop, bad-cop routine gets results."

He cracked a smile. "I heard her say to the owner that if they couldn't come to an agreement he'd have to talk to me again and after that it was all smiles and how can we make this right. Today, finally, two vegan entrees, imagine that. They found tofu in Hong Kong at last."

"It's a murr-acle," Selena drawled. She headed to her office, glad to still be in her casual jeans and soft, worn, fitted T-shirt. With the afternoon and early evening devoted to the casting rush with Hyde, she had a mountain of work to plow through, but nobody she had to impress with the full Selena Ryan Productions façade until then.

She was spread out on the sofa in her office, hip-deep in paperwork, when Kim knocking on the doorjamb got her attention. She realized she'd probably been there a while when an emphasis of bangle bracelets was added. And she was jangling her car keys in the pocket of her smartly tailored linen pants, looking like a woman with better things to do than knock and wait.

"Sorry. What's up?"

"I need to run over to pay a college application fee for Sara. I put it off too long and it's today or she misses the deadline. She told me she'd taken care of it, but…"

"So I'll see you at the audition?" Selena glanced at the clock—sure enough, it was approaching time to get showered and changed and make the traffic-challenging drive to Mirah's central casting offices, where all parties had agreed to meet.

"Yes, and I should have plenty of time to make it there and back to Mirah's. I'm going to put all the contract copies in your car so they're there in case Mirah wants to review something with you before I get there."

"Got it. Drive safe."

She went back to her paperwork for another eighteen minutes, then hurried up to the house bedroom to get ready.

Given the rising heat of impending summer, she would have opted for tailored trousers and a casual jacket, but facing Jennifer required careful attire. Plus she had to make it clear to everyone that she and Jennifer were *not* a couple. That meant very serious dressing. She started with her favorite blue because it made her feel comfortable, but passed over everything until she came to a complete power suit with the tailored narrow lines she wore to meetings with studio accountants. She mulled over a pair of Prada pumps that had been added to the closet only yesterday. Shoes, in Kim's opinion, mended almost any fashion faux pas. She had a point, Selena thought, as she stepped into the three-inch heels. The outfit went from power player to kick-your-ass. Knowing Kim, she'd probably bought them after Jennifer's visit with exactly that message in mind.

Mirah's Century City offices were humming with activity. Because Mirah took on only small to medium projects, the office was nearly always crowded with groups of hopefuls for quick casting calls. She wasn't surprised to see actors for some other project lining one wall. Many looked up eagerly, then away with disappointment. She wondered if that meant Hyde had already arrived. If so, she was a definite anticlimax.

She crossed the office and exchanged greetings with the receptionist, who pressed the door release so Selena could access the elevator lobby. Just as she pressed the call button, the door release sounded again and she recognized Gail Welles. Since Welles had no reason to know her yet she gave only a vague nod. Close-up she still wasn't sure if the opaque green of her eyes was real or contact lenses. A tickle of memory poked at her brain and it wasn't from the theater. Maybe some party? If they'd met before there had definitely been people around.

Somewhere between the second and third floors, with two more to go, Welles suddenly said, "You probably don't recognize me. I might as well just face the music."

Selena gave her a distant lifted-eyebrow look. So they had met before. Nothing was coming to her yet, though.

"I'm the waitress who dropped that food in your lap. If that's going to make a difference, then I figured I'd better just say something now and save everyone some bother. I'll leave if you say so."

Selena blinked. This was the woman she'd thought scrawny? It couldn't be. "You've changed your hair."

Welles nodded. "For the audition."

She'd also been the waitress when the photo of her and Jennifer had been taken. Had she taken it? No, be reasonable, she chided herself. She was in the photo. She couldn't have taken it. She hoped her face didn't look as flummoxed as she felt, though. Belatedly, she said, "That I know you from that other situation will have no bearing on the decision. It's forgotten."

"Thank you."

The doors opened and Welles waited for Selena to exit first, which was good because she was fighting down a powerful blush. She felt foolish for having missed it because Alan was right, she had a Face. She hadn't noticed the unusual eyes in the diner, and there was a grace to the way Actress Welles moved that Waitress Welles lacked. She supposed that if she'd met Welles in a production office she'd have remembered different things about her, like the jade-tinted eyes. The ill-fitting uniform didn't do justice to those long legs and strong shoulders. The waitress hadn't pinged her gaydar either, at least not much, but Actress Welles would have, even if she hadn't already known she was gay courtesy of Trevor.

One of life's little weirdnesses. Oh well, if the food-in-the-lap had been a ploy, it had nearly backfired—after all, she could have easily decided to be a bitch about it. Maybe it hadn't been a ploy, though. Maybe Welles was a better actress than she was a waitress. But now there were *two* potential actresses on the project with a prior history. Terrific.

She put Welles out of her head when she entered the large conference room, but she had a moment of panic wondering if Jennifer would recognize her. That wasn't likely—Jennifer was no more likely to take detailed note of a waitress's features than Selena was.

Jennifer was in one of her deadly jeans and slinky top combinations. The boat-necked blouse was the type that threatened to slide off one shoulder. The shade of rose was vibrant under the fluorescent lights, but didn't diminish the impact of her dark, glossy hair and bronze eyes one bit. She was, top of her head to the tips of her pink-tipped toes, a walking enticement to sin.

Under the watchful eye of Jennifer's agent, a nebbish fellow Selena respected as an agent, they exchanged hugs that Selena made sure left plenty of air between them. She shook off a shiver as the scent of Jennifer's subtle perfume filled her head.

Damn it all, Jennifer was *perfect* for the wife.

Welles entered and Selena found herself watching her, still curious. She introduced herself to Jennifer, who was polite in an appropriately distant way. Welles took it in stride, introducing herself to the next nearest person. She smiled and Selena almost smiled herself. There was something fascinating about the way the woman's face changed as she talked. Alan was right, every emotion was right there on the surface.

Jennifer was studying Welles—that was typical of her. Any female actress in her sphere was either an ally or a threat. There was no sign of recognition, though, and if Gail was smart she'd keep it that way. No reason for Jennifer—or anyone—to know she and Selena had already met. Nobody deserved the kind of innuendo that was so commonplace in the blogosphere—nobody except maybe that Weston girl.

She reluctantly admitted to herself that there was chemistry in the contrast between Gail's sharp edges and Jennifer's curves. This would be a *very* interesting reading.

She made the rounds to greet the assembled directors and assistants. She was chatting with the costume designer when Hyde and BeBe arrived. The flurry of sweetie-darling air kisses required some time to get through, but the moment James Sherman and his agent came in, Mirah called everyone to business.

"Thank you, let's get started. I hope everybody had a chance to meet everybody. Just in case, I'm Mirah Zendoza, the casting director. Our screenwriter, Delilah Connor, couldn't be here, but we've got Michael Story, the art director and Lee Lewis, the costume designer." She indicated each of the leads in their various areas, leaving Director Eddie Lynch to last. "Eddie's simply one of the best in independent film today. We're going to read three full scenes, so if the actors will take their seats, we can give it a go."

The four actors sat down on the far side of the conference table, scripts in front of them, water handy. If it hadn't been a setting that came with their chosen profession, Selena would have pitied them the formality of it. No props to play with, just the array of producers, directors and assistants on the other side, eyeing them with visions of posters and lighting, costuming and set design in their own heads. Probably disconcerting was Eddie Lynch's unblinking regard. He preferred an organic approach and wouldn't say a word until after he'd seen the product of Mirah's mixing of this group of people and turning them loose on these particular scenes.

By the time the little quiet fell before the first line, Selena's heart was beating hard. Some of it was simply being near Jennifer, she could admit that. Her remaining anger and all-too vivid memories of their passion were only part of the reason. Lamont and Butler were a powerhouse combination. They were visually riveting, and now she worried they would be too distracting and overpower the film itself. That left poor Sherman and Welles with the unenviable jobs of trying to bring adequate attention to their own lines without having to scream "look at me" as they did it.

It was plain in Jennifer's eyes—at least to Selena—that she knew this part would move her from the B-list to the A-list. She was just about there anyway, and a solid dramatic performance opposite a bona fide A-lister would cement her status. Butler looked appropriately smitten, but had been equally charming to the other actors. Sherman looked like he was trying not to throw up and Welles wasn't far behind him.

Mirah was good at her work. She started Welles and Sherman in a scene they had together, and the actors' voices steadied. When Hyde joined them at the end of the scene, he had found a blasé weariness that didn't take away from Sherman's obvious malcontent and Welles' quirky adoration mixed with desperation.

After the next scene, Selena's heart rate came down a little, and a deeply pleased flush threatened to take over. Hyde was slightly slouched, his gestures restrained, and with each moment he became more and more a man who ought to have had all he wanted from life but time and again found himself frustrated. It was good work, the kind of subtlety she had suspected he could bring to a role.

She had to hand it to Jennifer, as well. She had toned down the star power, only letting it flare as called for in the script. When she turned it back on, she dazzled and Hyde let his bemusement show. Selena hoped the look on his face wasn't how she looked when Jennifer got under her skin. Then Welles' brought in the envy and jealousy at just the right degree, leaving Sherman to fade to the background, sufficiently conniving to create a sense of a wild card everyone was failing to note.

It worked, it all worked. Or close enough that with rehearsal, direction, costumes, lights, art direction, sound effects, music and editing it would work. She thought of several notes she wanted to leave for the director and was grateful when the door opened and Kim slipped in, looking poised, though Selena could tell she was annoyed at being late. She was going to be working her ass off on the picture, so she deserved to see it birthed.

Mirah brought her back to the room with, "Let's do one last scene. Page forty-two."

Hyde grinned. "Am I finally going to get to kiss someone?"

"Behave," Mirah admonished.

Welles, who had yet to utter anything that wasn't in the script, said quietly, "I'll want practice at that."

"Flatterer." Hyde gave her a sidelong look.

"No, just a gay girl. I'm not used to five o'clock shadow."

After a scant pause Hyde laughed and Selena thought his amusement was genuine. "Is this where I swagger and say I'll convert you?"

Welles, with a lift to her lashes that was at once coy and sarcastic, said, "If anyone could, it would of course be you."

Jennifer, who had watched the exchange with cool detachment, shifted in her chair. "I think you'd want to kiss your wife, darling."

"Oh, I do, beautiful Jennifer, I do."

"Fine, nobody wants to kiss me." Sherman averted his face with a pout.

"We've had our fun now," Mirah said firmly. "Page forty-two, please."

Kim scrawled, "This is great!" and Selena nodded agreement. She kept her expression as aloof as possible, too aware that Jennifer was continually trying to make eye contact. Just because Jennifer didn't care if everyone thought she got parts by sleeping with people didn't mean *she* wanted to be thought of as someone who could be manipulated that way. How can someone trust you'll deal fairly with them if they think someone you slept with is always going to win? Hyde Butler had signed on to this project because of her reputation. She had watched a lot of lowlife operators make comfortable livings when she had been struggling every day to pay the bills and get a film out the door. Now her refusal to do it their way had finally given back big dividends. She was not going to let anyone in this room think anything about her had changed just because Jennifer was practically leering. Damn her.

Once again, she'd lost the joy of what was happening right in front of her, the magic of actors finding synergy, the crew looking for all the ways to make it work on the screen, and all because the business side was ugly and people like Jennifer Lamont dabbled in the mud and danced away clean as a whistle.

In lieu of ignoring Jennifer, she focused on Gail Welles. At least as far as she knew, Welles was not a conniving starlet. Maybe she had just dropped the plate. One thing was for certain—the girl could act. With each sentence the character of Georgette sharpened and defined. Her vocal shading grew increasingly subtle. Maybe, on top of having a Hyde Butler movie to give the public, she also had a newcomer worth enjoying. That was a good thing. She realized she was smiling, and summoned her aloof face again.

The last scene worked as well as the others, drawing genuine laughter from the assistants and agents. Even Eddie Lynch smiled.

When they were done, BeBe gushed, "Hyde, you are a genuine star," as she took Mirah by the arm, no doubt suggesting that before any decisions were made Hyde—meaning BeBe—had to give her opinion.

Her suspicion was confirmed when Mirah said quite clearly, "Selena, Eddie and I will make a few decisions the moment we get some time alone." She nodded at the door and the other directors and their assistants took the hint.

As they filed out, Hyde said, "For what it's worth, I'm happy with the ways things are shapin' up."

BeBe gave a vexed sigh, but unleashed a series of air kisses. Welles, with no agent to make assurances and pitches on her part as she left, merely shook hands with her fellow actors, then Mirah and last Selena. "Thank you for this opportunity."

"Your work was excellent," Selena told her honestly, liking the warmth and firmness of her handshake and the steady eye contact, nothing like Jennifer's sidelong glances. How could she have not noticed the waitress's unusual eyes? They talked as loudly as her voice, right now edged with excitement and anxiety. Maybe that color wasn't real, though up close she didn't see any signs of tinted lenses. "And you'll hear shortly which direction we're going."

When Selena, Eddie, Kim and Mirah were finally alone, Mirah said, "So, Eddie, what do you think? Can you work with that group?"

Eddie hadn't moved from his chair, and Selena had learned over the years of their collaborations not to let his stillness bother her. He'd move when he had reason to. "They're a bottle of nitroglycerin. Shake it wrong and it'll explode."

"Are you saying you can't shake it right?" Selena leaned against the conference table.

"I didn't say that." Eddie looked up, his expression mutating ever so slightly toward a smile. "I'm only warning about the potential. The two supporters are Mirah's usual fine work."

"Thank you." Mirah wearily sank down into a chair. "Sherman has stage credits that I respect, but I can't really take credit for Welles. She was a referral, and if you ask me, a gift from the gods. I think we're done casting the principles, then. Lamont is going to cost, but she'll sign anything reasonable. Her agent won't fuss—they both know what she gets is way more than mere money."

Kim ran her stylus under the beads of her cornrows, a habit she had when excited. Her grin was wide as she quickly tapped on her Blackberry. "I was getting goose bumps even though she's not on my favorite people list. But she works for this part. It's practically typecasting."

"You can work with her?" Selena knew perfectly well Kim's feelings about Jennifer.

"If you can, I can," Kim said. For a moment, all of the style and aplomb that Kim had crafted for dealing with the industry during the years she'd worked for Selena disappeared and she was just a friend, talking woman-to-woman. "But you only have to say the word and her name will never cross my lips again."

Selena loved watching a production come together, but this one would be spoiled by having to steel herself to spend time with Jennifer. Maybe it would get easier, if only Jennifer would direct the coy sex kitten act at someone else, now that she had what she wanted. She had to remember, too, that she had a unique perspective on Jennifer Lamont, but her growing number of fans saw her exactly the way her agent and publicist wanted her to be seen.

She gave Kim what was probably an unconvincing nonchalant smile of thanks. Glancing at the others, she said, "So at this point, all we have to do is linger long enough to make it look like we actually had to talk it over."

"I could order in dinner," Mirah said.

"I'd like to review the shooting schedule," Eddie said, "and finalize the plans for local hires in Spain."

As they discussed their next steps and devoured a few sandwiches and sodas, Selena realized she was surrounded by people who loved the movies as much as she did. If she stayed focused on the good, and stopped obsessing about the pettiness of some, she'd be better off. Gail Welles flitted through her thoughts and she smiled to herself, picturing both the confident actress flirting with Hyde as well as the waitress trying to scrub mayonnaise out of her hair.

Her resolve was tested by having to ignore not one, but two calls from Jennifer before she reached home. She did not want to know what Jennifer was after now.

Gail was winding her apron around her waist when her cell phone buzzed. She wasn't quite on the clock, though Friday evening traffic in the diner was already heavy. Since she'd been glued to her phone for the past twenty-four hours, hoping for some kind of word on the part, she fished it out of her pocket and checked.

It was Madeline. She steeled herself for disappointment and ducked into the kitchen to answer.

"I just got a package for you from Ryan Productions. You're being offered the part of Georgette in this movie—"

"No way."

"Would I make this up? You have to decide by noon Monday—"

"Yes."

"I haven't even read the contract yet."

"I would do it for free." She couldn't believe she sounded so calm with her heart was beating so hard she could barely hold onto the phone.

"Nonsense." Madeline sounded annoyed.

"I'll be in scenes with Hyde Butler." *I'll be in scenes with Hyde Butler*.

There was a silence and Gail was aware of the clanging of pots and pans behind her. She shifted to get out of the doorway.

"I wasn't aware he was a principal."

Had Madeline even tried Google? "Well, I'm very aware of it. Hyde Butler and Jennifer Lamont. I read with them."

Madeline's tone was growing warmer by the moment. "In that case, they're not paying you nearly enough. Ryan Productions has a rep for being fair, so you'll get the backend promised share of revenues, but they're not offering much more than SAG scale for the part itself."

The enormity of the moment sunk in, all at once. She had gotten the part, a great big *beautiful* part, with two big name stars. She had *earned* it damn near on her own. She wasn't going to lose it now.

Her voice didn't sound the least bit like a nice girl from Iowa. "Don't mess this up for me. I'll sign the deal as offered."

"But Gail, I know I can get you more."

"But you've just said they're fair, so how much more could you get before they think I'm a pain in the ass and go with someone else?"

"It's my job to get the best for you. I'll read the contract over carefully and advise you on whether it's a good deal. I already think the compensation is too low."

Trying hard to keep her volume down, Gail said, "I want to read the contract myself. And then I'll decide if I'm going to sign it."

Madeline sounded offended. "You have to let me do my job."

Maybe it was the accumulated three years of anxiety and frustration, or maybe comparing notes with the other auditioning actors. Maybe it was Selena Ryan herself and the casting director's cut-to-the-chase style. When she'd arrived last night she hadn't at first realized she was the only actor whose agent wasn't there, and only now did she feel the sting of humiliation that Madeline hadn't made the effort. Ryan Productions was no lightweight outfit. If Madeline had done even the slightest amount of research, she would have known that Hyde Butler was linked to the movie.

"You know," she said firmly, "it's late for you to start acting like an agent. You sent me on that audition without even checking out the production. So here's the bottom line. I can't afford to take a risk. I will listen to your advice but I'm making this decision. If you can't live with that, I'm getting new representation."

After a short silence, Madeline said, "I'm not accustomed to being lectured by a newcomer—"

"I've been your client for three years."

"If you'll calm down, I'm sure we can work this out."

"I'm perfectly calm." Gail realized she was, at least in that moment. "I can come by first thing Monday morning. I'm willing to hand-carry the contract to them, too. I want this part."

"I want you to have it too. I can see you at nine."

"Thank you, Madeline. I'll be there."

She stood in the doorway for a moment, her stomach about to

turn inside out. It really didn't matter what Madeline did. She'd go right around her and sign anything she had to for that part. Telling herself to take control, she looked up the phone number for Ryan Productions, wracking her brain for the name of the nice assistant who had arrived late. Stylish-to-the-last-degree black woman, lively eyes and smile… Katie, Kelly…

"May I speak to Kim, please? We met yesterday at the audition reading for *Barcelona*."

Her guess was rewarded by a brisk voice coming on the line. "This is Kim."

"This is Gail Welles. I'm sorry to call so late in your day. I just wanted to say that I just heard that you're offering me the part, and I will work out any detail necessary to make it happen."

The tone grew much warmer and Gail could hear a smile. "That's welcome news. I thought I'd have heard from your agent earlier today, so was wondering if there was some kind of problem."

How long had that contract been sitting on Madeline's desk before she'd even deigned to call Gail? "No problem at all. The signed documents will be in your hand if I have to walk there myself to deliver them."

"I'm looking forward to working with you then. As soon as everyone is on board we'll have a schedule for rehearsals and the local and Spain shoot schedules."

Spain…she was going to Spain? Good thing her passport was up-to-date. She thanked Kim for her time and hung up, feeling dizzy.

"Whenever you're ready to join us, Gail," Betty called.

Gail tried to snap out of her stupor, but she really thought she might faint.

Angel paused, plates lining both arms. "Are you okay? Because if you are, I could really use some help."

"I got a part."

"Great. I've got five tables waiting."

"I've got a part in a Hyde Butler movie."

"Okay, that's cool. Very cool." Angel paused. "Betty! Gail's gonna be a star!"

"Sure, kid." Betty left the counter with her customers-are-waiting look.

"A Hyde Butler movie."

"Really?" Betty gave Gail a searching glance, her expression mindful of a mother hen. "Honest? You get to speak lines and everything?"

"More than just speaking lines. I'm his wacky girlfriend. Jennifer Lamont is his wife." Gail still didn't believe it. She recognized this detached feeling as shock. Not as bad as when her parents had died. Strange to find out that it was sort of the same feeling when something really fantastic happened.

"Thanks for giving me time off yesterday," she added belatedly.

Betty waved her to work. "Be kind to me in your memoir."

"Count on it," Gail promised.

She tried to get into the rhythm of the dinner service, looking for the tables where no one yet had water and menus. At her first break she made the only phone call that mattered.

"I know it's late Aunt Charlie, but I've got good news."

"I was just about to take out my teeth," she said. "The moment the phone rang I knew it would be important."

"I got the part. I'm going to be in *Barcelona* starring Hyde Butler and Jennifer Lamont. I'm his girlfriend. It's a big part—not a star, but a big part."

"Oh, child." Aunt Charlie's breath caught. "I knew if you only got a chance, it would be fine. I can die happy now."

"Don't you dare. You have to be at the premiere. Promise?"

"I will do my best. I'll do my damnedest, in fact!"

And she would, too. After that, Gail floated through her evening and the weekend. She was no longer Gail Welles, waitress and wistful. She was Gail Welles, actor. So she still didn't have two pennies to rub together and lived off diner food and party appetizers. That was going to change, and soon.

She would live up to Aunt Charlie's dreams for her. In an odd way, she also needed to live up to Selena Ryan's faith that the woman who dropped a plateful of chicken and mayonnaise on her could deliver a crucial part in a movie. Selena did have a nice handshake, and when she truly smiled the way she had when the auditions were over, she was much warmer. Getting to know Selena Ryan, everyone on the picture, really, wasn't going to be a hardship.

Buzztastic # #

Boys and girls, did we tell you or what? Hyde Butler is doing an itty-bitty indie film, and Jennifer Lamont's his leading lady! Lamont we understand, after all, she and the executive producer have been sweating up the sheets. But why would Hunky Hyde join in? A lot of action heroes just have to find out they don't have the chops for Real Acting Parts. Is this Hyde's Waterloo? No one at Ryan is talking.

Other names we're seeing around the project are Jimmy Sherman, featured player at the Glenview Community Showcase. Sorry, we stopped typing to yawn here. Plus Gail Welles, pics of both below. She's trying but she'll never match up with Lamont. We get why Ryan would go for Lamont, who wouldn't? Poor Eddie Lynch, who has to make this mess of talent into some kind of picture. Let's face it, it's either another shot at the Big O for Eddie or a Big Egg that'll stink up the city for a couple of weeks.

Chapter 7

The look that Gail's agent was giving her plainly said that she was acting like a diva. From her perspective, this role could put her up in the top five of Madeline's success stories. Maybe she wouldn't make as much money as the shampoo actress or the dramatic doctor were consistently pulling in, but by the time *Barcelona* had finished its income stream, it represented a lot of free publicity and more than mere chump change.

In her opinion, the non-chump change entitled her to sit in her agent's spacious office, reading a contract, while Madeline waited. It was the most time she'd asked for since signing on with the agency. And that, she considered, was primarily her fault. She half-remembered a quip that power wasn't given, it had to be taken, and she'd given too much to Madeline and not taken enough for herself. Playing the daily part of a waitress in West Hollywood was not paying her dues, and she'd become perilously close to thinking it was. Without this chance she'd have gone home to Iowa very bitter and drained.

"This paragraph you've indicated to take out? About the assignment of credits in multilingual, multi-format, multinational subsequent distributions of secondary market contracts? Why is that not good?"

Madeline's frown deepened. "It's a standard clause that production companies put in and agents take out. The clause says that when they sell some other version than the initial DVD release that they will present the credits in whatever order they wish. Sometimes that's due to local legal requirements for disclosure in very conservative countries, but sometimes another performer's agent will have inserted a clause saying whenever the producer has that leeway, they move up to the top. I don't want you dropped to the bottom of the list unless it's legal compliance."

"Okay, I get that. So what you've put in says that regardless of edition or format, the previous clauses controlling presentation of my screen credit are in still in force. Okay. Thank you. I see how little things like that could get by."

Madeline's eyebrows unknitted slightly. She tucked silver-shot black hair behind her ears and gave Gail a world-weary look. "I'm trying to look out for you."

None of this is fun to her, anymore, Gail thought. How sad. "Can I ask why you didn't come to the audition the other night? I was the only person there without their agent."

"I didn't think you'd get it." Madeline seemed surprised by both the direct question and her own candor.

"Well, that's pretty honest. I guess I appreciate that."

Madeline removed her glasses and massaged the bridge of her nose. "You showed promise in your initial test, but most of the work in this town is commercials and small television parts. You don't look like their usual request. I apologize if I let the all-powerful image machine dictate how I devote time to my clients, but this is a business."

"And you don't get many calls for unvoluptuous, strong-featured character actresses."

"I don't. But that doesn't mean I don't know what a good contract is and isn't. Seriously, you will not be risking anything by asking for ten percent more upfront. They expect you to. That will put you substantially above the SAG minimum, and will also allow you to ask for more in subsequent negotiations with other producers."

Though her acting coach had said the mundane business aspects of film work could be talent-numbing, ignoring them would be professionally damaging. Movies were magic, but behind the scenes were decisions like this one. She needed the part, very badly. She would be eligible to apply for Screen Actor's Guild membership after two weeks on this project, and start earning the very important access to health and retirement benefits. Steady work, regardless of role, was key to being able to put day-to-day worries about the rent behind her.

"Okay…" She thought about it, asked herself what Aunt Charlie would do. For some reason she got an image of Selena Ryan in her head, a consummate professional, who took the work seriously and expected nothing less from others. "If you really think that it's appropriately professional to counter with a request for more upfront, then please, let's do that. I don't want to lose this part, but I don't want them to think I don't respect myself, either."

Madeline put her glasses back on, and Gail swore she saw a glint of approval behind the lenses. "Let me do that and then we'll messenger this over."

Get a part and your agent might actually respect you, she thought cynically.

"I'll take it. I'm going that way," she lied, "and I guess I'm nervous enough to not want to trust it to anyone but me."

With a glimmer of a smile, Madeline began marking up the pages. Gail excused herself to the restroom, then waited for a few minutes in the lobby. When the receptionist handed her the envelope, saying, "Here's the finished contract," she caught the envious look of a young man she had taken for an aspiring actor.

"Don't give up," she said to him, tucking the precious envelope safely under her arm.

He gave her an uncertain look in answer.

As she drove from Madeline's agency offices in Westlake to the far more posh Ryan Production offices in Beverly Hills, she wondered if she'd looked that scared when she'd walked into those offices at the beginning. Probably.

She'd never been north of Sunset Boulevard, which was funky with blast-from-the-past shops and the latest trends in youth fashion. The crowded boulevard and side streets gave way to wider, twisting roads, and she passed gated house after gated house, increasingly distanced from the street and each other. She hoped the address was right—these all looked like private homes. Occasionally, one had a discreet sign indicating some sort of enterprise was behind the electric gate. When she glimpsed houses through the foliage she loved the Spanish rooflines and second-story balconies. Most of the homes didn't look huge, but they had style and presence.

To her relief, when she turned into the cul-de-sac the Internet instructions had guided her to, there were only three houses, and all appeared to be businesses, well set back from the road. One was an art restoration business, the other said only The Beverly Agency so she hadn't a clue, but the last was Ryan Productions.

She pulled into the short driveway, rolled down her window and pressed the call button. In response to the tinny voice asking her business, she said into the box, "I'm delivering a contract for the *Barcelona* production."

The gate immediately rolled open, and after she was past it, the concrete drive turned just once and she parked in the circular driveway, making sure there was room for other cars to get by hers. She hadn't yet gotten out of her serviceable but rusting Corolla when another car came through the gate. She recognized the late model Prius from the day of the audition and was curiously flustered to know that Selena Ryan would be in the building.

A chic young woman in tailored slacks and a nicely fitting

113

sweater greeted her as she stepped through the door. "I can sign for your package."

She had only a moment to take in the cool terra cotta tiles, the high molded ceilings and the delicate sound of a fountain feeding an array of greenery on the other side of a huge central room. She could easily forget that outside the temperature was climbing toward ninety and the sky was not a color anyone would call blue.

Refreshed with one deep breath, she said, "I'm not actually a messenger. I'm the actor. Is there any way I could give this to Kim myself? Or put it on her desk?" She went for honesty. "I'm a hopeless newbie and paranoid something will go wrong."

The young woman rose from her chair, "Welcome to a Ryan film, then. Let me see if Kim's free. I'm Cecile, by the way. You are…?"

"Gail Welles."

"Oh!" Cecile's smile lit up her face. "If she's not tied up I'm sure she'll pop out to get it."

Dazzled that the receptionist seemed to know her name, Gail told herself to keep her feet on the ground. It didn't help that Cecile immediately returned saying, "Kim says to bring it back. Down this hallway, second door. Would you like some coffee or tea?"

"I won't be here long enough to enjoy it, but thank you."

"I'll put it in a To Go cup, save a trip to Starbucks. Coffee's my specialty," she added, with just a hint of pleading.

"Okay, coffee. Milk and fake sugar."

"You got it."

Two doors down, she was relieved to recognize Kim from the audition. She wished she could wear a skirt and bright layers so comfortably, and she was flat-out envious of the hair.

"Gail! It was good of you to bring the contract by. Have a seat."

"Thanks. Truthfully, I'm terribly paranoid something will go wrong."

Kim's smile was easy and welcoming. "I get that. When I

114

was given Selena's name as someone to contact for an assistant production job, about six years ago, I carried my letter introducing myself by hand too."

Cecile cheerfully delivered the coffee, accepted Gail's thanks, and tapped her headset to answer a call as she departed.

"This is a lovely office."

"Don't I know it. They'll have to carry me out of here in a box. I'm really happy you'll be on *Barcelona*. It's my first project all the way up to exalted producer status. That's in addition to an executive producer, an assistant producer here in L.A. and one in Spain."

Gail, feeling more comfortable by the moment, grinned. "You are all gods to me. You make movies."

"Don't let any of the rest of them hear you say that. You can say that to me all you like. So, you've brought me the contract?"

"My agent had some revisions. I hope they're all standard. She said they were. If they're not, if there's something that's going to sour this, she may not be open to negotiation but I definitely am. I guess I shouldn't say that."

Kim reached for the envelope Gail proffered. "Probably not." She studied Gail for a moment, then spread the sheaf of papers on her desk. "Let me look."

She flipped through the pages quickly with "hmm" and "uh huh" her only commentary. Finally, she closed the document. "These are standard push-backs. We'll revise it accordingly and send it over to your agent's office for signature. Probably get there tomorrow morning."

The wave of relief inside her was so huge she thought she might cry like she had sitting at that bus stop, so she sipped her coffee several times before responding. "This is really tasty. And thank you. I'm very excited about this project and will do my best not to be a pain in the keister."

Kim eased back in her chair. "How did you get into acting? That's not an idle question. Sooner or later we're going to be talking about the phenomenal Gail Welles, our discovery, and that's the kind of detail the press always wants to know."

"Allow me a moment to be boggled at the idea." Gail sipped again, collecting her thoughts. "I guess I should be better prepared for that kind of question. I put on and take off a dozen parts a day, but they're parts. I've never stopped to think about the role of Gail Welles, Celebrity."

"There are plenty who spend a lot of time planning their appearance on the Tonight Show or their acceptance speech at Cannes."

"I'd rather think about taking words and making them come alive. I can't remember a time when I wasn't thinking about how Scout walked in *Mockingbird* or the way Scarlett O'Hara pouted or Dustin Hoffman managed to wear a dress and look strong and fragile all at once. Sure, I'd like to play Portia and Medea, but honestly, I go to the movies and salivate over roles like Miranda Richardson in *The Devil Wears Prada*."

"In another fifteen years," Kim prompted.

"When I'm older, please yes. But I've always watched the character actresses. I'm not the…'Mr. DeMille, I'm ready for my close-up' type. I've been told I have interesting features, but never beautiful ones. It's not the face that launched a thousand ships."

Kim shot a look over Gail's shoulder. "A pretty face isn't the be-all-and-end-all, is it, boss?"

"No matter how I answer that, I'm in trouble with somebody, so I'll take the Fifth."

Gail, her pulse suddenly racing, turned to greet Selena Ryan. It was strange, truly, to see her not as a customer or a celebrity, and not yet as an equal. They were colleagues, working toward the same goal on the same project. Collegial, she told herself, that was how she was feeling. Striving for a normal tone, she opted for something banal. "It's a pleasure to see you again."

Selena set a folder on Kim's desk as she said, "Likewise." There was hint of a question in the hooded eyes. Gail had thought them almost black, but they were closer to dark chocolate.

"I admitted to Kim that I'm really nervous that this is all a dream, so I brought by my contract."

"Standard revisions," Kim said. "I'll leave it for you, for when you get back tonight. Though maybe not." She gave Gail a conspiratorial glance. "I don't want her taking post-studio-accountants-meeting rage out on the document."

Selena's gaze narrowed and Gail could tell she was a little annoyed at being teased in front of her, but that she truly didn't mind. She said something back, but Gail missed it, caught up in new insights. She'd studied the harried, tired businesswoman who sat in her diner. The Selena at the audition had seemed almost withdrawn. But in this environment it was as if Selena were coming out in colors. Her hair, not a particularly notable shade of dark brown, was certainly glossier in the natural light from Kim's window. The asymmetrical simplicity of the cut, just long enough to tuck behind one ear, suited her. The terra cotta floors might account for the glow in her cheeks, which had always seemed pale and drawn. Maybe it was just that she was in her element.

"You only have about twenty minutes before you need to be out of here," Kim was saying.

Selena gave Gail a nod as she turned to the door. "I'm wearing the Pradas again. Accountants."

Though her spirit was floating on air, Gail decided it was time to get her hinder out of Kim's chair. "Thank you for taking the time to see me."

"I look forward to working with you. By the way, I don't know if anyone told you, but you came recommended to us by Trevor Barden."

"You're kidding! How incredibly nice of him. Any suggestions on how to repay him?"

"With Trevor, make him proud, and speak kindly of him."

Gail shook hands, remembered to collect the coffee as well, for which she complimented Cecile on her way out. Kim's advice went around in her head, reminding her of Betty's request to be recalled kindly in the future. Funny that people thought they had to ask for that—being kind was easy. Why wouldn't she be?

She'd never aspired to be a princess, never gone through

a ball gown and tiara phase. But at that moment, skipping out of the elegant building, she felt like Cinderella. It didn't matter that her magical coach was a pumpkin of a car, or that she had another night at the diner ahead of her. She couldn't help but spin in a circle before she unlocked the door. Life was good, very good indeed.

Abruptly aware that there were a lot of windows facing her direction, she sheepishly slid into the driver's seat. She checked her reflection in the rearview mirror and told herself if she didn't stop grinning her face might get stuck that way. She had just enough to time to find the best chocolate chip cookie in Beverly Hills and deliver it to Trevor's office.

Selena watched Gail Welles' dancing departure from the grounds, not quite sure what to make of it. Gail was not a giddy ingénue fresh off the farm, but for a moment there, she had certainly looked like it. She'd been perfectly poised in Kim's office. Even at the audition she wouldn't have said Gail Welles away from her craft was fascinating, but it was turning out to be true. Waitress, actress, woman so happy she could twirl like a little girl. Which Gail was the real one?

What did it matter? She had studio accountants in her future, and a headache already starting. Ahead of her lay the difficult decision about partnering with a studio for the production of *Barcelona*. She didn't want to, but with the star power they were lining up, a studio's backing would mean more screens for the film and a bigger promotional budget. It also meant giving up control. It meant going to meetings with accountants and walking away pretty sure that some financial sleight of hand had reduced the bottom line, but equally aware that everyone whose interests she protected still got more than they would have by her going it alone.

The meeting was in downtown L.A., where insurance agents and CPAs gathered. She parked her car in the secure garage, and was extra diligent in checking the surroundings, even though she knew where the real sharks were. How long, she pondered, before someone said, "European sales weren't as robust as our first estimates" or, "Latin America just didn't warm up to this one."

As it turned out, twenty minutes.

She knew the big production houses brought their People to a meeting like this, but she wasn't a big house and she knew perfectly well how to use a calculator. In spite of the freezing temperature of the room and the long line of expectant faces watching her every move, she took her time going through the reports, asking lots of questions about why the final numbers were all four percent under projections. She double-checked the math—four percent across the board. Her notes from the last meeting said the economy had already been factored. Increase in piracy had already been factored, too.

Finally, she said, "So what you're telling me is that all your assumptions from six months ago were right, but the estimates were wrong. Industry-wide sales declines are exactly what you predicted, so why are the final numbers not closer to the projections?"

The array of suits blustered and even tried to empathize with her surprise over the reduction in the expected payout. She felt as if needles were being driven into her temples.

"I have performers, directors and editors to pay. I have to take 'they made a mistake' back to them. So you're going to have to be more specific."

The urbane, Armani-clad man closest to her, who was making her crazy with his smug awareness that there was nothing she could really do about their reporting, finally said, "I understand your position, but roughly four percent is not that big a deal."

Selena looked down at her quick calculations and the light bulb went off. "It's not roughly four percent." Fed up, she let her anger and disdain trickle to the surface. "It's *exactly* four percent. *Exactly* to the penny four percent in every single category. Did you think that because it's 'not that big a deal' I wouldn't ask for an explanation? You have none, and what an amazing coincidence, every market, exactly four percent."

She capped her pen and closed the folders. "Here's what you're going to do. You're going to put the four percent back in and consider it a penalty for your utter lack of subtlety at cooking the books."

For a rewarding moment, nobody seemed to know what to say. She pressed her advantage. "Really, did you think a little indie doesn't know how to apply a spreadsheet formula? Not only are you going to add back the four percent that disappeared from these numbers, you're also going to do it right away, or I will make sure that somebody up the food chain knows that's why I didn't even consider bringing you a Hyde Butler independent film for partnership. And now we're done."

She swept the papers into her satchel and stalked out in her Prada pumps, hoping everyone in the room had felt exactly where she'd just planted them. They'd kick back, she knew that, but for once she had said her piece. If they were going to lie about their numbers, they could at least try to make it a decent lie. Nothing annoyed her more than being thought stupid. It had felt really good to have a bullet called Hyde Butler in her gun, and finally get to be Barbara Stanwyck and pull the trigger.

Back in the car she headed for home, thinking she would catch up on tomorrow's To Do list. Later, a dip in the pool and a nap would probably take care of the headache. At least the relatively quick meeting meant avoiding the afternoon traffic. She clicked her headset on to call Kim and was disconcerted by what she thought was dead air.

Then a voice said, "Lena, are you there?"

Damn. She should just click it off and let it be one of those cell phone mysteries. "I'm here, Jennifer. What did you want?"

"I tried to reach you all weekend."

"Your contract is on the way. I don't know what else we have to talk about."

"Lena, we can talk about anything, can't we?"

She'd given Jennifer what she wanted. What, other than a little more icing on top to hide her ulterior motives, could this call be about? "I know you must have something specific you want to say, so please just say it."

"Meet me for a drink or something. It's awkward on the phone."

"So there is something you want to discuss. This isn't just a casual social call."

"Why can't it be both?"

"Because it's you and me. We have business. There's no social."

Jennifer actually laughed. "If you say so. How about a glass of wine and some tapas at Vin?"

Vin wasn't a bad choice. The owner actively discouraged staff Tweeting up who was in their restaurant. The diner where Gail worked had not proven to be in the least off the radar, and besides, she very much didn't want Jennifer to know that the actress she was going to be working with had been their waitress. Why had it even popped into her head as a choice? Maybe because Gail had twirled her way to her car. Selena couldn't remember the last time she'd danced because life was that good.

"Okay, at Vin. I need about thirty minutes to get there. And I warn you, I just left an accounting meeting."

She had meant to let Jennifer know she wasn't in the mood for games, but Jennifer purred, "I'll have to kiss it and make it better then, won't I?" before she hung up.

She managed to find parking just off Santa Monica Boulevard, which was a minor miracle. Her brisk footsteps slowed as she approached Vin—it had been so long since she'd been there that she'd forgotten it was a couples' place. It was too dark and moody for the after-work crowds, and the wine selection matched with small plates and seductive desserts were why she'd introduced Jennifer to it to begin with. She ought to have told Jennifer to make an appointment with Kim, just like she had when she'd first made contact. What had possessed her to agree to this place? Given the ambiance, she'd almost have preferred a hot dog on the Santa Monica Pier with paparazzi filming their every bite.

The entrance seemed clear of people with cameras, and

she saw no loiterers who might be eager to see who Jennifer Lamont was meeting with at such a romantic location. That was reassuring, but not a lot.

The maitre d' quickly escorted her to Jennifer's booth, cozy and discreet in the back of the restaurant. Jennifer already had a glass of wine and a plate of crostini with wild mushrooms—a favorite of Selena's—but both looked untouched.

"I thought we could share a merlot, then maybe try a shiraz or pinot," she said as Selena settled in.

"I won't be here that long." Selena tried to sound brisk, but the acoustics seemed to slow her words. "What is it you wanted to discuss?"

"I'm very happy to be working with you again." The gorgeous bronze eyes, in the low light, were velvet purple. "We were always a good partnership."

"Until you discarded it, yes we were." She crossed her arms over her chest.

Jennifer shifted against the back of the curved booth, moving slightly closer to Selena. Her black tunic dress looked as if it would drop off both shoulders with a puff of Selena's breath. "Do you remember what it was like before anyone knew about us? When we flew down to Cabo San Lucas?"

Selena refused to let her shiver show. She remembered that stolen weekend vividly. She'd been the first woman Jennifer had ever been with, and every sensation was a revelation. They had steeped themselves in sensuality, from the food they'd ordered, to the few hours out of their hotel room they'd luxuriated in the Mexican sun. Jennifer's rapture at the touch of a woman had been addictive. Selena had never been so sensually open in her own life. She'd given a lot of herself that weekend, holding very little back about what she liked and how exciting she found Jennifer, and it still hurt to know that it had only been a means to an end, nothing more than hooking up to get a part and calling the sex research.

"I'm not talking about the sex, though…" Jennifer's lips curved fondly. "The sex was certainly worth talking about. I remember the plans we made."

"I do too." They had been going to make lots of movies together, be as famous a partnership as Woodward and Newman or Goldwyn and Mayer.

"My next few roles were all meaty and good, and didn't rely on the audience believing I was straight. By the time I got another big part that did, I was, well, I was with Cary by then."

"Since Cary gave you the part, that was efficient."

Jennifer sipped the wine, then offered the glass to Selena, who shook her head. "I didn't plan it that way, but we both know that while you and I were an item, I was not getting leading lady type offers."

"Why are we talking about this now?"

"Well, it struck me that one of the key points of the movie is that our dear hero Elgin has two women willing to kill over him. Not only is she a beginner, the Gail woman is also a lesbian. When that gets out, no one's going to buy her in the part."

"I knew she was gay before she auditioned—she was a referral from a trusted source, with high kudos for comedic range. Comedy is key to Georgette, as well as the ability to make a lightning change to desperation and anger, which Welles does. The audience isn't supposed to be itching to see her in bed with Elgin."

"That's where I come in." Jennifer shrugged. "If you want to add that kind of scene, it'll hit big on YouTube."

Selena refused to picture it. "All the viewer has to believe about Georgette is that she's a bit unbalanced and not entirely trustworthy. Everybody loved Welles in the part." But why not you, Selena asked herself. Gail wasn't going to upstage Jennifer with the beauty-famished media.

"I'm sure she's quite a gifted talent, but in these times, homophobia is—"

"What do you know about homophobia, dear sleeping-with-men Jennifer?"

"It's just as virulent toward bisexuals, you know."

"When was the last time you told anyone you were bisexual?"

123

"What does that matter?" Jennifer curled one leg under her.

"Because right now, you're playing it very straight, and taking every advantage you can of the ease that puts into your life. Since I'm your only fling to the other side, I think that makes you straight, but with a documented experimental phase. A fact which only makes you more attractive to many men."

"Oh, I hate to disappoint you, but you're not the only fling. You got to be first, but not last."

Whatever you do, Selena told herself, don't let her see you bleed. Stunned by how much the admission hurt, she reached for the wine glass as a way to stall for time. She sipped, but tasted nothing.

"Well, if I thought that you genuinely cared about more than sex that fulfilled your need of the moment, that would be different." Selena supposed she could get angry, but between the headache, accountants and Jennifer's disturbing nearness, she suddenly only felt tired and too vulnerable. "When you actually stay with a woman or man longer than it takes you to advance your career through your liaison, then maybe I'll be ready to accept your claim to any kind of sexuality. Seems to me, sex is nothing more than a tool you've learned use, which is not the same as knowing who you are." No matter how much Jennifer's revelations hurt, I know who I am, Selena thought.

Jennifer ran one elegant hand through her thick hair. "Thank you so much for your wisdom, sensei."

"Why are we having this conversation?" *You want something, and not just to hurt me*. Idiot, how did you think she'd behave here? It didn't help that she was remembering the first night in Cabo, when they hadn't slept until morning.

"I'm concerned that the Gail woman is a bad cast, that's all."

"So you said." Selena nearly added, *But Gail acted circles around everyone else at the auditions*, but something inside went *click*. It wasn't that Gail was unconvincing if the viewer knew she was gay, it was that Gail was utterly convincing, regardless.

She gave Jennifer a long, considering look. Jennifer had never made a secret of her desire for the kind of parts that led to Oscars and other statues. In terms of age, at thirty-three, she was ripe for it. Thinking back on the audition, Gail Welles had disappeared the moment each scene started. Hyde was talented, but so much larger than life that he might always be Hyde with many viewers. Same with Jennifer. Sherman, the fourth principal, was solid, but nothing like Gail. And there was the rub. It wasn't looks, sex appeal, amount of screen time or any of the usual competitive reasons. It came down to talent. Jennifer was not secure enough to welcome the competition for critical attention.

"Your head hurts," Jennifer suddenly said. She pressed the back of one hand to Selena's forehead. "You've got migraine lines."

"It's not a migraine." It was all Selena could do not to flinch from Jennifer's touch. It was all she could not to melt into it either.

I really should have found some cheap, meaningless sex. Jennifer was using every skill she had, and would take it to the bedroom if she thought it would win her what she wanted. To Jennifer, the sex would be meaningless, but there was nothing cheap about it. It had a price. Selena knew if she gave in to the pounding in her pulse and the thirst for kisses, it would be very cheap, but far from meaningless.

That was why they weren't together, after all.

"I really do have to go," Selena heard herself say.

"No you don't." Jennifer kissed the side of Selena's mouth so lightly it might have been just the whisper of her breath.

A glance downward confirmed Selena's suspicions that under the dress Jennifer wore nothing. Minute, clear ties across her back were all that held it on, and Selena knew from experience how to shred those, how to pull a delicious dress like that down, how excited it made Jennifer when she was possessive and hungry, and took her all in a flash fire.

The small voice saying, "You'll hate yourself in the morning," didn't stop her from kissing Jennifer back. There was nothing sweet about it. It was eager and deep, eliciting a throaty moan from Jennifer, who moved close enough for Selena to feel the swell of firm breasts against her arm.

"Gail Welles is not negotiable," she said when their mouths parted.

Jennifer pulled her back for another kiss, slower and more thorough. She gave a slight laugh when the kiss ended. "Since we're going to make out and talk business at the same time, what if I said I won't sign if she's part of the picture?"

Selena knew she was just about to fall off a cliff, but her reflexes as a producer pulled her from the edge for just a few moments. "Then you don't sign."

Jennifer's eyes were very dark, like they always were when she was aroused. Or was that just good acting? How much of this passion was just a show? Or was playing a lesbian a part she could get into it, for long enough, and really enjoy?

Her gaze focused on Selena's mouth, but when Selena said nothing more, she whispered, "Damn you," and kissed Selena again.

This is doomed, this is crazy, this is nothing, Selena told herself, even as she indulged her fingers in the longed-for texture of Jennifer's hip. She slipped one arm around her, pressing her against the leather of the booth, and kissed her with bruising heat.

Then she managed to get to her feet, hoping that her own dizziness wasn't apparent to Jennifer, who looked dazed.

"What was that?" Jennifer put her hand to her mouth as if to feel Selena's kisses.

"That was what you gave up."

Pradas don't fail me now, Selena prayed. Just get out the door and run for your life.

She didn't feel safe going home, nor being alone, and had no one she could call who would just listen and not tell her what she already knew. She was being a fool over someone who'd hurt her, and her libido was doing most of the thinking. She could even hear Kim now. The lecture would start with, "Girl, doesn't your back already have her footprints on it?" and go from there.

126

Maybe because Gail Welles' name had come up during the disastrous assignation with Jennifer, Selena found herself wending the Prius toward the diner. She knew it wasn't a good idea, but there was no reason, really, for anyone to notice. She did need some dinner and her stomach was pouting over the wasted crostini with wild mushrooms. That other parts of her were pouting even more loudly than her stomach was irrelevant. Everybody told her she was getting too thin, so why shouldn't she sublimate with food? The diner was safe for her on her own, it would be okay.

She parked the car in a rare open slot in the diner's tiny lot, and rested a moment. Her suit felt sticky and tight, probably because parts of her were still swollen. The Pradas, put to such good use terrorizing accountants and the only dignified touch to her panicked retreat from Jennifer, were killing her feet. Her chest hurt, but pressing a hand to it didn't locate a source for the pangs that had started when Jennifer had said she'd been with other women since dumping her.

A glance in the rearview mirror added to her feeling like a hollow shell. Some ego you've got there, she thought. She dumped you because a man had what she wanted, and knowing she was capable of that, you thought she hadn't had some lesbian nooky on the side? She's got a worthless soul, and yet you placed value on her secretly pining for you.

Loser.

So.

Sometimes, the Ice Cream Fairy whispered, *it's okay just being a woman*. Selena Ryan could stay in the car, she decided. Lena was getting butter pecan with hot fudge.

She pushed aside the various chargers and work accoutrement that always cluttered the passenger seat, and found her gym bag. She tossed the heels into the rear seat, squirmed out of the suit skirt and pantyhose, then gratefully pulled on cropped yoga shorts. After a quick glance to assure herself she was alone in the parking lot she whipped on a simple cotton tee in place of her blouse. Socks and gym shoes completed the transformation.

There was no sign of Gail when she went in, which was probably just as well. Gail Welles did not need to know that the leading lady was scared of her talent. She badly wanted to tell someone about Jennifer's behavior, though. You should have found a therapist by now, she told herself. Everybody in L.A. had one, didn't they, in lieu of friends who'd get you drunk and listen to your tales of woe all the while making rash promises of avenging the wrongs committed against you only to be forgotten by morning under the weight of a healthy hangover? If she'd done that after Jennifer had dumped her, maybe she wouldn't be so achingly aware that she wanted Jennifer's mouth *there* and her hands *there*...

Ice cream.

The familiar Latina took her order for a chili dog and a sundae. Selena studied the menu as if she'd never seen it before. It's just a relapse, she told herself. Jennifer was a drug, and she was craving a hit, that's all.

The menu's powers of diversion were all used up, but she didn't want to check her phone. Not right now. If she talked to Kim, she'd spill her guts up to and including her hand under Jennifer's dress.

The low-voiced conversation on the other side of the partition sorted itself out and she could distinguish two voices—one was her waitress, and the other possibly Gail.

She was about to stand up and say hi, when Gail said, "I'm so glad it's slow tonight. I can't keep my mind on anything."

"You just got your big break. I'm impressed you even came back to work."

"I am going to make in the guaranteed eight weeks what I'd make here in a year, that's true, but I have to save as much as I can. What if I don't get another part?"

"How could that happen?" That was a new voice—possibly the owner, with her edge of a smoker's rasp. "You're going to be a star now."

"You can go a long time in between parts, and let's face it, I don't have the T-and-A quality most parts call for. I'd be happy playing an uptight doctor on some drama at this point."

Which would be a waste, Selena thought. Gail would look squished on the small screen. The big screen would let her stretch out those long arms, and pour off the myriad of emotions she put into a single scene.

"After dues and taxes it'll still last me a long time, and maybe Aunt Charlie can stop paying for my trips home, and I can find a slightly better apartment. I'd like to send her money for once."

"You're lucky in your aunt. She's been your guardian angel." Selena's waitress appeared with the hot dog and the condiment caddy. "I'll be back with your ice cream in a bit."

The dog, after she slathered it with relish, was hot and salty, and such simple fare she felt steadied by it. So she'd shared a few hot kisses with her ex, like a whole lot of people eventually did. Maybe if they'd been in a motel room they'd still be there. Maybe part of her still wanted to be there, but the truth was she'd walked away. Done it once and would do it again, if it came to that.

"So I hope it's enough notice," Gail was saying. "Once I start rehearsals in two weeks, I won't have the energy for two jobs. I'll get paid weekly for eight weeks guaranteed, and if the shoot runs long, I get paid more. Plus I get paid if they pull me in to fix anything during editing."

"It sure sounds exciting, kiddo. When you finish up, if nothing brighter has come along, you check back with me. If I've got an opening, it'll be yours."

Gail's voice was slightly choked. "Thanks for being so good to me. You've been great."

"You're a good kid. Not like this troublemaker."

Selena smiled as her waitress feigned indignation at the slur. She hoped her ice cream arrived soon.

"—And I never dumped food on anybody, now did I?"

Gail laughed. "No, that was my act. Know what's totally bizarre—did I tell you? The woman I dumped all that food on is the executive producer of the film. Small world, huh?"

"Really? She's right over..."

129

The voices dropped considerably and within sixty seconds, Gail appeared with Selena's sundae.

"Hi," she said shyly. "Angel said you were here. I'm sorry I didn't see you come in." Gail set down the saucer with the tall sundae glass along with a long-handled spoon. She had a funny, anxious, awkward expression on her face.

"Might be just as well. I'm having a face plant into ice cream. I'm not sure you should see me like this."

"I'll avert my eyes."

Selena laughed. Now that she was bothering to look, Selena was thinking Gail's eyes weren't actually jade, because at the moment they appeared turquoise, or maybe that was the light. She realized Gail was lingering as if she wanted to say something. "What?"

"It's just...acting lessons don't include this situation. I'm so incredibly grateful to you—"

"To Mirah, not me. I was just there at the end applauding her genius. To Trevor Barden." The point mattered to Selena, though she didn't want to name why. She wanted appreciation and respect, but not gratitude.

"To all of you, then. I will make the most of the opportunity. I won't let you down."

She thought Gail was sincere, if it wasn't all a gee-shucks farm girl act. She had a refreshing spoonful of butter pecan slathered with just the right amount of hot fudge, and decided that Lena, eating ice cream, could give the whole cynical bit a rest and take Gail at face value. "Are you busy? Can you sit for a minute or two? I'm sure you have a million questions."

"It's pretty slow. I guess it'll be okay for a few minutes." Gail slid into the small booth opposite her, looking as perfectly at home against the fading vinyl as Jennifer had against the leather at Vin.

They couldn't be two more different women, Selena thought. Just as quickly she realized she liked this one much better. "What would you like to know first?"

"What happens next, I guess."

"What happens next is your signed contract gets copied to all concerned. Kim will send you a packet of information about the shoot schedule, where you have to be and when, how you'll get there, and a bunch of phone numbers. Then Eddie Lynch and the screenwriter will have the scenes and their scheduling laid out for you in about a week. You'll do script run-throughs until Eddie wants you moving around, get measured for wardrobe, get made up for light checks, all that boring, important stuff. Do not bring a friend to take pictures." She cracked a smile. "You might as well tattoo newbie on your forehead if you do that."

"Thanks, I'll remember that." Gail looked to one side as if she were writing a note to herself on the inside of her eyelids.

It would be fascinating just watching her read a book, Selena thought. "There will be a shoot photographer, and you'll end up with plenty of stills for your portfolio. Can I ask you a somewhat impertinent but very relevant question?"

"Sure."

"You do kiss Hyde several times, once quite passionately. Is that going to be hard for you?"

Gail blinked. "Why would it—oh, you mean because I'm gay. Well, I have to admit the only guys I've ever kissed were in character for productions back home, if we don't count Mitch Conroy in the fourth grade. His nickname was Butch. I think that's what confused me."

Selena couldn't help a shout of laughter. "I had to date a couple of guys just to see what that was like, but I grew up in Hollywood and when it just didn't seem to work out, I had plenty of role models to suggest maybe I was looking on the wrong side of the species."

"Do you mean you happened to live here, or did you grow up in *the* Hollywood?"

"My father was a producer."

"Oh, how interesting."

"Not really. He was never bad enough to be Ed Wood or good enough to make more than short reels. We spent some time in Mexico making movies there." Those years had been the best, there'd been lots of money those days, and not a lot of yelling. When they'd moved back to Hollywood she'd been two grade levels behind her peers, though, and reintegrating had been difficult, especially when her father and new wife weren't concerned about her traumas at school. "Nothing you'll find at Netflix. He might have been good if he hadn't been a drinker."

"I'm sorry to hear that, I mean, I've got a cousin with an alcoholic parent and it's not easy."

Maybe it was the ice cream. The butter pecan was going right to her head. She felt a little dizzy and Gail had a warm smile. "My dad's in Wikipedia."

"Well, that's something. At least he's remembered."

It wasn't hard to believe Gail was from the Midwest. Looking on the bright side, saying something positive. "Not for filmmaking. He cooperated with HUAC. Voluminously."

Selena watched emotions ripple over Gail's face. Surprise, shock, distaste. To spare her the need to think of something comforting to say, she went on, "He was young, sure, and came in right at the end, but he wrote down people's names at parties and was thrilled McCarthy knew his first name. They gave him somebody as a Person of Interest, and he'd hang around them, taking note of friends and what was discussed." She hadn't really known the extent of his cooperation into the communist witch hunt in Hollywood until after he'd died. It had been a shock to find out that in addition to his untreated alcoholism he'd been an informant against people who thought him a friend, adding a seamy layer to her already disjointed and bewildered understanding of him.

"For someone who wanted to make movies, he never saw the big picture. I don't think he really understood he was getting ahead by ruining other people's lives, and even his masters didn't respect him. I don't know if he started drinking after that or was already inside the bottle, but he never stopped trying to break people so he could use their bodies for ladders. He wasn't a nice person. My brother and I were pretty much on our own after our mom died—none of his girlfriends or subsequent wives knew what to do with us. I'm afraid when he was completely broke and looked me up I wasn't very nice."

"What else were you supposed to be?"

A person could drown in those not-quite-jade eyes, Selena thought. "What would someone from Iowa do?"

"Find a home, put him in it and visit."

She shrugged, had another large spoonful of ice cream and told herself this little heart-to-heart was bordering on inappropriate contact with a hired player. Not that there was a written rule, just her own rules. And she lived by her rules, for good reason. "I didn't visit. But we've gone a long way from my question. Can you kiss Hyde Butler? Millions of women will envy you."

Gail's pensive expression deepened. "It's not...I mean, when I'm playing a part I'm not making out with the other actor. I'm the character kissing a character. Georgette has seriously warped hots for Elgin. That's not a problem for me to portray. Hyde Butler doesn't strike me as the kind of guy who has to think I have the hots for him personally, or the kind of guy who'd get some gamey jollies out of insisting on retakes."

"That's not my impression of him either," Selena admitted. "Don't let that laid-back southern boy charm fool you, though, he's high intensity."

Gail nodded vigorously. "Oh, I could tell. His energy sits right inside his chest, and all through his shoulders in a big, brilliant ball."

Selena had worked her way down the sundae glass far enough to unearth a second layer of hot fudge. It was helping her composure and the ache in her chest to talk about movies. Gail's grounded approach didn't seem to diminish her wonder and excitement about the process. "What do you mean by that?"

"My drama teacher in high school, years ago, showed us photos of a lot of famous people and pointed out how each of them had their energy zone. It's the spot where the audience tends to look the first time they walk into a scene. He tested us with the stars like Hepburn, John Wayne, Anne Bancroft. All sorts of charismatic people, like Capone and, yeah, Senator McCarthy.

The class wrote down where they first looked when the picture came up and there was a lot of similarity to our answers. Katherine Hepburn, it was all around here, for example."

Gail cupped her jaws and moved her hands down her throat. "Tight for dramatic parts, and bigger, more like sitting on her shoulders when she did comedy. John Wayne, it was all down on his hips, Cary Grant right over his heart, Bette Davis…" She gestured meaningfully over her own breasts. "And her energy flooded upward to her whole face. The really big stars, the energy zone moved when they were in different roles. Jimmy Stewart's was all over the place. Hyde has his in his chest, between his shoulders, coiled up like a snake. If he can loosen that up, let some of that energy drift up toward his eyes, that would really give him some range."

She stopped short, coloring slightly. "Oh. Listen to me, I take it all back. I don't know anything, and I've surely got no business telling someone like him how to act. I won't do it to his face, I promise."

Selena licked her spoon. Butter pecan was the best drug ever. "It's okay, I won't tell. What about the rest of the cast?"

"Jim Sherman has it all down in his belly, like Peter Lorre and Steve Buscemi. Jennifer Lamont it starts at her naval and flows downward, because…" Gail swallowed hard. "I mean, I'm not… it's just… She has an amazing store of sexual energy, like Monroe, who could pull it toward her face and carry off innocence along with all that sex appeal."

Selena was too far gone on the bliss of ice cream to stop her face from flaming in response. She managed not to say, "Don't I know it," while Gail looked mortified.

"I forgot," she stammered, "that you two…"

"It's fine," Selena assured her. "You're right."

"She's very beautiful, and I'm not saying I don't notice that, of course I do, you'd have to be blind not to, but I'm not lusting after her or anything like that." Gail clamped her mouth shut and stood up. "Well, I should get back to work before I say anything more stupid than I already have."

"No worries, Gail, really. I asked."

Selena was amused at Gail's impolitic candor. She might have a few bumps with the press if she didn't learn to rein herself in sooner, but that was a skill that could be learned. And she was absolutely right. Jennifer's sensuality wasn't just an act. Maybe that was the right approach, now that she was at the bottom of her sundae glass. Analyze Jennifer, think of her as an accumulation of skills, not a woman. Easier to think about her as a kind of Monroe archetype, not warm, breathing flesh and blood. It didn't hurt to tell herself that if she'd fumbled her way any higher under Jennifer's skirt she'd have found a zipper and underneath was the bloodsucking lizard alien who'd happily toss Selena on a river of lava and walk over her to safety.

She felt better for chatting with Gail, that was for sure. Gail had an actor's ego, no doubt about it, but it didn't seem to fuel itself anywhere but from inside. Part of her wondered if in this day and age an aspiring actress from the Midwest with an elderly aunt who believed in her could really exist. It was safer, wasn't it, to presume it was all an act, but every minute in Gail's company only confirmed that she was thoughtful and maybe even kind. It was hard to picture her picking up a plate of food with the intention of slopping it into someone's lap. Impossible to imagine her sizing up potential bed mates and the advancement they could offer.

Oddly, it lingered in her mind that it might be safer to imagine Gail just another actress with designs on her next part. Did she really have something to fear?

She was nearly to her car when she heard Gail call her name. The parking lot was not very well lit, but there didn't seem to be anyone loitering around.

"Your phone," Gail said, panting slightly. "I'm so glad I caught you."

"I can't believe I didn't immediately sense it wasn't attached to me."

"I dropped it in the gravy, but I've wiped it off." Gail held it out.

There wasn't enough light to see her face, but Selena heard the teasing note. "Gee, thanks. I'm going to crave mashed potatoes every time I make a call."

Their fingertips brushed as the phone went from hand to hand. Gail's laugh filled Selena's ears with the same warmth that radiated from their fleeting contact.

"See you in just a few days," Gail said, backing away. "Well, more than a few."

"I know," Selena said. "I'm looking forward to it."

Over her shoulder, Gail said, "So am I."

By the time Selena backed out of the parking space, Gail had gone back inside. Through the window she could see her chatting with a customer, that easy smile curving her lips. The image lingered for the drive home and returned when she was finally settling into bed. The little part of her that said perhaps she ought to focus her thoughts elsewhere was shushed by the rest of her and she fell asleep still hearing Gail's laugh.

Buzztastic # #

Why all the mystery about Hyde Butler's new project? When people won't talk to us we know there are secrets! It's a big rush, too, like someone's preggers. Jennifer Lamont might be back with her ex, but it wasn't that long ago we saw her dancing to all hours with the man in her life, director Cary Castle. Maybe the gals are going to be baby mamas, courtesy of Cary? Let's keep an eye on Lamont's waistline. There's got to be a reason for the big hurry to film and bringing in such risky unknowns for the bit parts. We've scraped the bottom of lots of barrels looking for any news on Gail Welles. How did she catch Selena Ryan's eye? And does Jennifer know?

Next up! Click over to this head shot no star wants out there. That's right, we've got the close-ups of the family's reaction at watching Daddy go to jail for possession. Again.

Chapter 8

After that intense but very informative conversation with Selena, Gail didn't expect any repeats, but she caught herself more than once checking the booth Selena always chose, remembering the conversation and her odd sense of ease and connection. Selena's story about her father was pretty awful, but she still loved the movies despite the dark history in her family. When she'd talked about shooting schedules and the way the process worked she'd relaxed and smiled easily.

There were no repeats, though, and life went on much as before, for over a week.

The first indication that her day-to-day existence wouldn't be the same was answering her phone while she was trying on clothes at the Nordstrom Outlet to find a reporter from *Variety* at the other end of the line.

"I—I'm right in the middle of something. Can you call me

back in five minutes?" She didn't want to sound like a dunce, and she didn't want to embarrass the production. She didn't even know if it was okay for her to talk to the press.

The reporter reluctantly agreed and Gail quickly called Kim.

"Sure, you can talk to the press. Your name is already rolling around on the gossip Web sites, mainly because they don't know anything about you. If you're not sure who you're dealing with, just refer them to Ryan Productions' main phone number. The first thing to know is the magic phrase 'off the record.' Anytime a reporter or blogger tries to draw you into chitchat, you should say something like, 'We're going off the record, right?' There are some slimes who'll chat away then ask you something really personal and you think you're off the record and next thing you know your brand of tampon is the news. And some who won't care if you do say it's off the record. Seriously, avoid the gossip bloggers who don't represent print media. They're not all evil, but enough are that it's hard to trust any of them. And it's totally true that there's print media that's full of hip, thin people who think anyone not them is fair game for humiliation on anything they can think of."

Gail sat down on the dressing room chair, feeling a little overwhelmed. "Do I have to talk to them?"

"Of course not. But anyone from *Variety* you probably should. I know the name, he is who he says he is. Keep your answers short. Don't volunteer information, but be friendly and firm. Anything you want can be deemed off-limits—that is totally up to you. Doesn't mean they'll stop asking, but just keep saying whatever subject they're prying into is off-limits."

"Okay. It's not like I want to run around doing interviews. I don't even know how this guy got my number."

"They're masters at that sort of thing. Last magic phrase, and it's a good one. Let's say someone asks you about a co-star's drinking problem. Maybe he's got one, maybe he doesn't. Avoid a yes or no answer. Just parrot back, 'What are you talking about?'"

Gail echoed, "What are you talking about?"

"It's a lousy sound bite," Kim said. "Any off-the-wall or rude question it's the perfect response. So tell me about Hyde Butler's womanizing."

Gail hesitated, then said firmly, "What are you talking about?"

"I've heard Jennifer Lamont is into naked body painting."

"What are you talking about?"

"Selena Ryan—what a bitch. A total slave driver, isn't she?" Kim's voice bubbled with suppressed laughter.

"What are you talking about?"

"You know what people say about her."

Gail laughed. "What are you talking about?"

"You got it—hi, boss," Kim said, her voice slightly muffled.

Gail could make out the crisp tones of Selena's voice, slightly raised in protest.

"Just giving Gail a lesson in handling the press. She got her first call."

It sounded like Kim dropped the phone, then Selena came on the line. "Do what Kim says."

"I promise I will." She realized how much she enjoyed the low timbre of Selena's voice.

"Did she tell you about the party you're coming to on Saturday night?"

"I was about to," she heard Kim say in the background.

"A *party* party?" She pictured Selena at the audition, in those incredible shoes and form-fitting suit, sophisticated and professional without being pushy or flamboyant. "As in swanky?"

"Swanky. Here, Kim will tell you more."

Swanky meant serious dressing. She looked at the pairs of designer slacks and jeans she'd found on discount. It would take all of them to meet Selena Ryan's definition of a swanky little black dress.

Kim came on the line saying, "If you need an advance on pay, that's doable, it's in the contract. Just tell your agent."

"No, I'm fine." She'd start getting her larger paychecks before the credit card bill came. With the contract actually signed she finally felt like she could dip into the last emergency reserve she had, the one she'd held back to buy a ticket home.

"There's a great little consignment store in West Hollywood, kind of off the beaten track. Has lots of vintage wear, and you might think about that kind of look. They made lots of clothes for tall girls with no hips in the Sixties."

"Thanks, that sounds like a great idea." She eagerly wrote down the name. Vintage meant it didn't have to be the latest and most expensive style to be fashionable. She conceded that ground to Jennifer Lamont.

When the reporter called again, she strove for charm and poise, and gave her first interview to the press while sitting in a department store dressing room. She expressed her enthusiasm and awe, her admiration for the rest of the cast and crew, and how she hoped to hold her own with such wonderful performers. Afterward, not sure she'd done okay, she distracted herself by buying several pairs of jeans and trousers. To appease the credit card gods, she traded down on the blouses to fresh, brightly colored T-shirts. At least they would be unfaded and workmanlike.

It was early yet, so she decided to tackle the consignment shop on her way home. As she was looking up the address on her phone, she got a text from Kim.

"You did good," it read, and it had a link to a *Variety* article.

Already? But there it was, *Rising Star Gail Welles on Her Big Break with Hyde Butler*. It read okay, she hadn't embarrassed herself. Wow. So that's how fast fame could happen, she mused. It would do well to remember that fame went away just as fast. She sent Aunt Charlie a text with the link—there was an aide at the residence who would help her view it. That would be a thrill for her, to call the bridge buddies to the screen to see Gail's name in big letters.

It took a little time to find the shop in West Hollywood, but she had a good feeling about it when she took in the brilliant pink paint around the door. The window featured a mannequin in a flapper's dress with beads down to her knees. If a gay man didn't run "Christopher's Elegance," she'd be very disappointed.

The older man at the counter put down his book and studied her over his glasses. "Did you want an outfit or do you need to pee?"

"Outfit. Though in a while I might…"

"Don't move."

He set down the book, squaring it to the edge of the counter, then carefully paced around her at a distance, goatee twitching. "How tall are you?"

"Five-nine and then some."

"And then some, indeed." In a flurry of activity he selected a dress, black, a handbag, sequined silver, and a pair of ankle boots that looked very small. "Put these on."

He gestured toward the back of the store.

Both amused and bemused, Gail obeyed. Once she'd set down her things, she looked at the dress label—Chanel. Oh my lord, genuine Chanel. She should have recognized the trademark large buttons, the square cut, even the banding around the hips, all classic, vintage Twiggy. She'd never pull that off. Would she?

Incredibly, the dress did fit. To her own eyes, though, she looked like a drinking straw in a well-made dress. She put on the little boots, which zipped on but looked like authentic Victorian button-ups. She liked them very much. She even liked them with the dress. How strange that two vintage pieces paired this way actually looked stylish and modern. But overall… She sighed.

She went out to see how it looked in the better lighting of the main store. Her helper was waiting.

"If you're going to walk like a field bovine this will never work. You're wearing *Chanel*."

Okay, Gail thought, not taking offense, if you can't impress this guy, you won't impress Selena or anyone else. She straightened her shoulders and walked toward the mirrors like she was meeting a friend.

"That's better. Have you any idea, any idea at all, of how many women I have watched try that dress on and not one of them could wear it. Who *are* you?"

She laughed and looked at herself the mirror. She was getting used to it. "I'm a lucky actor who just got a good part, and I have a swanky party to go to."

"Lots of beautiful people? Then this is the dress. Nothing intimidates like Chanel."

"Can I look around a little?"

He made a helpless gesture and returned to his book. "It's your time."

She was looking at a men's pinstripe suit, sort of the 1930s mobster cut, when he appeared at her elbow. "Thinking of genderbending?"

"I've had people tell me I'd look good in less feminine clothes."

"Do you want to be less feminine?"

"No, but I want to look good."

"Well, I've seen butch come and go in all the different forms. There are women who put on men's clothes and look like men and that suits them. Sometimes they change their name and anatomy and I learn to call them Mister and life goes on." He spread his arms with an elegant shrug, and Selena noticed that his fingers were gnarled with what looked like painful arthritis. "But you're not one of them. You put on that suit you're not going to look butch or andro or whatever label you prefer. You're going to look like a woman in a man's suit, which is not the same thing. Your prerogative, but it's hardly fashionable. Now, this suit…"

With dramatic flair he drew her across the store to the women's suit rack and pulled out a jacket. The pinstripes were diagonal and the jacket buttoned all the way over on the side. The lapels were thin, the trousers seamed for a straight cut.

"This suit will start a riot. You could be the latest trendsetter. And you'll look more feminine than ever, like Dietrich. Well, not like Dietrich, you're very adorable I'm sure, but not Dietrich. In her mode. It would be a good signature style for someone just getting her name out."

Gail touched the fine wool. "It reminds me of the kinds of

143

suits that all the women Girl Friday characters would wear in the screwball comedies."

"That's it exactly." She received a glance of great approval. "On you, the shoulder pads need to go, I think. I can do limited alterations. I cut cloth for Columbia's costume department for decades and can still manage a thing or two with a needle."

He suggested she continue with the adorable boots as footwear and when she stood in front of the big store mirror, jacket buttoned, she couldn't help a pleased flush. What gay friends she'd had in Iowa had always said she was butch and shouldn't fight it, but it never quite felt right. Lack of boobs did not a butch make. This suit, though cut with many masculine lines, made her look even more like a woman without being girlish or frou-frou. She didn't feel like a drinking straw with feet.

"You must be Christopher," she said as she held out her hand. "I'm Gail. And I'd like to try the Chanel on again."

A half-hour later she carried the dress, clutch and shoes to the car, well-pleased. The second time around she'd seen that it flattered her in all the right ways. When she could afford it she'd come back for that suit and a promised viewing of Christopher's collection. He had, but wouldn't sell, one of the three identical dresses he'd sewn for Katherine Hepburn during the full shoot of *Guess Who's Coming to Dinner*. She felt positively blessed by his eye for fashion and enjoyed the time spent with his reminiscences. It was almost like having her own Queer Eye on her side. She was reassured that she wouldn't embarrass Selena, and that mattered. It mattered a lot.

"Ellen," Serena said sincerely, "you are too good to me. Thank you so much for hosting this at the last minute."

"I've done nothing. Your party guru sent over a crew and took care of everything. I spent this afternoon having a facial and a manicure." Ellen Spelman drew Selena out to the spacious back patio, which was set up with low tables and chairs, a half-dozen food stations, all under brightly colored umbrellas providing shade from the evening sun. The bar was draped with a black cloth emblazoned with the *Barcelona* film logo.

Beyond the polished granite flagstones was a sparkling pool and banks of ferns and trees so thick she had no clue where the fence might be. A quintet was playing something Moorish she recognized as Lorena McKennitt's work and everything looked inviting and relaxing.

After that run-in with the studio accountants, she'd decided to eschew a partnership with a big studio. They'd come back with a report that was better fudged, and restoring 3.95% of the revenue. The .05% was basically an accountant Up Yours.

In her gut, she knew this film was going to be big, and it would be her highest revenue earner ever. It was going to exceed her expectations, and she didn't want to read in the press that it had failed because the numbers some studio executive had pulled out of his behind had been designed for a Hyde Butler blockbuster, not an independent film with a hard-to-classify comedy-mystery story.

"Why don't you go up to the room where you left your things and get dressed? I can handle this," Ellen urged her. "Kim will be down in a few minutes, I suspect."

As if on cue, Kim appeared in an authentic Spanish kaftan of a deep midnight blue. Assuming her first role as a producer she had opted for a full scale makeover. Cornrows had been combed out and straightened, then wrapped in bands of silk. Selena was still getting used to it, but there was no doubt that she looked elegant and poised. "Boss, go get dressed. You look like a hobo."

Feigning mock offense at the dismissive look at her jeans and tank top, Selena tripped happily up the stairs. As nervous as she was about taking money from people who had invested with her before, she felt better than she had in a while. Even the prospect of seeing Jennifer again didn't give her a lot of pause. Maybe those kisses and being the one who walked out had been just what she needed.

She wasn't afraid to wear a cocktail dress that showed some skin, and she didn't need Pradas to get through the night. Crushed patent pumps would do just fine. She repaired her make-up, decided to add a little highlight to her eyes and headed back to the patio. It was a new project, and Jennifer Lamont be damned. They were going to make a *fine* movie. She had to resist the impulse to do a little dance step and thought of Gail and her open-eyed wonder. She might be much older and wiser than Gail, but it didn't mean she couldn't twirl too.

The first half-hour was everything she could have hoped. Everyone knew one another, if only peripherally, and asked her questions about the timeline of production in ways that indicated they were seriously considering buying in. She normally would have planned this night for months, but getting Hyde on film in a few weeks rather than after his next picture had been the smarter move. She was trading on her reputation big-time, and yet she knew she could deliver.

She was chatting with Ellen about replenishing some of the food trays when Ellen said, "Who's that?"

"Gail Welles, the newcomer I was telling you about," she said after a glance.

Ellen gave her a strange look and Selena realized her voice had gotten a little breathy. She cleared her throat while she wondered where on earth Gail had found a dress that showed off her long legs to such perfection. She looked again, then said to Ellen, "She's a woman of many surprises."

"I'll say. If that isn't Chanel I'll eat a tablecloth. Quite the find, Lena m'dear. She's very eye-catching."

Eye-catching was apt. Selena made her way over to greet her, aware that she was somewhere between staring and tongue-tied. There was no trace of the scrawny waitress. She was more aware than ever that in many ways, she had no idea who Gail Welles really was. Certainly she hadn't expected this tall, confidant woman wearing couture and rakish, flirtatious boots.

She greeted her warmly, with the usual Hollywood air kisses, and her hand was on Gail's shoulder long enough to realize she was trembling. Gail's face was unusually closed, frozen in a mask of relaxed composure, but the opaque not-quite-green eyes didn't reflect the smile on her lips. She was scared to death,

Selena realized.

"James and I arranged with the car service to arrive together," Gail said, gesturing behind her. "His wife is home with their new baby. Thank you so much for sending a car for us."

She greeted James with what she hoped was equal alacrity even though she was still finding it hard to stop looking at Gail. Events like this were easier for men, as always. Once they passed a certain bar for quality, any dark suit would do. James looked suitably stylish, examining everything out of the corner of his eyes. She introduced him to Ellen's husband and checked on Gail, who was chatting with Ellen. Those two in safe hands, she greeted other arriving members of the crew, glad of Mirah's easy charm with people and Delilah's sharp wit. Eddie was a man of few words, but everyone in the room knew his credentials.

It was a typical well-organized Hollywood fundraiser, no chance of being a brawl. It risked being somewhat of a bore, but that energy changed the moment Hyde arrived. Selena had watched it happen before. The attendees quickly fell into two camps, the group that rushed him, eager to be introduced, and those who hung back, far too sophisticated to stargaze. They were in a definite minority, and all of them capitulated when Jennifer breezed in just minutes later.

Selena faded to the background and let the stars do their voodoo. They shone like beacons with that indefinable quality that brought fans to the theater and made an ordinary story amazing.

When someone asked Jennifer if she was having a boy or a girl, Jennifer laughed with delight, pulling her dress tight against her washboard abdomen. "The gossips will make up any lie to suit themselves. Next thing you know they'll have me married to Hyde and doing martial arts movies."

There was general laughter. Selena had seen that ridiculous claim, and was glad Jennifer had put it to rest with the investors. Most of them weren't film people, but if they had heard that rumor, they might have wondered if it was true.

Delilah appeared at Selena's elbow to murmur, "Butter

wouldn't melt in her mouth, and you know it."

"Ancient history," Selena said.

"She brought a friend with her."

"Really?" I don't care, Selena thought. Finally, who Jennifer might be seeing no longer mattered.

"At the bar, chatting up Gail."

She glanced that direction and did a double take. "She brought a woman?"

"Said the blondie was someone she was mentoring. Has some horror movie lined up."

"I know the blondie." She really couldn't believe her eyes. She quickly told Delilah about the incident leaving Hyde's party.

"In that case, they deserve each other, don't they?"

"Except that I don't want that Vivienne Weston creature anywhere near this project. Not as anyone's personal assistant or so-called unofficial understudy, nothing."

She sighed, knowing she'd have to deal with it. Had Jennifer somehow found out about Vivienne's encounter with her? What was Jennifer up to now?

Watching that lowlife of an actress talk to Gail was a lesson in opposites. While Weston glittered like overpolished brass, Gail was shining steady and pure, a quiet star. As she surreptitiously watched, Weston tried to take a phone photo of someone in the crowd, but Gail put her hand in the way, and said something that made Weston stow the phone.

How had she ever thought Gail capable of the same kind of low tricks Weston would try? Jennifer had poisoned her toward actors, that was for sure. They weren't all like that, and she shouldn't have thought she'd never be romantically intrigued by one again. Oh, hell...

Horrified at the direction her thoughts had taken, she forced herself to focus on the party. So Gail Welles was new to the inside of filmmaking, so new she thought every aspect was a treat. So fresh she could literally dance for joy. So what if being around her was proving renewing in unexpected ways, it had nothing to do with feelings outside of their professional relationship, and all the mayonnaise and chicken and butter pecan in the world didn't change that.

Feeling off balance, she realized Hyde was going to leave. He'd stayed the fifteen minutes she'd asked for, purely as a favor to her, and she gave him a sincere hug as they walked to the door.

"I really do appreciate this."

"Enlightened self-interest," he said.

"Liar. You're in danger of being found out as a nice guy."

"You slander me. I thought better of you," he quipped as he went out the door to his waiting car.

She knew that once Hyde left, Jennifer wouldn't linger either, and she'd take that Weston creature with her. She hoped so, since she hardly wanted another tête-à-tête with either of them. She didn't make it back to the patio though.

Jennifer was lounging against the patio door. The light from the setting sun limned her body under the thin black silk. "Have I done my part?"

"Yes, and I thank you." Behind Jennifer she could see Vivienne Weston still next to Gail at the bar, chattering away.

"Hyde got a hug. I saw it."

Selena shook her head. "Not tonight. And your little friend, I have firsthand experience with her attempting a slick bit of blackmail. There's no way she's getting any kind of role in the film or behind the scenes. She either has endless *chutzpah* for showing up in a room where I am, or she really doesn't know who she tried to rope into her little blackmail scheme."

Jennifer left the door, a small frown creasing her forehead. "Really? She's someone I met, seemed genuinely eager to learn the ropes. Kind of fun."

"I don't care if she's your latest pet or project, I don't want her near me or G—anyone. She was trying to take pictures out there."

"I'll take your word for it, Lena. Seriously." Jennifer was only a few feet away now. "Thank you for the warning."

When she took one more step toward her, Selena made

herself not retreat. "Are you leaving? I need to get back to the party. It's time for the pitch."

"I don't have to leave. I was thinking maybe you and I—"

"No. That's not going to happen."

"I'll send Viv home with my driver."

"No. We're not doing anything together but make this movie." She was aware of voices near and didn't want to set anyone's gossip mill in motion, especially not investors. "I have to go back out there now."

"There's no way you kissed me the way you did and it didn't mean anything."

Selena stepped closer so she could lower her voice. "It was goodbye. Please take your pet with you when you go."

It was a good exit line, and she used it as such, sliding around Jennifer to rejoin the party.

Not that she hadn't met some perfectly lovely people, but as Aunt Charlie would say, trash was trash. Gail didn't know who this woman was, but she had already gone from *talkative* to *leech*. She'd admitted she was there only as Jennifer's guest, then she'd tried to take pictures. Now she knew how easy it was for all those Hollywood gossip sites to get photos from inside parties.

As the leechy woman babbled on about her big start in pictures, some slasher movie where she had a line and then about ninety seconds on screen in the shower, Gail had to remind herself that a month ago she'd have been happy with a part like that. She knew how frustrating it was to get anyone to look at her seriously. Even if she had the money and desire to do it, she'd stop before grapefruit-sized enhancements, though. The woman next to her hadn't and was proudly displaying the surgeon's handiwork.

She let her attention wander, hoping to catch someone's eye and have an excuse to walk away. She watched Jennifer go through the wide open French doors where Selena had disappeared a few moments earlier with Hyde. From where she stood, she could see them moving closer and closer together, as if they were irresistibly drawn magnets.

Were they an item again? The gossipmongers certainly thought so, though the next day they had Jennifer with someone else or pregnant. She considered the way they had been in the diner, Jennifer exuding sex appeal and Selena looking like misery. A lover's tiff? At the audition she hadn't gotten any sense of an undercurrent, though. Selena had been briskly professional. She was such a reserved woman, until the overdose on ice cream the other night. Gail would bet a dollar that the butter pecan nose dive had had something to do with Jennifer.

She was spared making any further conversation with the leech when Jennifer returned to the patio and gestured. Her companion immediately went to heel. Gail glanced at Selena, catching her just before she wiped a look of distaste from her face. Was Jennifer using the little blonde to make Selena jealous? How…high school drama.

Well, anyway, she hoped not. Selena was too complicated and intelligent to have anything to fear from someone as shallow as that. She looked again toward Selena and found that Selena was looking back at her. Their gazes locked. She started to smile, but it didn't happen. All at once she was sitting in that little booth, and there was no one else in the world but the two of them, talking about the things they loved over ice cream.

Selena blinked and the moment was broken. But Gail's heart kept beating fast. "It's just the dress," she muttered, only to have their hostess, who had paused at the bar, give her an odd look.

"Are you enjoying yourself?"

"Yes, Ellen, very much," Gail assured her. "Everyone has been super. I'm not much good with names, though. I hope if I meet any of them again, I'll remember."

"I didn't catch the name of the woman you were just talking with."

"Neither did I. She asked me a lot of questions about how I got started, where I was working, how I got the part, whose phone numbers I had. She seemed very pleased that her name was in all the blogs, but I'd never heard of her." Gail realized that James was getting ready to leave, so she thanked Ellen for the lovely evening and went to join him. She had been very glad not to enter the party on her own. She hadn't quite gotten to his side of the patio, near the doors, when Selena stopped her.

"Going so soon?"

"James and I used the same car," Gail reminded her. "I took the whole night off, though. Did you need me to stay?"

"Trevor Barden isn't here yet, and he'd like to talk to you, I'm sure. I'll make sure you get home."

With a few words it was all arranged and after saying she'd see James on Monday when rehearsals began, she turned back to Selena, who was comparing notes with Kim.

Selena looked up, her dark eyes full of intense silvery lights, and Gail was again seized with a breathless vertigo. It didn't scare her. Well, maybe a little. "This is the boring part of the evening, but if you wait here, you'll see Trevor come in. I have to go pitch now."

She found an out of the way chair and gratefully sat down. The boots were fun, but pinched her toes. From where she was she could watch Selena working the crowd, then was glad to be tucked out of sight when Selena asked everyone to sit down for a few minutes.

"First, thank you all for coming. I know it was really for Ellen's hospitality rather than any great love of film—" She paused to encourage polite applause acknowledging Ellen. "Perhaps a few of you were eager to meet the stars of our film, the incredible combination of Butler and Lamont. *Barcelona* will be a wonderful movie, in the tradition of *In Bruges* and *Fargo*. Offbeat, funny, about a unique place in the world, with a great cast and crew. With Eddie Lynch directing," she gestured into the crowd, "how can we go wrong?"

After pausing for more polite applause, she went on, "I hope you also got to meet the other crucial members of the production team. Our screenwriter and casting agent are both amazingly talented contributors, and my own production staff is committed to creating an entertaining, talked-about movie— within budget."

There was laughter as Selena grinned. Gail loved watching her talk, the economical gestures with her hands, the vivacious gleam in her eyes were full of her passion for the project. She loves what she does, and Gail could appreciate that. How had she thought the woman in the diner was miserable? Selena was warm and vibrant, and the halter cut of the dress showed off the graceful curves of her neck and shoulders.

"When you go," she was saying, "we have a little memento for you, and you'll also find the usual portfolio information about the financial backing and shares available. I hope you'll join us on this adventure." Her smile flashed in the lights and Gail was dazzled. "It's going to be a terrific one. And now, the bar is still open and I hope everyone will enjoy the rest of the evening."

Gail realized belatedly that she'd been joined at her table. "Trevor! Selena said you'd be here."

He gave her a warm smile as he unbuttoned his sport jacket and relaxed in the chair. "I had to see it for myself, Gail Welles, rising star. I saw your name in *Variety*. Does this beat waitressing?"

He did seem genuinely pleased, Gail thought. "It does. I can't tell you how grateful I am. This is all because of you."

"I made a phone call. The rest was up to you. But thank you for the cookies, and feel free to drop more of them by any time."

"Can I buy you a drink? Selena spared no expense, so I can afford the best."

He grinned and agreed. Gail led him to the bar, where the cute bartender was very attentive, remembering that he liked martinis. Their progress was slowed by several people stopping her to chat, and she found herself explaining several times, trying to make each sound just as fresh and interesting as the first, that she was indeed an unknown neophyte, pleased and awed to be part of the production.

"You're handling that well," Trevor said when they finally escaped the bar area with their drinks.

"Thank you. It's all a little unreal. The *Variety* thing took me totally by surprise. And all that stuff in the online tabloids—that's just crazy."

"It'll make you insane if you care what they say. Nobody has ever shown me that their tripe affects anybody's box office or ratings, and only people you don't want to work with anyway look at that sort of stuff before they consider casting you. Their dirt is all about degrading women's looks and speculating on which women are prostituting themselves for work, but when the movie's a hit, all the credit goes to the straight men. They only time they mention gays is when it involves sex." He gave a nod toward the largest knot of potential investors. "Those are the people you really have to care about if you stick with indie projects. The people with the money."

"Well, that's always true, isn't it?"

"You'd be surprised by people who think they can take twenty million from a group of investors and not owe them a thing back. Selena's not one of them. If she was, they wouldn't be here and you wouldn't be the nearly famous Gail Welles. In TV, it's all about the bottom line every week. Ratings every morning, instant feedback. Stick with movies." His smile was rueful. "You only have to deal with results months and months after you've moved on to something new."

"Unless you're Selena," Gail observed. "She's dealing with it every day."

"That's why she gets the big bucks." He held out a hand as Selena approached them. "You are looking wonderful as always, Lena."

Gail loved the glow all around Selena, who gave Trevor an affectionate kiss. "I think I can finally have a glass of wine."

"Gee, Trevor, you look fantastic," Trevor said in mock hurt.

"The lady needs a drink," Gail said. "Then she'll be nice to you."

Selena gave her an amused look, tinged with something else Gail couldn't name. She lingered for a few minutes, and thanked Trevor for referring Gail before moving back to the other guests.

Gail, subtly guided by Trevor, moved through the investors one more time, listening to the kinds of things people said and admiring Trevor for his sheer aplomb. She was working on it, trying to learn fast. After about twenty minutes, Trevor admitted he had another party to go to and bowed out, leaving Gail somewhat bereft. The guests were starting to leave but she had to wait for Selena to be free before she could find out how she was getting home. There was probably a spare car.

Selena spent some time talking to a silver-haired man with an impossible tan and Gail decided she'd had enough snacks to risk another drink. The cute bartender, with a perky pony tail, bright eyes and a tight-fitting vest, suggested a vodka and cranberry juice, and Gail went along. It evolved into a tasting between various vodkas. Gail was trying to decide if she liked Grey Goose or Belvedere better when she realized Selena was heading her way. Most of the guests had gone and the other bartender was starting to pack up the bottles.

"Enjoying yourself?" Selena's glance included the bartender and the row of little shot glasses in front of her.

"I was sampling. Taste testing." Gail hoped she didn't sound drunk. She didn't think she was, though she felt really quite… good.

"When you're ready, I can give you a ride home."

"Sure, now is good."

"That is, if you need one." Again, she glanced at the bartender.

"Yes, I do." She didn't think the bartender was hitting on her. She looked, got a wink, and was very confused. Cute women like that never noticed her. Hmm—be in the movies and suddenly everyone decided you were attractive? That hardly seemed fair, she was the same person she'd been a month ago, without bad hair and clothes from a discount store. Wasn't she?

"Here," the bartender said, pushing a napkin toward her. "If you should need someone to tend bar for you."

Gail took the napkin, saw that it had a name and phone number written on it. She put it in her shiny silver clutch, trying hard not to blush. She didn't know if she succeeded, but Selena was smiling brightly.

"I live on the edge of Silver Lake and Westlake, toward Dodger Stadium," Gail explained as they walked toward the front door. "So feel free to have the driver drop you first. You must live closer than that."

"My house is just behind the production offices, actually." Selena led the way down the front walk. "And I don't use drivers unless I have to. I'll give you a lift home."

She was caught off guard at the idea of Selena seeing where she lived. "You could drop me at the diner and I can get home from there."

"Nonsense." Selena produced a key fob and kept walking.

The chirp from a car just two away startled her. She recognized the sleek hybrid from her visit to the Ryan offices. It suited Selena, the spare lines, but it was hardly the conspicuous consumption type of vehicle most Hollywood types drove.

She opened the passenger door only to find a dress bag on the seat.

"Oh, hang on." Selena came around to her side of the car. Even though Gail stepped back, their shoulders brushed. "One of Kim's shadows brought my things out to the car for me."

She watched Selena shift the garment to the back seat, unsuccessfully trying not to stare. She edged toward the seat, but Selena muttered something and leaned in for more of her belongings. Again, their shoulders brushed, then Selena's hip and Gail's thigh made lingering contact as Gail tried to get out of the way. Selena emerged with a collection of cables, a laptop bag and a gym bag, all of which she stowed in the backseat as well.

"There. I tend to spread my stuff out in the car."

"I won't tell you what you'd find in mine, starting with the donut wrappers." Gail hoped it didn't look as if she'd been staring at her executive producer's bare back, admiring the line of her spine and the way the halter of her dress cupped the front of her body.

She snuggled into the passenger seat. It was comfortable, even though there was some kind of attached pullout shelf under the dash that reduced the room available for her knees. Obviously, Lena was not used to passengers. Gail found that somewhat reassuring, though she wasn't willing to think about it much. She tried to put that all out of her head. Before she realized it was a stupid question, because the answer was emblazoned on the dashboard, she asked, "This is a hybrid, right?"

"Yes. It can be disconcerting not to feel the engine vibrating when you're at a stoplight." Selena buckled up and then they pulled away from the curb.

"I can imagine." She watched the gates of the enclave open to let them out, then glanced across the car at Selena.

Hands lightly on the wheel, she seemed absorbed in driving.

"It was a nice party." She hadn't a clue what else to say.

"Thank you. I'm glad you enjoyed it. Especially that last bit."

"Oh, you mean the bartender? She was nice."

"And flirting with you."

Gail shrugged. "I guess. I'm not used to it."

"I don't think she was sure she was your type, but you seemed to be hers."

Gail laughed. "I haven't dated enough to have a type. Between working and college, then working to save money to move here, and working and auditions…"

"Nobody in all that time? You're what, thirty?"

"Thirty-two. I didn't say nobody. But nobody serious. And they were all women in theater, no common trait between them except for that. I guess if I have a type, it's someone who loves something the way I do."

The exclusive enclave behind them eased into the busier boulevards of Beverly Hills. Climbing one last crest, the radiant night vista of the Los Angeles area spread out to the dark horizon.

Gail let out a sigh. "It's so beautiful. I know it's all electricity we ought to be saving and air pollution from all those cars, but it's beautiful."

"And that's not the best view either."

"Where would that be?"

"Mulholland Drive—it's a shot used in movies and TV all the time. You'd recognize it right away. Would you like to see it? It's not that far off our route. You don't have a curfew, right?"

"No, not at all. But I feel bad that you're already taking me halfway across the basin only to have to turn around and drive right back. You could get me a cab at any of the hotels."

"It's okay, Gail. I need to unwind, and I like to drive." Selena glanced across the car at her, dark eyes illuminated only by the lights from the dashboard. "I have one niece and I took her to see it last year because it's the quintessential L.A. vista."

Gail concentrated on breathing and telling herself that her palms had no right to be sweaty. Selena saw her as a protégé, maybe, like a niece, and that was good. Of course thinking *Aunt Selena* was just so wrong, it was not at all how she felt, which was nothing but admiration and gratitude and respect. Nothing more.

How many shots of vodka had she had? The tastes had been just a few sips, but she was having an enormous amount of difficulty keeping her gaze off Selena's hands.

At the moment, those long, agile fingers were dancing over the buttons on the radio. A rock song Gail didn't know filled the car. Selena tapped the glowing display and the volume lowered. "This is from the latest Levi Hodges album. I am really hoping he agrees to do our theme song."

"That would be really cool," Gail agreed. "I have to admit that the diner plays lots of great sock hop and Motown, so I'm not up on what's hot."

Selena tapped the radio until the display read "50sR&B." "Big Girls Don't Cry" was halfway done. She was used to hearing it while serving waffles and corn dogs. Now she was sitting next to a beautiful, interesting, charming woman, on the way home from a Hollywood party where she'd been an actual invited guest. She needed to remember that Selena was with Jennifer, probably, who was everything a Hollywood starlet ought to be, all the things Gail wasn't and never would be.

"Even on a Saturday night," Selena muttered as they slowed for the interchange between the Santa Monica and Hollywood freeways. Traffic crawled for about five minutes, then resumed its normal speed. Instead of heading south, Selena went north, and before long she took the exit for Mulholland Drive.

"It's quite funny," Gail said, "but a friend and I parked our cars at that park-and-ride lot at the exit back there and took the bus to here, then we walked up the road to these stairs." She pointed. "When we walked up those stairs it seemed like forever. All for some free food and a few hours of not feeling like we waited tables. Know what was at the top of those stairs?"

Selena gave her an indulgent smile. "What?"

"Trevor Barden. He'd seen me audition, badly, but asked if I'd read another part for him and here I am. Even if this is the first and last movie I ever make, here I am."

"It won't be the last, Gail. You don't have to worry about that."

"That's very nice of you—"

"I'm not an idle flatterer," Selena said firmly. "There are dozens of things I could have said, but it's the truth. Keep your life clean and you'll always be working."

Gail blinked hard to hold back tears that were a mix of pleasure and uncertainty. Her thoughts and feelings were jumping around like her pulse. "I'll try to keep my feet on the ground. I think it's harder for women like Jennifer, actually. She must be terrified of wrinkles and sags. I've got nothing to sag and I think the older I get the more interesting my face gets. My drama coach—before I moved out here—said I wouldn't be truly handsome until I was at least forty."

"Your coach may have a point. Ellen had the right description, tonight. She said you were eye-catching."

The music changed to "Who Wrote the Book of Love" as Selena effortlessly navigated a hairpin turn.

"Eye-catching? Maybe in this dress. I had to have a gay man's help picking it out. How stereotypical is that?"

"I don't think Ellen meant the dress." They veered off the road into a parking lot. "Here's the overlook."

They glided into a parking space and got out of the car. Selena pointed out where film crews could set up. "Using that position, and putting just a few cars in the shot, it always looks like a little out of the way corner. You never see this." She gestured at an explanatory marker, unreadable in the dark.

The wind was whipping up, and Gail held back a shiver. In spite of the valley heat, there was a little bit of chill in the air at this hour. She followed Selena through the parked cars, joining a number of people at the railing.

It was breathtaking. Glowing like a lamp was the Hollywood Bowl, and just over there the mountain spelled H-O-L-L-Y-W-O-O-D. W for Welles, she thought, and right below them the Hollywood Freeway dove straight for the heart of the high rises in downtown L.A. Everything glittered green, gold and red, alternating with white, like tiny stars. Several sets of giant spotlights were tracing the sky.

"Thank you," Gail said. "You're right, I've seen this a million times, just never with my own eyes."

"It's the kind of view that inspires people in their love affair with Los Angeles. You're above all the…reality. This is an illusion, like the movies."

"I used to think I wanted to live in a movie," Gail said. "Life's easier in the movies."

"What changed your mind?" Selena shifted to face Gail more directly, and Gail made herself look toward the distant lights to avoid staring at the alluring curves of Selena's shoulders glowing ivory in the starlight.

"I realized that in the movies, people are always on a journey from the beginning to the end. They don't get to stay in one place and be happy, right there. Hold a moment in time and just be happy. Soon as they do, it's either time for the credits or the scene changes and it's another day. On the other hand, when the moment is sad, the movies stay there forever, and they add a great soundtrack. My folks died when I was in high school. No wise mentor arrived out of the blue, and I didn't have an awesome soundtrack to cry to. I just…moved on, finally."

"Is that what you want when you're grieving? To move on?"

Gail tore her gaze from the distant twinkling lights. Selena's regard was serious and steady. "How long you stay in the grief is a kind of testimony to how much you loved, isn't it?"

"Then I loved her a lot, didn't I?" Selena blinked, then rushed on with, "Did I say that aloud? Oh, lord, just forget about that. You'd think I'd actually had that glass of wine."

Gail was certain Selena was blushing, though it was hard to tell in the mottled light. So much for thinking of her as The Boss or The Producer or some other title, anything but a woman with all the flaws and fun and mistakes anybody could make. She and Jennifer had broken up for sure? Or maybe it was a long on-again, off-again affair in the off phase.

Now Lena—no, Selena—just looked nervous and was glancing at her keys, probably wondering why on earth she'd bothered to bring some clueless neophyte up to here to see the lights. There were a few couples kissing, plenty holding hands. That wasn't why Selena had brought her up here. Instead, they were talking about death and broken hearts.

Death and broken hearts was safer than anything else, she scolded herself. She didn't bring you up here to make out. So what if you can picture this moment in a movie, it doesn't mean she can. In the movies, sure, you'd be kissing the girl now, somehow, the romantic location throwing all common sense to the wind. Irresistible attraction and it's going to work out just fine if you kiss The Boss or The Producer or The Women You've Only Talked To For Three Hours Total, right, only in the movies does any of that nonsense ever work out. You're tipsy and she's feeling blue about Jennifer Lamont, bombshell sex goddess. So you can stop licking your lips every time you look at her. Like a kiss would fix that.

She shivered and studied the view.

"You're cold."

Gail nodded and next thing she knew, Lena had slipped an

arm around her and the shivers stopped. She wasn't cold at all. She couldn't breathe, in fact. The top of Lena's head nestled against her ear and it would take only the slightest effort to lean in for a kiss. There was starlight dancing in Lena's eyes and Gail adored the way Lena was looking at her. Part of her hadn't a clue who Lena saw, but she wanted to be the woman who put warmth in those eyes.

A car pumping bass squealed past the overlook with a skitter of a thrown can added to the noise. Lena jumped, then looked around at the cuddling couples. Was she realizing, just as Gail abruptly was, that the other couples were all male-female?

"It's late," she said.

"Yes," Gail agreed. She sighed because for just a second she had thought the tossed object had been aimed at them, the two lesbians standing far too close together. The other couples resumed pitching their woo, but the jolt of reality had separated her and Lena—stop that, she told herself. Selena, Selena, Selena, or you'll call her Lena for real. Maybe the reality jolt was for the best, though, but someday Gail would like to live in a world where she didn't look over her shoulder because she was holding another woman close. The promising moment was gone beyond recall, for all the wrong reasons.

She followed Selena back to the car and was glad to be out of the wind. "Thank you for driving me up here. L.A. is full of contrasts."

The inane remark deserved no answer, and Selena made none. The Hollywood Freeway bore out the truth of her words, lined with big box stores and auto dealerships with marquees still glowing, though shopping hours were over. As they got closer to Dodger Stadium the streets narrowed, the houses shrank, then warehouses and strip developments of offices and storefronts were interspersed with apartment buildings.

Nothing of any import had been said since they left the overlook, and Gail hoped the evening didn't end with a working girl trolling the car. She had Selena stop at the Lorelei Arms' front steps.

"It's not much, but it's home," she said.

"We lived in a place a lot like that when I was a kid."

"Safe and clean." Gail shrugged. "The colorful neighbors, no extra charge."

"See you Monday morning?"

"Bright and early." Time to get out of the car, she told herself. For a moment she couldn't make herself move. Finally, she put her hand on the door, but stopped when Selena said her name.

"Thank you."

"For what?"

The smile she got was as enigmatic as the explanation. "I'm not sure."

Scant minutes later, tumbling into bed, Gail was certain she'd made a fool of herself. She'd practically drooled on the woman. Her body was suddenly obsessed with the fact that she'd been celibate for far too long. Certain parts were definitely perking up, saying, "Remember me?" If she had any sense, she'd call that bartender and go on a real date with an available woman who thought she was "eye-catching."

If she had any sense.

By the time Selena locked the door of the pool house behind her, dropping her clothes where she stood, she was shivering with fatigue. The party had been exhilarating and exhausting. A drive had been the perfect way to unwind.

She wasn't the least bit unwound.

A hot shower drained what was left of her energy and she went to bed, wrapping her arms around the body pillow, willing herself to sleep. She had so much to do, a film to make a success. Tonight, she hoped she'd raised enough to post security for a full-scale enterprise loan. She'd owe a lot of people their money's worth, and they'd invested with her because they all trusted Selena Ryan would do right by them.

Doing right by them didn't include developing a schoolgirl infatuation on an actress in the production. A *young* actress, eight years younger, an entire world younger. Gail had no right to be guileless and thoughtful. No right to make Selena feel renewed and refreshed. No right to make someone as jaded and heartsore as her think that her arms around Gail instead of this pillow would fill the holes in her life.

It's not as if it made any sense. They didn't really know each other. Thank goodness Gail had been a bit tipsy, or she might have realized, as they looked at the view and talked about life in the movies, how much Selena ached to take Gail with her to some place else, uncomplicated and full of sunshine, where they could touch and laugh and tell their secrets, complete with a soundtrack during the more lyrical interludes. It made no sense that she looked at Gail and wanted movie magic to be real, just once.

Gail was something special, everyone but Jennifer seemed to agree on that. And that was all—a special performer. A kind and decent person, and not something to be used for her own fantasy escape or some delicious, quick sex on the side.

She was just hungering for something she couldn't have. Shouldn't and wouldn't have, not right now. Rehearsals started early Monday morning. It was Kim's baby. She didn't even have to show up. If she had any sense she'd go to the office instead.

If she had any sense.

Buzztastic # #

Newbie Gail Welles has a case of major awe for co-star Hyde Butler in the upcoming indie flick. We tried to get The Butler to answer a few questions about Gail, but he's too busy playing craps in Vegas. Pics next page. That's some armful he's got there!

Usually summer means less dress-up and more dresses off in Tinseltown, but not this summer. We've got photos a faithful site user sent us from a posh event last night. Check out the Armanis! Is that the Luscious Lamont leaning on a captain of industry? Last we heard he's married. What about her galpal ex—an ex all over again? That's what's so fun about the bi-babies, everybody's a potential hook-up! When J.L. hooks up, we'll let you know!

Chapter 9

Five-thirty Monday morning might as well have been three a.m. Gail rubbed her gritty eyes and hoped the car turning the corner was coming for her. All the working girls had gone home. The smell of things she didn't want to identify lingered in the air, hinting that the day would be hot and humid. Her head wouldn't have been quite as thick if Angel and Betty hadn't popped the cork on champagne after the diner had closed last night. She was wearing the gift of a suede jacket that everyone had chipped in to buy her, and even more grateful for it in the slight pre-dawn chill.

It was her car, had to be, though she followed Kim's instructions just as she had Saturday night. She asked to see the driver's orders from Garcia-Zimmer Security before she got in, and once in, she texted that she'd been picked up. It was a little disconcerting having a specific security protocol, but apparently it was a necessity. A little vigilance took away a lot of stress. The theater's street parking wasn't enough for everyone, too, and the production company couldn't guarantee their cars wouldn't be vandalized. Whatever the reason, she was glad not to be driving herself when she could barely keep her eyes open.

The Carlisle Theater stage door was repaired, and one of Kim's assistants checked her in. She wasn't the first or last to arrive. Jim was already sitting in the front row, coffee mug cradled on his chest. The casting director was there, looking as much in need of caffeine as Gail felt. Kim was outright cheerful by contrast, obviously that most dreaded of creatures, a Morning Person.

It wasn't ten minutes before Hyde arrived. He looked as if he'd come from the gym, hair wet, brimming with energy. As he teased everyone but Kim about not being morning people, Gail heard for the first time his light drawl. It was downright charming.

They were supposed to start at six with script readings while the sound crew began their checks. Tomorrow the lighting people would flit all around them as they rehearsed. By Thursday the costume folks would measure them and they'd start blocking and prepping the scenes to be filmed in the Carlisle—which was most of them—in the order most advantageous for use of actors, technicians and finished sets. The balcony and wings would be lit and dressed for sets, with a nearby apartment building adding additional exterior shots, which made the make-up people very anxious. It was like a jigsaw puzzle, and Gail's plan was to show up when she was supposed to, stand where she was told and do the lines she was given. She hoped to feel more at ease by the time they were actually shooting.

Focusing on the work would also put her feelings about Selena into the proper perspective. At least that was what she was telling herself.

But nothing was getting underway when Jennifer still hadn't arrived by six-fifteen. At six-twenty she finally walked in. The director, who had been pacing, said, "Thank you for joining us," before asking the actors to settle themselves at the table on the stage and prepare for scene thirty-one.

"Coffee first," Jennifer said.

"Darling lady," Eddie said, "you may have coffee if you promise me to get your clocks repaired. We can't start late every day. I know you know this."

"Dear Eddie," Jennifer cooed. "I promise to be good."

Hyde hunkered down in his seat and snored loudly. Gail decided it was wise to ignore the early morning tensions.

Finally, they got underway and several hours later, Gail was hoarse and felt badly over-rehearsed. Fortunately, they got to move around while the gaffers taped cables into place. In the midst of being clucked over by a technician, she realized that Selena had arrived, but had no idea how long she'd been there.

It only took about five minutes to realize Selena wasn't going to make eye contact with her. Okay, that was probably for the best.

It still hurt. It wasn't as if they'd done anything untoward, or even borderline, regardless of what she'd been wishing for. They'd had a couple of personal conversations away from their professional ties. That was all. And if that was all it was why wouldn't Selena look at her, and why was she herself so desperately trying not to care? Did Lena's avoidance mean she had realized Gail's attraction and was embarrassed?

When they broke for lunch, provided by a catering company, Selena was talking intensely with Kim and Eddie. Gail took her salad and soda over to where Jim was eating and they talked on and off while he texted his wife at work. It was gratifying when Hyde joined them, asking to see pictures of Jim's daughter and posing a few polite questions about their backgrounds. Gail tried not to notice that Jennifer had sat down with Kim and Lena. She was thinking like high school, and putting stock in cliques, which was a waste of energy. She focused instead on Hyde, asking him how he got into acting.

"I took drama in college as a way to get what I thought would be an easy pass. I was into sports. Period." Hyde got up to sort his trash into the appropriate garbage and recycling bins. "I was bitten by the bug then, but the sports scholarship was king. Then I blew out my knee and rent mattered and I ended up sellin' air conditioning. Some film company came through to shoot in the national forest nearby, and they had auditions for extras. I did a walk-on, someone asked if I could talk and next thing I knew I was a local lumberjack. Dog of a movie, but you have to start somewhere."

"I feel very lucky where I'm starting." Gail wrapped up her trash, absorbing the reality that for the next eight weeks she wasn't going to have to worry about having something to eat. The crab salad had been delicious. "This isn't going to be a dog."

"I don't think so." His easy grin was infectious and she found herself smiling back. "And you're part of the reason why. I was wondering if you could show me that thing you do, with your shoulders."

"What thing?"

By the time he'd gotten her to demonstrate what he meant and Gail tried to get his extremely toned physique to slouch, she was standing on a chair behind him, pushing down on his shoulders.

"You've got too much muscle for this and your posture is just way too good," she said. "Pretend you've got ten pounds of plates and food on each forearm." She pushed down harder but his shoulders would not budge.

It was not perhaps the most auspicious pose when the director called, "Places!" and without missing a beat added, "Children, if you're quite done."

Hyde laughed and grabbed Gail by the legs, carrying her up to the stage on his back. Jennifer gave her a look that plainly said Gail was behaving like a gauche newcomer and Gail felt her face flame. Kim seemed slightly scandalized. Horsing around was pretty common in the theater as part of getting to know each other, but evidently things were different in film.

A quick glance at Selena didn't help one way or the other—her indulgent gaze was on Hyde. She seemed genuinely amused, and only showed alarm when Hyde let go of Gail's legs without warning. "Don't drop her!"

Gail landed easily, but darned near dislocated her shoulder imitating a gymnast's dismount.

"Ten," and "Nine-point-nine," were shouted from some of the crew members and fortunately, everybody then went about their business.

"You're a good sport, Gail." Hyde thumbed open his script.

"Just one of the boys," she quipped.

"Hardly." He gave her one of his intense looks. "I'm not one to step on your sexual politics. I know perfectly well you're a girl, but I'm kind of glad I don't have to treat you like one."

Gail sort of knew what he was trying to say. "Just treat me like a person—a person who isn't ever going to want to jump your bones."

She was aware that Jennifer was joining them on stage, but other than shifting to allow her into their circle, Hyde continued his conversation with Gail. "I was even thinking that in my next picture, I'm a married guy trying to save his wife, totally in love with her, but for reasons that make sense to the other people, I'm to have a bombshell sidekick I pick up along the way. So I'm trying to figure out how I'm not supposed to have sexual chemistry with her. I say we make her a lesbian, then she can be a totally hot babe femme I get to treat like a person, not a potential conquest. It would be a different way to do a not very unique story. I know some actresses who'd love to play it, too. And way easier on me."

"You poor man," Jennifer said. "Such troubles you have."

He gave Jennifer a lopsided smile, and Gail watched the way his entire demeanor subtly changed. For whatever reason, he felt he had to treat Jennifer "like a girl." He'd never scoop Jennifer up the way he had her, without it meaning something more. He'd called it sexual politics, but she called it human nature. Jennifer clearly ate up his flirtatious attention, making her history with Selena seem like the piece that didn't quite fit the puzzle. Jennifer's fluid sexuality aside, Selena didn't seem the type to respond to all the coy eyelash flutters—but maybe once upon a time she had been.

"Really, folks, we need to get back to work," Eddie said. "Back at the table, please—"

"Hang on, Eddie." Selena joined them on stage. "I just wanted to let everyone know that the producer on our Hong Kong production just came down with swine flu, so I'll be away for at least a week, probably more—but at the other end of the phone except when I'm in the air. Kim is your go-to producer and you couldn't be in better hands. So be good, and no worries. I know producers lie for a living, but I'm telling the truth, you're a fabulous ensemble working with the best crew in the business."

Under the cover of murmurs of agreement, Gail was thinking she'd spent the last week fluttering on the inside because she'd see Selena every day, but so much for that idea. It was for the best, because nearly initiating a clinch on Saturday night had been foolish and unprofessional. She was just being silly. Time to get down to the work, focus on the part, be a star, get paid and do Aunt Charlie proud.

They were in the middle of a scene when she saw Selena head for the stairs that led down to the stage door exit. Even though she had turned away for a cue, she swore she knew when Selena had left the building.

A long plane flight to Hong Kong meant Selena got lots of work done while her body still thought it was the workday. When the evening was waning, Los Angeles time, the enforced inactivity and solitude provided too many hours to stare out at the dark night and wonder why it had been so hard to leave. Walking out of the Carlisle she had felt she was going to miss something she was unlikely to experience again. Maybe it was just a fine production coming together, all things clicking the way they ought, making magic for the screen. She couldn't wait to see the dailies.

She wasn't so self-deluded that she didn't know she missed watching Gail work. She had loved watching Hyde transform into a big kid, clearly enjoying himself in the low-tech production where a green screen wasn't his most frequent staging. Gail seemed to bring that out in people, and she would miss watching her blossom into a full-fledged star, confident of her part, breathing life into Georgette and driving Elgin to madness with her possessive deviousness. Yes, she would miss that, and it was a shame. It was one of the reasons she loved producing movies.

But there was something else... Every time she recalled the way Gail felt next to her and how much she had yearned to lift her lips for kisses, she had to admit that lust was in play. It was undeniable. But there was something else changing when she was around Gail and now it would stop while she was away. And maybe not start again. She felt an ease around her, like they both spoke the same, rare language. She'd been deeply pleased that the crew seemed to respect her. Was it that she was taking a risk on an unknown and so wanted it to turn out good? Maybe all she was hoping for was a validation of her judgment.

Trying to grab a few minutes of sleep somewhere over the Pacific, she knew that she wouldn't sleep while she thought about Gail.

Maybe being halfway around the world for a little while was the best thing.

After stopping first at the hotel where Todd was cooped up with his misery, she went on to a tense meeting with the director. Michael tended to think every bump in the road would ruin his picture, and losing his producer counted as a huge bump in the road. She sympathized—the entire picture was Todd's baby, a project he'd brought with him when Selena had opened the firm to him. She knew little about the ins and outs, only what overflowed from Todd onto Alan's or Kim's desk and then flowed on up to her. Generally, it hadn't been much beyond keeping expense tabs, nonsense with caterers and a last minute switch of a location shoot.

After a good venting of his various anxieties, Michael calmed enough to bring Selena up-to-date on the day-to-day issues.

Two agents representing two actors unhappy with some aspect of the production were both hinting their clients could come down with the flu too. A critical secondary player had a growing waistline, evidently a few months more pregnant than they'd all been led to believe. A screenwriter was about to jump off a bridge because a performer was refusing to utter certain reprehensible lines, and there were a thousand other small matters from transit for location shoots to telling the accountants to pay the local wage taxes on time to avoid a shutdown. In other words, the usual producer's woes.

Michael didn't even know the Mender's Guild had sent an English-speaking negotiating representative not four hours after Todd had been reported as sick, stating their agreement for services had been with the person Todd, not the company Ryan Productions, and had to be renegotiated with her. As far as Selena knew, a mender was the person who stuck duct tape on something until a real repair person could be found. Invariably, the members of such guilds were related to the other craftspeople, making employment by the picture a family affair. With Kim tied up on *Barcelona* and Alan better suited than she was to hold down the home fort on his own, she'd been the logical person to keep Todd's production moving. The shoot was supposed to close in six days, and now they were two full days behind schedule. In terms of their budget, that was huge.

So here she was, thinking increasingly longing thoughts of the production she'd left behind, where the actors still liked each other and none of the usual woes had yet to emerge.

Finally checked into her hotel, she called Kim. "Yes, I made it, I'm alive. It's just the usual million chickens pecking all at once. How are things at the Carlisle?"

"Wonderful. Eddie actually smiled today. He wants to start with some camera work tomorrow afternoon, which is early, but the principals are comfortable. Mirah's got the rest of the cast lined up starting next week. How's your Internet connection there?"

"Pretty good, it looks like. I ought to be stable enough to

log in and watch the dailies. It'll keep me sane." She gazed out the window at the chaotic Hong Kong skyline. It looked like it would rain later, oh goodie.

"The smartest thing we did was cast Gail, you know. She's like a breath of fresh air. Everybody likes her, except Jennifer."

"Has she been trouble?" She hated to think of Jennifer unleashing one of her games on Gail.

"No, just a feeling I have. She asked me, very friendly, how we managed to discover a jewel like Gail. I told her she'd been recommended by another producer and she went away."

Good thing Jennifer hadn't recognized Gail from the diner, then. Jennifer around Gail—it made her nervous. "Well, keep me posted. It's eleven a.m. here. What time is it there again?"

"Eight p.m., the night before."

"I'm sorry I called you so late."

"Now you know why Todd is always so cranky." Kim was laughing when she hung up, but Selena was really glad she hadn't waited until any later in her morning to call.

If she had it right, she'd wake up the day after tomorrow and there would be dailies posted on their corporate site for her to review. With that to look forward to she ordered room service, had a shower and made herself stay awake through a series of phone calls, tackling one problem after another. When the sun finally went down in Hong Kong her head was on the pillow. Already swamped with sleep she nevertheless pictured Gail clinging to Hyde's back, her face lit with glee.

She could still hear Gail laughing, all the way on the other side of the world.

"Cut!"

Gail put a hand on her stomach. "I don't know why I can't get that line. I am so sorry."

Eddie looked neither upset nor reassuring. Gail was getting used to his unchanging Zen-master aura. "Keep going instead of stopping. If you flub, start over. The film editor will get the right one."

Gail ran through her grimaces and shakes, working her frustration out of her face. She'd been okay for going on a week now, so it was embarrassing to stop everything cold with a silly little line she couldn't say properly.

"Break it into phonetic pieces," Jim suggested.

The two secondary actors, who played the parts of local agitators for independence for the Catalan state, looked tired, and Gail was willing to bet that the tap of heels in the theater was Jennifer, who ought to have been doing her scene at this point.

Under her breath she muttered, "All we have to do is tell the bank we're having a great run. They'll never expect—*suspect*. They'll never suspect that we're not actually selling any tickets. They'll never suspect...suspect *suspect*...never suspect, *ver sus ver sus*," and on for several more iterations until the syllables lost meaning but her mouth would form them in the right order anyway. "Never suspect," she added one last time.

She nodded at Eddie. "Okay, I think I have it now. I'm so—"

"Don't apologize. Just do it."

She nodded. Everybody backed up into their starting positions, and she waited for her cue to launch into her long, rambling speech on how easily the theater would launder money for such a noble cause.

She didn't get it right, but taking Eddie's direction, she simply started over as if nothing was amiss, and that time she got through it. When Eddie called, "Cut," she wanted to go limp. "Holy crap, I don't believe I got it."

Jennifer's heels were loud on the boards. "Funny the things that'll trip you up, isn't it?"

"I didn't see that one coming. I thought I'd flub the first scene we did this morning."

"It's probably the pace." Jennifer gave her a surprisingly friendly look. "This is snappy dialogue, faster than you'd do in theater, and the tongue can get twisted."

"I hope I get used to whatever it is. I feel bad keeping everybody waiting."

She faded to the seats behind the lighting control boards,

waiting for her next scene and still fascinated by the process. One of the mesmerizing things about watching was the interplay between the Steadicam operator and the dolly grip. The cameraman's attention was completely focused on what he could see through his lens, so the grip silently guided his footing to avoid stumbles that would jar the take. It was like a *pas de deux* taking place while the actors said their lines.

Jennifer and Hyde, with the two businessmen, were now filming a scene from almost the end of the movie. By the end of the day the two businessmen would be done with their contribution, and the scenes making full long shots of the Carlisle stage would also be done. They'd film scenes in the wings next.

During the take Kim caught her eye with a silent wave. She waited until the shot ended before moving.

"Selena wants to talk to you. Use my phone—take it out to the foyer."

Her heart abruptly pounding in her ears, she hurried up the aisle so she could clear the sound zone before the next take started. She wended her way through the two curtains of black fabric that kept the light inside the theater the same regardless of time of day, and found herself alone in the theater's dilapidated foyer.

"Hi?"

"Gail. I just wanted to tell you the dailies are great. Kim said you were having a rough morning so I thought some encouragement was in order." Lena didn't sound as if she was on the other side of the planet. The call was clear enough to hear the weariness in her voice.

"Thanks—that's really nice of you. It just a silly line I couldn't get my mouth to say. Everyone has been so kind to me."

"I'm glad to hear it."

There was an awkward silence, then Gail thought to ask, "How's Hong Kong?"

"Crowded and noisy, full of great food and interesting people, but not home. We were at a thousand-year-old ruin yesterday, which was fascinating."

"Isn't it two a.m. there or something like that?"

"It is. I had to have a long dinner with one of the stars. I don't often get to call at this hour so—"

Gail plainly heard a yawn. "And now you need some sleep."

"I do. It just felt nice to connect while you're working instead of getting up every morning to see dailies knowing all of you have already headed home. Good to hear your—everyone's voices. In the background."

"Get some sleep," Gail said. "Or did Kim need to talk to you again?"

"No, I was done."

"Good night then."

"Good night Gail."

Gail was gazing at the blank display, bemused and pleased, when someone spoke right behind her.

"Is that Lena?"

She turned to show the phone to Jennifer. "It was, but she hung up. She said the dailies are great."

Jennifer's brow knitted slightly. "How kind of her to call you to say so. Lena can be so considerate."

"She's very easy to work for." Gail didn't know what else to say.

"I'll tell her you said so when we talk." Jennifer's smile was indulgent. "If it comes up. We usually talk about other things. You know how it is."

"Sure. Of course." Was she being warned off? She was just being paranoid. Jennifer couldn't know how she felt, not when she didn't know.

"And we're onto the next scene," Jennifer went on, as if Gail hadn't spoken. "We nailed it on the first take, did a second for insurance and you're up again."

"Oh."

"I'll give Kim her phone back."

Gail handed it over, not without misgivings, but as soon as her scene was done, she'd make sure it had indeed been returned. She hurried back to the stage.

Selena groaned when her phone rang even before she got into bed. Had Kim thought of one more thing?

Not Kim's bubbly voice, but Jennifer's silky purr. "Darling, how are you?"

"It's after two in the morning, Jen. Let me get some sleep."

"I know it's late. I just thought I'd wish you pleasant dreams."

"Thanks. Goodbye then." She didn't expect Jennifer to go away that easily, but it was worth a try.

"It's so curious that you'd make such an effort to get a message to the supporting actress. I'm human, Lena. I can use words of encouragement too."

"Who I talk to and why isn't your concern."

"That it's not me certainly is my concern. Everybody on this picture has a bigger piece of you than I do, and that includes your little discovery."

Selena rubbed her aching eyes. If she put her head down she'd fall asleep. "You and I have too much history for me to blow the usual producer's smoke at you. You'd know it for what it was."

"I'm not asking to get pats on the head. How about a little showing of respect for what I'm doing here?"

She could picture Jennifer, her eyes almost about to tear up. It's all a lie, never forget. It's about her and she wants something. And she can't have it.

"The dailies look great. The ensemble works, and you are definitely one of the reasons why."

"Why thank you. Was that so hard?"

"Can I sleep now?"

"Wish I were there to tuck you in, darling."

"Goodbye then." This time she snapped her phone shut, not waiting to see if Jennifer had anything else to say.

She settled under the cool sheets, an arm across her eyes. In three days she got to go home. In three days she wouldn't get herself up an hour early to go through the dailies. Sometimes she watched scenes twice, tracing the grainy outline of Gail with her eyes. In three days it wouldn't be Gail Welles on her computer, but the real Gail she would look at. She wouldn't be reduced to scouring the latest stupid blogs for hints of how Gail was getting along.

It had been weak to call and her excuses flimsy, but it was her birthday and she was a long way from home, and alone. And forty. And her gift to herself was Gail's voice, not speaking lines, but talking to her. It shouldn't have mattered so much. She didn't understand how she could yearn for it. She ought to be happy that, unlike last year, she hadn't spent her birthday weeping over her broken heart. No, this involved her heart all right, but the similarity ended there.

"Happy birthday to me," she whispered to the dark.

Buzztastic # #

Finally, after more false leads than a Hitchcock flick, we know where Hyde Butler is spending his days. All you lovers of all things Butler, head down to the Carlisle Theater for stage door fun! You're sure to see Luscious Lamont there too! Warning, you're only going to have burritos and tacos at the local diners.

We've already got exit pics up from this afternoon with Hunky Hyde signing autographs. There's the mysterious Gail Welles hiding behind sunglasses. Who dressed her in jeans and a boy's T-shirt from Target? Rumor is Welles is the real love interest in this movie, which makes us wonder what the message is. The Butler likes Gangly Gails instead of Juicy Jennifers now? Not to worry, he's always nearest J.L. when they leave the shoot. Who wouldn't be warm for that woman's form?

Chapter 10

Greetings and welcome homes took time, as did even a brief update meeting with Alan before Selena could escape to the pool house for a badly needed shower. She was only going to stop in at the Carlisle long enough to say hello. That was all. She needed sleep and with Todd firmly back on his feet and two days from his cast wrap party, she had no concerns lingering. The *Barcelona* shoot was moving along at a strong pace and didn't need her hand in any of it but she was going to drop in, nevertheless.

Just for a few minutes, she promised as she lathered shampoo into her hair. Only to tell everybody how great they'd been so far, she practiced as she shaved her legs. No power suit for this group, besides she wasn't staying long. The mid-summer temperatures made light, simple clothes the best choice, and it had nothing to do with the fact that it was just faster to pull on jeans and grab a silk tank top. A little mousse in her hair and a quick blast of hot air and she was in the car, wishing she were already downtown.

Being in Hong Kong had made her appreciate L.A. traffic. She didn't curse once on the drive, and made the distance in good time.

"Hiya, boss!" Kim met her at the bottom of the stairs leading from the dressing rooms to the stage. "You're a sight for sore eyes."

"Back at ya. How is everything?" Don't look for Gail, she told herself, as she followed Kim up the stairs.

"We are officially one and a quarter days ahead of schedule, but I'm not telling. There are a few minor story changes that came from concerns during shooting and we'll have time to implement them."

"Great."

A woman called out her name in greeting—not Gail, Jennifer.

There was a flurry of activity. She ducked around unfamiliar lights and the sound engineer's board. When she'd left the crew had just begun to bring in the workstations. It was hot, and the industrial fans didn't help much between takes.

"Stay right there," Jennifer called.

She'd only gotten as far as the buffet table. Suddenly all the crew was around her, singing something in a cacophony of keys and rhythms. Finally, the last line of "Happy Birthday" was discernible and she had to laugh when Jennifer whisked a cloth off the buffet table to reveal a large sheet cake covered with creamy white frosting. Decorated liberally with red hearts, it read *Happy Birthday Selena* in lavender script.

"We're so sorry we weren't with you on your birthday," Jennifer said.

"Is that red velvet cake?" Her stomach growled.

"I remembered." Jennifer handed her a cake knife. "You get the first piece."

It was easier, occupied with a task, not to look for Gail in the crowd. "Any excuse for cake, I guess."

"Got that right," one of the gaffers agreed.

She cut herself a small piece with lots of cream cheese frosting.

She wondered how it was Jennifer had remembered—she hadn't on the phone.

She handed a second piece to Jennifer, saying a gracious thank you for her thoughtfulness. "I remembered," she added, indicating the small slice with almost no frosting, Jennifer's preference.

Gail was standing just to Jennifer's left she realized then, but before she could recover her wits enough to cut a Gail-sized piece reflecting her lusty appetite, the caterer took the knife and shooed her away. Gail moved into the line waiting for cake and Selena found herself talking to Jennifer, but it wasn't long before Kim drew her away to talk shop. The cake was delicious—not the best red velvet she'd ever had, but rich enough, with tart cream cheese frosting, that she wanted to go to Georgia for the real thing.

"Now that everyone has had their sugar rush, actors please resume looking haggard and hot and the rest of you to places." Eddie, sporting an incongruous smear of frosting on his upper lip, was having trouble resuming order.

She sat back in the seats with Kim, watching the make-up artists scurry around the actors gathered for the brief shot in the orchestra pit. Then a series of Steadicam shots of Hyde crossing the area were taken, with the lighting adjusted for morning, late afternoon and night effects. Then he and Jennifer paired up to do more walking in the theater shots, then Gail did her stint, back and forth, until there was plenty of variety in different lighting for the film editor to work with.

"You're in time for one of the make-or-breaks," Kim said. "Let's watch on the monitor, because we can't crowd the shot."

It didn't take long to figure out which scene Kim meant. Gail didn't look nervous, though she had to be.

"I have to say I was worried about it because Gail's not into guys, and maybe I'm not enlightened enough but I wondered just how good an actress she was," Kim said. "But now the problem is that Hyde pretty much sees Gail like a little sister. They're madcap together."

Filming just to stage right, using a set of rolling stairs as the main prop, Elgin and Georgette argued about the best way to keep the money, evade the people they'd duped and not split it with Elgin's wife.

"I never understood what you saw in her."

"Baby, come on. Just look at her. You know what I saw."

"How could she be any good for what you need? She's had so much Botox she doesn't even sweat."

A low, naturally sexy laugh from Hyde reminded Selena why he was such a hit with women. Elgin backed Georgette to the stairs, leaning into her. "If we give her some cash, she'll go away. And we can go back to the way we were."

Georgette's hand knotted into the back of Elgin's shirt and it was clear that she was pulling him down as much as he was pressing her into the stairs. Her height was perfect for the pose, and it was definitely visually sexy. One powerful arm lifted her effortlessly to him for a lingering, masterful kiss that left Georgette gasping. Then he backed away, the knot of shirt in her hand finally pulling free.

"Do you promise?" Georgette rose to lean unsteadily on the railing. "We can just go back to the way we were?"

Already off camera, Elgin answered, "Of course I promise Gail."

There was a silence and then Eddie yelled, "Cut!"

"Slap me upside the head!" Hyde returned from just offstage. "I can't believe I did that."

Eddie gave the flustered Hyde a distant smile. "It's only an audio flub."

Gail said, "At least it wasn't me this time. Do you want to do it again?"

Eddie was nodding. "Yes, though that was perfect—you got it all. There's a genuine spark there, but she's losing him and she knows it. So one more, to be sure, then I want alternative angles in pose."

Kim looked down at her notes. "What do you think?"

"That worked well," Selena said. "I can only imagine how

it'll look with Jennifer and Hyde, but the fact that he cares about Georgette in spite of her nuttiness is there. It's important."

"His fatal flaw, actually liking the women. Poor fellow." Kim got up to say something to Eddie but Selena stayed in her seat, happy to just relax. Her tummy was pleased with cake in it, and she loved the sounds a live set made when everyone was working.

She woke not a long time later, her neck in a terrible crick. Kim gave her an amused look. "I couldn't bear to wake you."

A quick glance at her watch and the stage told her they'd moved on to shooting a nearly equivalent scene with Jennifer and Hyde. Elgin, the hapless philanderer, would make the same promise he'd made to another woman only hours earlier in the timeline of the film. The shot captured the contrast between his choices, and set up his demise, because now everybody wanted the beleaguered con man dead.

She rubbed her neck. "I feel every bit of forty, let me tell you." She glanced around casually, trying to spot Gail.

"I think she's below, in the mayhem of the dressing rooms."

"Who?"

Kim leaned back in the seat with a look both sympathetic and impatient. "Who you're looking for. You think I've worked with you for more than six years and don't see what you see?"

"It's not—"

"I know that. Look, I like her a lot, but I'm going to take a page from my mentor's playbook. That would be you. Don't mess up the balance here. If you and Gail become some kind of item it will change things and I'm not sure in good ways."

"I know—"

Kim put her hand on Selena's arm. "You're both perfectly nice, underneath all the personas you have to carry around."

She had to laugh. "Perfectly nice? I threatened people's jobs last week. And I'll do it again next week if I have to. That Weston creature, I told her I'd get her blacklisted, basically, and you know how I feel about that sort of thing. Sometimes I don't feel nice."

"Gee, yesterday Gail actually yelled at the dresser who

dropped a curling iron in her lap. What a bitch."

Thinking of chicken and mayonnaise, Selena grinned. "And I bet she said she was sorry for an hour afterward."

"Basically." Kim nodded in the direction of the stairs to below stage. "*Please* don't mess up my drama with drama. I will be your biggest supporter, in about six weeks. Keep it simple until then."

"Define simple," Selena muttered. She didn't feel like explaining to Kim that how she felt and what she wanted were incredibly simple. Basic. And terrifying if she thought about it. It was a simple joy to watch Gail work. A simple need to want that smile to come her way. A basic and simple ache for the energy and easy sweetness of Gail to wrap around her like a blanket of warmth. She'd sworn she'd never fall for an actor again, and yet she looked at Gail and an inner voice whispered, "She's safe. It's okay, she's safe."

Why did this have to be so overwhelming right now? It wasn't fair to be torn between all the people counting on her to make this picture a success and the urgent feeling that Gail would slip through her fingers if she didn't do something. So much for Selena Ryan, big-time producer. She was wallowing in a load of self-pity over actually having good, positive feelings about someone. *Crybaby*.

She made herself wait until the day's shoot was done, and Eddie was busy overseeing the digital technicians as they loaded up the dailies and did backups to make sure nothing was lost. Though everybody still said *film* it was a thing of the past, and the computer side of the operation was something she understood just enough to know she had to hire people who knew far more than she did.

She decided she could risk looking for Gail and headed downstairs to the dressing rooms. Most of the below-stage area had been pressed into service for storage, but two rooms were where the actors got made up.

Halfway down the stairs she spotted Gail talking to one of the make-up artists. Gail glanced at her, but it wasn't with the warmth she had expected. Maybe she was stressed about something.

By the time she reached the bottom of the stairs Jennifer was there. For a change, her smile was friendly, but not overly flirtatious. "How was the cake?"

"It was a nice surprise. Thank you again for putting that together."

"After we talked I could have kicked myself for forgetting it was your birthday."

"I was too tired to know the difference," she lied.

"There's an art house premiere I wanted to see tonight. Slip in the back, grab some popcorn. Interested?"

It had once upon a time been their favorite impromptu date, but the idea had zero appeal. Hell would freeze over before she did anything casual with Jennifer. "I'm exhausted," Selena said. "I fell asleep out there. I'm crashing as soon as I get home."

"Another time maybe."

Mindful of the many listening ears, she could only say, "Maybe," in response. There were only two more weeks here, two more in Spain and regular encounters with Jennifer would stop. She was a little surprised, but not at all unhappy, that Jennifer took the refusal with a casual shrug. She watched her leave the theater and felt her spirit lighten.

The bang of the stage door had been steady as performers and crew left. The woman Gail was talking to seemed to be finding more and more topics to discuss. Then she realized, duh, that there was plenty of body language suggesting they weren't just talking shop. She hesitated, watching how relaxed Gail was as she leaned against a crate while they chatted. Her conversation with Kim still looming in her mind, she told herself that she could wait until the end of the shoot to make any more intense contact with Gail. It made sense. It was what Selena Ryan would do and whenever she was in this building, that's who she was.

She watched the cute make-up artist, no doubt with several more piercings in addition to the half-dozen Selena could see, flirt with Gail—a shoulder lifted as she laughed, a shy glance at the floor followed by a toss of lush dark hair. Butter Pecan Lena was asking what if, in the meantime, Gail found someone else, like the vivacious woman she was talking to right at this very moment? Well, if she finds someone else that easily, she can't be all that drawn to you, Selena Ryan argued back. So you should see if that flirtation goes anywhere, and keep your mouth shut and hands to yourself, right?

She was spurred out of her frozen contemplation of Gail by Kim's voice from above stage. "Selena, are you still down there?"

"Yes," she answered.

Gail finally looked in her direction again. And it was as if she hadn't been gone for ten days, as if they were standing on Mulholland, looking at the view. There was a place inside her where this woman could be and it hurt that it was empty. One hand was holding onto the banister like a lifeline, and the other was curled as if holding Gail's. It made her feel foolish and it felt like a lie, because she wanted to do far more than merely hold Gail's hand. Her mouth was the only part of her that was dry.

She had loved Jennifer. It had been real. But falling in love with Jennifer had been exciting and heady, abandoned and very, very sexual. She hadn't been terrified to feel, and looking at Gail she was scared for both of them.

Kim came down a few steps to peer at her. "Do you want to see the dailies? They're cued up."

Somehow she managed to tear her gaze from Gail's. "You know, I thought I could make it, but I'm dead on my feet. I'll just fall asleep again." The make-up woman was finally leaving. They didn't kiss or seem to be making a date. "I'll look at them in the morning, but I'll make plans to join you tomorrow afternoon too, so I can get back on the right schedule."

"You got it." Kim disappeared into the theater above them and Selena was abruptly aware that she was almost alone with Gail now.

Gail hadn't moved, but instead of relaxed she was gripping the crate as if it were an anchor.

She left the base of the stairs to make her way around the

boxes and racks of clothes that cluttered the hallway. With every step she tried to think of something to say, but words weren't forming. Gail's eyes were shining with emotion, but whether it was pleasure or dread, she couldn't tell, which was disconcerting. Usually, with Gail, she knew exactly what she was thinking.

When Gail stepped back, she stopped. There was no music to tell her if this was a beginning or an ending. Her heart felt stretched, but she couldn't tell if it was growing bigger or about to break.

Maybe that was why she was so scared.

It wasn't up to her.

When Selena didn't say anything, just stood there gazing at her with an expression Gail could only describe as sad, she wondered what it was Lena was afraid to say. Neither of them owed the other an explanation of her private life, but maybe that was it—Lena didn't know how to say she and Jennifer were together again. Knowing that, why did it feel like her skin was shivering off her bones the closer that she got?

"How was Hong Kong?" Lame, but staring in silence was making her sweat.

"Busy."

"Are you with her?" Oh my lord, Gail thought, how could you ask her?

"Who? Jennifer?" Lena shook her head. "No. We're… No, not for a year. I never know what she's after."

"But she…"

"Did she say we were?"

"I guess not," Gail said. "Not in so many words."

Lena rolled her eyes. "Typical Jennifer. About to head home?"

They're not together, Gail thought. So why does she look so funereal? "Yes. My driver's outside."

"I could take you home."

"I don't think that's wise." Okay, she hadn't meant to say that either, but it was the truth. Obviously, she had no control over the brain-to-mouth connection at the moment.

"You're right."

Two men with lights emerged from one of the storage rooms, giving the two of them annoyed looks as they made their way through the crowded space. Gail hoped she wasn't blushing. They were just talking, after all, nothing…illicit.

Maybe not in reality, but her brain was one big illicit zone every time she let herself get lost in Lena's dark, luminous eyes.

"You're right," Lena said again. "But I—let's go in here. I feel like the whole world is watching."

"I know what you mean," Gail said. She followed Lena into one of the side rooms, which was haphazardly stacked with crates and coils of spare electrical cable and mounds of movers' blankets that had protected the sound equipment. "I don't know what we have to hide, but it feels like no one should know we even talk."

"It's that I don't fraternize. I mean the last time I did was Jennifer, but we were already dating when that picture got underway." Lena stared at the ground as if gathering her thoughts. "I don't want anyone hinting you didn't earn this part through the regular channels, or that I really use the casting couch after all."

"Why would they assume that we're…"

Lena looked up and Gail lost her train of thought. After a moment Lena said, "That's why."

"I'm sorry I'm embarrassing you, I don't know why—"

"It's not just you. Gail, for heaven's sake." Lena glanced around the tiny room. "It's just us. Can't we be honest?"

"You start."

A smile hovered at the corners of Lena's lips. "Can we agree that this is mutual?"

Her heart was twisting in her chest, elation to heartbreak, with every beat and she could only nod.

"And now isn't a good time to figure anything out?"

Now wasn't a good time and yet it felt as if now was their only shot. They'd walk back out that door and between investors, bloggers and Jennifer, there wouldn't be any room out there for them. Lena had already taken a risk starting this conversation, though. After clearing her throat, Gail found her voice. "I feel like I'm going to break wide open."

She heard Lena's breath catch. Her eyes shimmered with emotion, but she made herself look down at her feet because those eyes were dark waters she abruptly realized she didn't know how to swim.

Lena's voice was hardly above a whisper. "I missed you. I've hardly gotten used to you being there and I missed you terribly."

Don't look at her, Gail thought. Don't risk it. It can't be true, and it won't last. But what her brain said was prudent her eyes didn't obey. She stole a look at Lena, was undone by the naked desire in Lena's eyes.

"I don't understand," was all she could think to say.

"Neither do I. I don't get this at all."

Gail shuddered as Lena's index finger brushed her forearm. "Don't," she said automatically.

Lena pulled her hand back. "You're right."

She was turning toward the door, and Gail panicked. It seemed like such an unlikely place, and so few moments to actually think about it, but it would change everything, her whole life was off the tracks regardless of whether Lena left or stayed. "Wait, I didn't mean for you to go."

"Gail, please. You were right."

"I can't send you away."

Lena's voice was suddenly thick with tears. Looking over her shoulder, with one hand on the doorknob, she said, "I can't walk away. So we're stuck. Here in this dusty, no place of a room. One of us is going to have to make a decision."

"Okay," Gail said. Who knew what any character she'd ever play would do, who cared what someone she'd never be would do either. This was her choice. "Then I'll decide."

She slid her hands over Lena's hips, was awed by the shiver that rippled through them both as she wrapped her in her arms from behind.

The painful thud of her heart eased. Lena relaxed into her arms with a quiet noise of pleasure. There was no reason to move, hardly any to even breathe.

Then Lena turned in her arms.

The brush of Lena's lips… For one moment all the fear melted. Gail had nothing to fear from the kisses of any woman. The exquisite softness, the tenderness—welcome, and treasured. She kissed Lena back, and time was irrelevant. She brushed her nose against Lena's before kissing her again, languid and slow and feeling so right.

Lena's arms tightened around her and one more searching kiss, no longer so soft, made Gail dizzy. When Lena rested her forehead on her shoulder, Gail held on tight.

"So this is mutual, right?"

Gail gave a little laugh. "I'd say so."

Lena gently pushed her away, took a step back. Turned the knob. "Wait for me then."

"Yes," Gail said, though she hadn't a clue if Lena meant now or until next week, or after the movie was done. Her mouth was tingling with fire.

"We can…here." Lena gestured at the room. "But I don't want this. I want more for you. Better for you."

Gail nodded, and hoped that was the right response. Her clothes felt so tight she couldn't think.

Lena took a short, sharp breath, and held up a hand as if to ward Gail off, though Gail hadn't moved. "I want to claim you, out in the light. Not here. Like we're ashamed. I don't want to read in the blogs that you and I are—" Her voice broke. "Are having a *Sapphic shag*. I don't want you tarnished. You deserve better."

"Why is this all about me? What about what you want? What you deserve?" You deserve better than me, Gail thought. "The bloggers will say whatever they want, anyway."

"The difference is we know what's true. I raised the money for this film with my reputation. I can't have another shagfest with one of my cast—any leeway I had with people got used up by Jennifer. I survived that because it was lies. My reputation won't escape when it's truth and it's all I have."

Lena's eyes filled with tears. She said again, "It's all I have. Who would rather deal with Selena Ryan versus all the vultures in this town."

Gail wanted to protest but she was already recalling how many times, even offhandedly, she'd heard Ryan Productions referred to as fair and reasonable.

"Wait for me," Lena said again.

Gail pressed a hand to her heart. "Until when?"

"Until I deserve you. Because right now I don't. I'm—"

"What are you talking about?"

Lena's breath was coming so short and fast her shoulders were shaking. "I signed the contract that hired you. I know how to fire you a hundred different ways your agent never thought of. I can snap my fingers and ruin you."

"But you wouldn't." Gail took a step closer, not understanding a thing Lena was saying.

"No. I wouldn't. But I could. I have all the power here. And if I did what I wanted to do, right now, it wouldn't be right."

"It feels right, Lena."

"God… I love the way you say my name." Lena closed her eyes. "Please let me go."

"I'm not keeping you here," Gail snapped. "Go, then."

"Wait for me." Now she gazed at Gail, tears shimmering in her eyes.

"I will."

Lena began to pull the door open, but Gail pushed it firmly closed. Lena's gasp exploded across Gail's skin, igniting the fire she was trying so hard to put out. She kissed Lena with all her pent-up hunger, hands slipping around the slender waist, then up the back of the thin silk.

They arched together, rocking against the door. Gail knew something had given way inside her and she didn't want to turn back. Lena was not the one making the moves. She pushed her thigh between Lena's legs, loving the moan of response and how

193

Lena seemed to melt even more into their kisses. Her hand under Lena's shirt, she traced the lines of her ribs.

A tug and a step backward let her pull Lena down to the padding of the movers' blankets. Pressing Lena into the coarse fabric drew a shuddering gasp of response and she rested on one elbow so she could explore the column of Lena's throat with her lips. The combination of a sweet perfume and vanilla from Lena's hair filled her senses as she nuzzled at the soft earlobe.

She closed her eyes because her vision blurred. Her ears were filled with the quickening of Lena's breath as they shared another kiss. Lena was like liquid under her, encouraging the depths of their kisses.

We may never get another chance, Gail thought desperately. It would never work, out there, but right here, right now, they could both surrender. She cursed her inexperience, worried she was being too bold.

When her hand closed on Lena's breast the sensation was electric, crackling along every nerve. Lena groaned into their kiss.

"Please," she whispered, but Gail didn't know if that meant *stop* or *more*.

She listened to her own pounding heart and pulled up Lena's tank top so she could bury her lips between the soft, full breasts. Nothing better, nothing softer, nothing stronger. Sweet, burning fire danced between their bodies and sparked from Gail's fingertips as she traced the planes of Lena's stomach.

Their bodies found the best way to fit without the need for words. Gail loved the responsive shudder when she pressed her thigh between Lena's legs. She slowed long enough for another deep, connecting kiss, then fumbled with the buttons on Lena's jeans. Right here and right now she had no thought but to give Lena pleasure, to take away the fear, to be, for just these few minutes, the right thing in Lena's life.

"Gail…" She might have added *don't*, or it might have been a long moan, but Lena's body rose to her touch. Rose again and again, opened to her caresses until Gail covered the hoarse, sharp shout of climax with her mouth, not believing that it had happened so quickly.

Lena relaxed, and for a scant few heartbeats they gazed at each other. Gail brushed her nose affectionately against Lena's and they both whispered, "Thank you" at the same time.

Lena's smile was tremulous, and she began to shake her head, but Gail kissed her before she could say that they shouldn't have done that and shouldn't do it again.

Her own words came, she didn't know from where, but they were the truth. "Just so you and I are clear, you are not the only one in charge when it comes to this. I get to say yes too. No matter what else we may ever be to each other in public, the only power you have over me is what I give you."

Lena squeezed her eyes shut, nodding. "You know we can't do this."

"We already did."

"I know. God, Gail, what you do to me…"

The soft, wondering gaze faded before Gail was ready for loss of the warmth. "This can't be. I can't ask for more. Not right now."

She slipped out from under Gail and buttoned her jeans. Gail thought for a moment she would leave, just like that. But at the door she turned back, her face flushed, eyes burning. "I want you," she said as if against her will. "But I can't have you."

"Yet," Gail whispered, but Lena was already gone.

Gail rolled into the hollow where Lena had been, the fingertips that had stroked Lena pressed to her lips. Lena had asked her to wait but instead she'd seduced her in this sordid little room, on these musty blankets. But it wasn't enough to make her sorry. She would never regret it. They had been perfect together, had those few intimate moments where the world was just the two of them. It was better than never.

She meant to comfort herself, to make the best of it, but it didn't stop tears from spilling down her face.

Buzztastic # #

Give it up, girls! Hyde Butler is out of the country and won't be back for weeks. Official word is for the location shoot of the sure-hit Barcelona, *but we've heard a romantic Spanish villa is the home away from home and Luscious Lamont is staying there too. Meanwhile, we've got some shots of the outdoor filming here in L.A. just before they wrapped the shoot. If life imitates art, newcomer Gail Welles is desperate for bedroom time with Hyde, but J.L. just won't get out of the way.*

We know those aren't the pics you've been waiting for, though. We've got the originals of Viv Weston's screen debut and it involves lots of soap suds and her very fine assets. Click the link and feast your eyes, of course only if you're 18 or older. Wait until Hugh Hefner sees these babies!

Chapter 11

"Okay," Hyde said. "Who thought arriving at three p.m. in Spain in August was smart?"

Gail said nothing, but he caught her accusatory look anyway.

"I had to go to that party," he protested.

"Yeah, yeah, yeah. Carry my suitcase."

He laughed and did indeed lift her carry-on bag down the short stairs to the private runway. Gail followed him, shading her eyes. The only vehicle in sight was their shuttle which was a relief after fighting her way out of the Carlisle through fans and paparazzi every afternoon for the entire last week of filming there. The crowds had added to the stress of butterflies and lead in her stomach—butterflies when she remembered the feel of Lena against her and lead in the many moments Selena didn't make even eye contact. Now Selena was back in L.A., and Gail didn't know when she was scheduled to join them, if ever.

It was hot here. Not just run-for-the-air-conditioning-before-we-break-a-sweat hot but trapped in Jiffy Pop-on-the-fire hot. The humidity wasn't bad, but it was more than she was used to. She hoped the private residence the production was renting for their weeks in the country was all Kim had said it would be, including a pool, shaded gardens and her own bedroom with her own shower. It would be pure luxury.

She quickly used her phone to take a picture of the sleek plane that had brought them nonstop from L.A. to Barcelona and forwarded it to Aunt Charlie. Behind the plane there was a banner saying, "Bienvenidos a Barcelona," which ought to be good enough for her friends. When they flew home, she was diverting to Iowa on the production's dime, too, as a bonus for the production being well ahead of schedule and under budget. The charter here was another upgrade from usual indie film financial restrictions. It had been surreal, playing cards with Hyde, getting some sleep in a seat that turned into a bed, unlimited food… No wonder celebrities got hooked on first-class treatment.

In no time, Hyde, Jennifer, Jim and she were ensconced in the much cooler air of the shuttle. Kim and Eddie had arrived three days earlier, along with the heads of the key departments, the lead lighting, photography and computer technicians, plus the camera operators who were most familiar with the equipment they brought as well as what they could rent.

"Hit me if I look like a tourist," Gail said to Jennifer.

She was trying hard to be as friendly with her as she was to everyone else, but it wasn't easy. She was afraid that in trying to look as if she wasn't deeply aware of Selena's every move that she'd made it all the more obvious how much she cared. Jennifer was no fool, even though Gail found her actions confusing, to say the least. After reading up on all the nasty gossip that had surrounded the Selena-Jennifer break-up, she didn't for a minute believe that Selena had dumped Jennifer. And the innuendo that Selena had reneged on a contract for personal revenge, just like her HUAC informant father had turned on his friends, was sickening. Pragmatically, she understood why Jennifer had the part, and that must have been hard enough on Selena. Why would all those bloggers think that they'd ever get back together?

They were professional liars, she reminded herself. What she knew was that over the last week everything Jennifer said to her was increasingly double-edged.

"Happily," Jennifer said, her arch tone undercut by a smile.

Her oblique hints that she and Selena were seeing each other again had stopped, making Gail wonder if Jennifer had ever been hinting to begin with. Lena hadn't been around all that often anyway, arriving late in the day for the dailies. Twice Gail had made sure she was gone before then. Gail missed her, wondered if her absences were usual for a production or if they were about her. Kim didn't seem to think anything was amiss.

So she was waiting. Days and days in Spain ahead of her, it didn't seem so hard. But a minute didn't pass when she didn't wonder if Lena was happy about something, or frustrated, or thinking of her. There were no text messages, no hints or reminders of their encounter in the room below the Carlisle stage. She had only her memory of what she'd felt, and hoped Lena felt, to keep her from thinking she had made it all up.

Still, she was aware that Jennifer watched her, and if the hostility wasn't about Selena, then what could the issue be?

Their shuttle skirted the edge of the sprawling city, climbing into amber-crusted hills. The final turns to their temporary home gave them a gorgeous view of the Mediterranean Sea, shimmering blue in spite of the summer heat. Though there were a few high rises along the horizon, most of the city was only a few stories high, shining white in the blazing sun. To the south of their villa was Mt. Tibidabo. She hoped they would get enough time to be able to explore—the Church of the Sacred Heart overlooked the entire city. She hoped to see Gaudí's Sagrada Familia and the other fantastic architecture. Her guidebook was stuffed with sticky notes of all the things she didn't want to miss, including a harbor cruise. To come all this way and not swim in the Mediterranean seemed like sacrilege.

The villa came into view and Gail grinned. It reminded her of the Ryan Production offices, only much larger, and the massive front doors were set far back under an overhanging balcony draped with vines that were studded with tiny pink flowers.

Kim, looking cool and comfortable in knee-length shorts and a wrapped tank, was waiting for them at the edge of the shade, gesturing them to come inside out of the sun. "If you change your skin tone, the continuity people are going to have fits and the make-up people will be in an uproar. No sunlight. We'll have awnings and umbrellas at the outdoor shoots and please, if you go out anywhere slather on the sunblock."

"Hello to you too," Hyde said.

"Sorry." She gave him a hug. "I'm in worrywart mode. Before you all scatter, meals are served here in the villa at six a.m. and six p.m., with late supper at eleven. Food will be provided on locations as usual. Our time is short, so please don't get food poisoning by trying the paella at a street vendor. We have an excellent local chef who will make you the real thing. I've already put on two pounds."

Jennifer groaned. "Great, more wonderful food to turn down."

"The fresh fruit is divine," Kim assured her. "One last thing. I know we discussed this before we left the States, and Hyde is already used to it. Go nowhere without an escort from Garcia-Zimmer. They have vetted all of our detail, they're all bilingual and while Spain is a very friendly place to American tourists, anyone with celebrity is at risk for kidnapping. Besides," she added with a gleam in her eye, "they know great places to shop and the best ways to get around. They're here to make your stay here safe and pleasant, so don't duck out on them, okay?"

The last bit was directed more at Jennifer than anyone else, and Gail wondered if Jennifer had a history of going off on her own. Well, she was relieved to have someone to ask for help. They were here to do their work, first and foremost, so she didn't want to waste what little sightseeing time she'd have on getting lost.

Released by Kim to put their things in their assigned rooms, Gail fell in love with the house. The interior also reminded her of Ryan Productions offices, with terra cotta tiles cool to the feet and eyes, and banks of ferns making the air moist and earthy. The central courtyard, with a sparkling pool, was shaded by a white awning, painted on the underside with brilliant diamonds of gold, black and red. Gail Welles of Des Moines, Iowa, lounging in a Spanish villa, she told herself. Who would have thought it?

She unpacked her not very exciting wardrobe of shorts and T-shirts, took a welcome shower and then tiptoed around the courtyard taking photos for Aunt Charlie. Hyde caught her at it, and took some photos of her against the backdrop of walls draped with tapestries or studded with mosaics.

Dinner was delightful, with everyone in good cheer. The esprit de corps on the picture was exceptional, they all agreed, and she hoped she wouldn't end up spoiled. She played a hand of Hearts with Hyde—in their running game he owed her thirty-seven million dollars, since they'd played for a hundred thousand a point. He was on a tear and she lost ten million before it was all done. It was nearly ten o'clock, and she supposed she ought to force herself to sleep. Jimmy and Jennifer had played pool with Kim, but they'd all gone to their rooms at nine. The wake-up call at five would be brutal. Her body said it was only one p.m., though, and she just didn't think she could sleep yet.

"That was bloody," she commented to Hyde about his run of luck with the cards. "Spain agrees with you."

"I've been practicing on the side so I don't eventually owe you my entire future earnings." He picked up his wine glass and strolled out to the courtyard, which caught a lovely night breeze rising from the sea. "That is a beautiful moon."

She joined him on a stone bench. "I thought it would look different on this side of the world, but it doesn't."

"It's the same wherever you go, just varies by the amount of air pollution. We've all got the same moon to look up to."

They sat in a companionable silence for a bit, with Gail breathing in the fragrant air. When Hyde spoke, it was in a low voice, as if he feared being overheard.

"What's the state of your heart, Gail? Have you got any advice for an old man?"

He was half turned away in the dark, but she knew his question was serious. The blogs were constantly reporting on his jaunts to Vegas or being at some party with bodacious babes, but she'd found him to be anything but a playboy.

"First off, you're not old. In Hollywood years, you're still a baby for a male of the species. Second, who is she, and why does she make you feel old?"

He chuckled. "Her name is Emma and she's thirty-seven."

"Not that much younger than you."

"She mountain bikes and climbs rocks and snowboards. It exhausts me just to look at her photo albums. And when she's not doing that, she's a dentist. Nothing to do with this crazy business we're in."

"Maybe that's good. Good for her and you."

"You bet. When's the last time a showbiz marriage worked? But my agent reminds me that I'm Hollywood's most eligible bachelor, and that sells tickets."

"Does that mean you shouldn't have a relationship that people know about?"

"According to BeBe, yes. If I must have one, then it should be someone within the business, which is guaranteed to fail and my female fans will pity me all the more. BeBe's good at what she does and her entire focus is making me money. Happiness isn't her job."

"So, how much money do you have?" She shifted her position to face him sitting cross-legged. "Tell the truth. Is it a tonnage, ridonculous or oh-my-freakin'-god?"

He laughed. "Somewhere between tonnage and ridonculous, I guess."

"So you've got your kids from your first marriage covered for college, and new shoes, right? You're building that house in Montana, and already have a condo in Vegas and that lovely place in Miami. I mean—how much happier would you be if you were all the way to oh-my-freakin'-god amount of money in the bank? I've never understood why some executive making a hundred million dollars a year wants more. Isn't that enough? So maybe some women will decide if you're hooked up with somebody they're not quite so hot to see your pictures. How long can you go before you notice the pay cut? Will it matter if the whole while you're happy?"

He turned his face to the moon again and Gail admired his profile. She liked Hyde, a lot, and hoped they stayed in touch after the movie, though it was probably unlikely. They'd move in different circles. She'd never have his fame and fortune.

"You remind me of Selena," he said. "Sweet-talking me about happiness being more important than money. You'll both ruin me."

She was gratified to be compared to Selena in any way. "Well, in my case, it's not like I have a choice between fame or fortune in front of me."

"You will," he said.

"Making independent films where we don't blow stuff up?" She stopped herself. "I'm sorry. I'm not belittling your other work."

"It pays a ridiculous—make that a ridonculous amount more. But I have to admit this has been refreshing. Like a return to an acting workshop because I get to work with serious craftspeople. No digital effects and posing in front of the green screen. And because it moves fast and there's no huge delays to set up pyrotechnics, we're working every day. So no parties all night because there is nothing else to do."

"I've loved working on this picture."

He gave her a sideways grin. "Well, remember your own advice. Go for the girl that makes you happy and screw the money."

If only that choice was within her power, Gail thought, then she worried that Hyde suspected she was pining for Selena. "Well, we should get to bed, and I bet you want to make a phone call."

He turned his face to her, eyes crinkled with laughter. "Yeah.

I miss her a lot. And I really wish she were here."

"Dentists—she's got patients."

"She lives in Miami. I may have to stop there on my way home."

"I hope you do." Gail got to her feet and sighed. "Time for bed, dude. See you at breakfast."

She made her way up the grand staircase to her room. She would love to call Lena and tell her about the moon. So Hyde thought show business relationships were all doomed. The Sedgwick-Bacons and Newman-Woodwards were rare, that was for sure. But she didn't want a dentist. She wanted Selena. They couldn't fail if they didn't try, and there was always that possibility that it could be a real happy-ever-after for them, just like in the movies.

She repeated that to herself as she got ready for bed, hoping to believe it.

The heat took its toll. Though they were plied with water and fruit juice all day, and shaded at every turn, the sheer amount of standing around waiting for technicians to set up shots left Gail feeling wrung out at the end of every day. After a delicious dinner it was all she could do to drag herself to bed. The first week was a blur and she was glad of the approaching weekend. As much as she wanted to sightsee, a day of sleeping followed by napping was very appealing.

It was well after nine when she woke up her first Saturday in Barcelona. The chef and staff had said a casual buffet would be available most of the morning, so she pulled on shorts, a tank top and ball cap to head downstairs. She was in the dining room before she realized Selena was there, and it was too late to shower, do something about her hair, even put on clothes that flattered her more.

Lena looked as if she'd just arrived, a suit jacket hanging over the back of her chair and two heavy satchels of papers at her feet. Kim was very animated about something and Selena was nodding as she listened.

All Gail could think was that Lena's eyes were weary, her forehead creased with faint lines, like the woman she'd first met at the diner.

Kim noticed she was there. "It's okay Gail, just shop talk."

Lena turned in her chair. "Good morning."

"I slept in." Oh, way to go, Gail, she chided herself. Newsflash from the Oracle of Obvious.

Lena was staring someplace just above Gail's eyes. "I'm sure you earned it."

Trying not to be hurt that they couldn't even share a glance, Gail tried for a joke. "Can I get you something while I'm up? Chicken, mayonnaise, relish, on a plate, not your lap?"

"No thanks," was all Selena said, even though Kim looked confused and curious.

Gail mouthed swear words at herself when her back was turned. How could she be so stupid? She gathered her composure as she selected an array of fruit and a nice granola cereal, with a decadent slice of the custard-soaked, then fried-to-golden-perfection bread that the staff made every morning. To her, it was screaming for maple syrup, but the fresh citrus marmalade in its place was proving addictive.

She was going to sit at the far end of the table, but Kim gestured to her. "Join us, Gail. I was telling Selena about the restaurant shoot, including the wardrobe malfunction."

"Jennifer was a good sport about it, but the shoot didn't go well after that," Gail said. She tried not to dribble juice from the orange she opened all over herself, but it was so ripe and luscious it nearly exploded in her fingers. "We were all in a funk."

She wouldn't look at Selena while they chatted. She was afraid of what she wouldn't see, that there would be no recognition in the depths of Selena's eyes, that she'd see only Selena looking back, and not the Lena who had melted under her with abandoned desire.

They chatted for a while, straying from shop talk to news and weather. Just as Gail was wondering why Selena didn't go up to her room to change and rest, the door chime sounded.

"I bet that's Levi," Selena said, rising. "Can someone find Eddie?"

"Levi?" She glanced at Kim, who was quickly texting.

"Levi Hodges. He's doing a song for the soundtrack. Nothing was certain until he got in touch with Selena a couple of days ago."

I'm screwed, Gail thought. I'm going to meet a rock-and-roll god and here I sit, unwashed, uncombed with orange juice all over my hands.

When the tall, lanky Levi Hodges strolled in with Selena, scratching his sparse beard, she could only think that he gave Hyde a run for the title of sexiest man in the villa. She was totally and completely outclassed.

Fortunately, nothing more than an introduction was required of her. In short order, he produced his iPod and plugged it into a small set of speakers Kim had set up. Eddie, having clearly slept in as well, joined them. Once he had coffee, Levi pressed play.

She liked the industrial grind right away. There was a mechanical clack and slide that was woven into the bass line while Levi's grungy voice told a story of rolling in circles, rolling forward and back, hoping to move on but falling off the track. She didn't catch some of the words, but she liked the beat, a lot.

Eddie was immediately as enthusiastic as she'd ever seen him. Gail saw Selena relax into a pleased smile that she shared with Kim.

"That was exactly what I was looking for," she told him. "It's perfect."

Levi let out a gusty sigh. "I was worried, because it seemed so easy. We played here and I seemed to hear the rhythm everywhere. Even when we got to Prague I was still hearing it." His gaze strayed to Gail, as if curious as to why she hadn't chimed in.

She found her voice. "I really liked it. It's kind of stuck in my head in a good way. I love the way you worked in the skaters."

Levi grinned. "I was hoping someone would hear that. Skateboarding is huge here. People come from all over to do the four-stair in front of the Museum of Contemporary Art."

"I read about it in the guidebook." Looking at Eddie, she added, "It wasn't far from Convent dels Angels. Kind of cool, the medieval convent and the skateboarders in the same area—if you like that kind of juxtaposition, I guess. Every skater on the planet will want to do a video to this song."

Eddie got a faraway look. "I think I'd want this for the opening credits. And I'll talk to the local casting associate to see about hiring skaters. Frankly, I was getting worried with only Gaudí as a motif. Gaudí and skateboarders, now that I haven't seen."

They all fell into rapid consultation and Gail faded into the background, and finally escaped to her room to shower and find fresh clothes. She made something tidy of her hair, then went back to the dining room, but it was empty. Okay, so Levi Hodges would think her a total waste, but what did she care. Selena obviously had other plans for her first day too. She wasn't going to linger hopefully. She'd ask the house amanuensis if there was an escort available to take her to Gaudí Park. It was on her list and a perfect short trip. The photographs she'd seen of the twisting and curving walls, encrusted with the artist's brilliant trademark mosaics, were inspiring.

She hadn't made it to the concierge's little desk when she heard her name called. She knew the voice, and every nerve jumped.

"How do you know so much about skateboarding?"

Selena had changed out of her suit and looked perfectly at ease in knee-length white shorts and a shimmering short-sleeve shirt of the pretty blue that looked so good on her. Gail made herself look at the floor, and it took a real effort.

"I don't know much except that we went by it a couple of mornings ago. There were guys flying in the air, like three and four feet off the ground. Skaters came into the diner too. Generally, a pretty nice breed of people."

"High praise. Where are you off to?"

"I thought I'd sightsee." Don't ask her, she can't go with you, Gail warned herself. She just got here. She has work to do. She's not…yours. Not yours to ask.

"On your own?"

"I'll take an escort, I promise." She risked a look and found Selena gazing at her.

"That's not what I meant. Okay, though…"

For just a moment, everything Gail could have wanted was there in Selena's eyes. A longing ache that equaled the one she felt. Her blood felt molten and her stomach flip-flopped at the memory of Lena's mouth on hers and the smell of Lena on her fingertips. Then Selena blinked and it went away.

"We finish shooting end of next week," Gail said.

"I know. I go back to L.A. on Tuesday."

"Oh."

"You're stopping in Iowa on your way back, aren't you?"

"Yes. To visit my aunt."

"Good. Enjoy the visit."

She didn't cry, though she badly wanted to, as Selena walked away.

Buzztastic # #

All the mysteries surrounding the hot new flick Barcelona *and the sizzling hotties in it are solved. Pics from the location shoot in Spain all over our page. Luscious Lamont is positively popping out all over—oops! Thank you loyal reader for that one! And who's this we see all cozy with The Welles? We know G.W. has a hot scene with H.B. in the movie, but it looks pretty hot with this blonde cutie too! Galpals on the set?*

Rumor has it Levi Hodges pitched a new groove for the Barcelona *soundtrack. Remember you read all about the Butler-Hodges connection here first! With Butler, Hodges and Lynch all working on it, how can it miss? Buy us our tickets now!*

Chapter 13

It was hard to keep her mind on invoices and projections, but staying closeted with Kim to go over expenses all weekend kept Selena from prying again into how Gail spent her time. She hadn't expected it to be so hard just to look at her. If she looked once it felt like she couldn't stop at all.

Gail had stayed out Saturday night with Hyde and Jennifer, but over Sunday brunch she'd managed to stay appropriate as one of many listening to their adventures involving a night visit to the Sagrada Familia, a sizeable bribe to get inside the cathedral after dark and climbing a construction scaffold for pictures of the city's nightlights.

Nobody would attach any significance to her shocked but amused laughter as Hyde recounted Gail's quick thinking, when cornered by a security guard, in producing a Sharpie marker and offering a Jennifer Lamont signature on the guard's chest.

Jennifer even said she was traveling with a Sharpie from now on, because there was no telling the trouble it would solve.

The stab of memory at the trouble Jennifer had been in that had cost them their relationship was definitely still bitter, but it wasn't the same kind of pain she'd carried around for a year. It faded even more as she watched Gail's hands tracing patterns in the air, trying to describe the figures on the outside of the cathedral's unique spires. She knew those hands, knew their strength, knew how they could play across her skin or reach her hungriest places.

She forced herself to cut up a pear so she could breathe again.

"Hopefully nobody got pictures of us, or we'll be all over that horrible website that's obsessed with us," Gail said. "They turned a bug flying into my eye into a clinch with the dresser who was trying to fish the thing out. Do they really make money from ads, so much money that it's worth lying for it?"

Selena was glad to be busy with her hands. She'd seen that photo and her mind had known that it was all tripe, as usual, but their faces had been so close together and the other woman was so cute—she hadn't been pleased to discover she could have a stupid jealous fit. Gail was not a fickle woman, and not likely to have a casual fling, so there was no reason for her anxiety. She knew if they had just a few minutes alone she would be reassured. They'd also probably end up having sex again, and that was the problem.

"They must," Jennifer said. "Given it was my boobs they flashed all over, I'd like a cut of the revenue. At least they finally pulled the picture, but now you can get it everywhere else."

"Imagine the field day they'd have if we'd gotten arrested last night," Hyde said. "Jim, you should have come with us."

James shook his head. "Yeah, sounds like a bundle of fun. Actually, I don't know how you guys found the energy. I was out cold at eight."

"I should have been," Gail said. She got up to refill her coffee cup. "Anyone else want some?"

211

There were several yesses, and Gail circulated the table, pouring from the carafe on the sideboard. "Sugar? Cream? Be sure to leave a tip, now."

Helpless to do anything about it, Selena watched Gail top off Jennifer's cup with waitress efficiency. Maybe Jennifer would miss it—after all, it was likely common knowledge that Gail had waited tables, like half the actors in Hollywood.

Luck wasn't with her, or maybe it was her own expression that made Jennifer give her an especially close look before she turned her gaze back to Gail returning the coffee carafe to the sideboard.

"I knew that I knew you from somewhere," she said to Gail. "You were my waitress at some point, weren't you?"

Gail flushed. "Maybe. Maybe I was hoping you wouldn't remember in case I had an off night."

It might have passed with a laugh if Gail hadn't then given Selena a look that screamed *help*.

"Wasn't it at a diner in WeHo? Remember, Lena? You took me there after that museum gala."

A little silence fell. There was nothing for it but the truth.

"Yes, I remember, and Gail was our waitress. I didn't recognize her." It was the truth, just not the whole truth.

"I was sweating bullets worried that either or both of you would remember me. It was very awkward."

"Some guy has a blog about my selling him a broken air conditioner." Hyde reached across Jennifer for the basket of fruit.

"So when did you figure it out, Lena?"

Jennifer wasn't going to let it go.

"I didn't. Gail reminded me."

Jennifer was framing another question, but a startled gasp from Kim distracted them all.

Selena leaned toward her. Kim was deadly pale. "What's wrong?"

"I don't know."

It was the last thing Kim said and the world went into slow

motion. She pitched forward into the table and rebounded, crashing like a limp rag to the tile floor. After only a few moments she began to convulse, the heels of her sandals drumming the floor.

Selena couldn't move. Her arms wouldn't obey her.

It was Jim who got to Kim first, shouting, "Someone get a cushion and call 9-1-1." He pointed at Hyde. "Help me turn her on her side. It's all we can do."

Kim's seizure abruptly stopped and Selena realized she'd been holding her breath. "Is she—"

"Damn it, she stopped breathing."

Selena had a flashback to long ago school lessons on emergency first aid. Jim seemed to know what he was doing. She hadn't yet been able to stand up. Jennifer had dashed out of the room and now she was back with their concierge, who was speaking excitedly into the phone.

One-two-three. She could hear Jim counting under his breath.

Hyde said, "What's that?" and she still couldn't stand up to look.

"It looks like a spider bite," Jennifer said.

"It does, and it's still swelling," Gail agreed. "This could be an allergic reaction."

Jim, in between puffs and counts said, "I think it's anaphylaxis."

"They say five minutes," the concierge said. "In España, there is doctor in ambulance."

Finally, Selena managed to get on her feet. She felt helpless and absurdly useless, of no worth whatsoever when Kim was perhaps dying right in front of her. She thought of a million pointless things, like boiling water and if praying would mean anything from someone who hadn't been inside a church in years, and if God would prefer Spanish prayers from here, but she didn't know Spanish and none of what went through her mind was any help to anyone. She was frozen, and all she could see was Kim's lifeless face.

Jennifer pointed out the irregular swollen mass on Kim's leg, just above her ankle. She had a flashback to *Spiderman*, another useless response in an emergency, what the hell good was a movie right now? But her gaze traveled over the flooring under the table, then further out until she spotted the lifeless remains of a spider. It looked perfectly ordinary to her, not radioactive, but she upended a glass over it.

"Did you find the one that bit her?" Gail was at her side, steady and solid.

"I don't know. But maybe it'll help."

A siren blared into Selena's numb awareness, and a flurry of activity resulted in all them being ordered out of the way. It was said in Spanish, but there was no mistaking the meaning. It took a few tries to get someone to listen to long enough to explain about the spider, then they were unceremoniously shoved into the adjoining living room.

"Please, God, don't let her die." Selena wasn't sure she spoke the words aloud.

Then Gail put her arms around her and she breathed in safety and warmth.

In a few minutes the doctor appeared and explained something to their concierge. Jim, whose Spanish was passable, nodded along.

"She's going to be okay, probably," he said. "They've given her a general serum for allergic reaction. But he's worried because she may have fractured her skull when she hit the floor. There's a lot of swelling."

The concierge added, "The spider is common, most people have itches, but Señora Kim very bad reaction. Someone go with her to hospital, yes?"

"I will," Selena said. She wanted to cry with relief, though a fractured skull sounded very, very serious. "Though I'm useless. Jim, you were amazing."

His rakish features were drawn with worry. "Gail waited tables. I was an EMT all through college, and I still roll out for calls one weekend a month. Sweet Jesus, I hope she's okay."

"I'll go with you, Lena," Jennifer said.

"No." Consequences be damned. Kim could have died, and still could, and what did her stupid rules and stupid pride matter? "No. I want Gail."

A hospital in Spain was much like one in Iowa, Gail thought. Half the labeled items were in Latin and meant nothing to her anyway. Warning signs were in red, and she had had enough basic Spanish to know that *cuidado* basically meant *don't be an idiot here*. Still, it would have been helpful to Lena if she spoke Spanish, and she cursed her monolingual limitations. Their security escort arrived a few minutes after they did, which did help a lot, even though his English was taxed by trying to translate some of the medical jargon.

Within thirty minutes of their arrival a doctor came to update them. With fits and starts, he explained that Kim's head injury was a small fracture that would mend in time, and she would be held overnight to make sure she didn't have a concussion or any kind of residual damage from the seizure. The doctor was more concerned by her reaction to a bite from a fairly common European spider. If she had been bitten when she was alone, it likely would have been fatal.

"Then she's going home as soon as she can fly," Selena said firmly. "Nothing is worth risking anyone's life." She flipped open her phone, then laughed with chagrin. "I was calling Kim to have Kim get Kim a flight home."

"Maybe you should call her daughter," Gail suggested. She handed over another tissue she'd scrounged from the nurse's station.

Lena dabbed at her eyes. "It's the middle of the night, and no reason to alarm her family out of a night's sleep when they can't board a flight until it's morning there. And I'll know more. I'll wake up Alan in a few hours and he'll set things in motion. Maybe her daughter and mom can fly here."

"Will we have to close down the shoot for a while?" Talking about details seemed to be helping her focus. Gail had been afraid more than once that Lena was going to pass out.

"No, I can finish it." Lena gave Gail a confident, bright smile that lasted about two seconds. Then her face crumpled and Gail pulled her close.

"She's okay. It's going to be okay."

After minute, Lena muttered into Gail's shoulder, "Everybody says life is too short for this or that. Well, it's too short not to hold you. Too short not to have told Kim how much I treasure her as a friend."

"You get a Do Over, then."

"How did you get so smart?" There was a long, loud snuffle in Gail's ear. "You've probably never even been stupid enough to get a broken heart."

"I haven't cared about anyone enough to chance it is all." She tightened her arms, and would have said more and probably kissed her for comfort, but over Lena's shoulder she saw Hyde's unmistakable tall form, even though he'd donned a skater's cap and sunglasses. Right behind him was a crowd of cast and crew. "We have company."

Jennifer didn't miss that she'd been holding Selena. Gail swallowed nervously. She asked herself what, realistically, Jennifer could possibly do to them now that everyone knew, something that wouldn't be cutting off her own very pretty nose to spite her equally pretty face. Was Jennifer really foolish enough to run to the gossipmongers just for spite?

Holding Lena tight against her had felt like the one thing she'd been born to do. The only thing that even came close was getting lost in a part. It was like the magic of movies come to life, for real, for her. She wasn't going to let Hollywood high drama rob her of it.

Lena updated the group on Kim's status and praised Jim again. "Your quick action probably saved her life. And we have to get her out of the country as soon as possible. I'm hopeful her daughter or mom will be able to fly here and escort her home. If not we'll send one of the security detail home with her, to make sure she is taken care of every step of the way. I know we're all badly shaken by this—"

Her voice broke and she put her head down for a moment. Gail ached to hold her again, but the situation was inflamed enough.

"We'll hold off shooting for a few days," Eddie said.

"Kim will get on her feet and beat us with a bedpan if we do that." Hyde shook his head in further emphasis. "No, the least we can do for her is land the plane safely without her."

Selena laughed. "Hear, hear. I'll be sticking around, and we can do this. You are all such a group of professionals that there's no question we can't proceed. Kim will take up the reins stateside the moment she's able."

Eddie nodded. "Well, it's Sunday then, and I'm up for the beach."

"Tanning's a no-no. The actors can't go to the beach," Jennifer reminded him. "So you're on your own. I'll stay here a bit."

Gail was relieved when Hyde also opted to linger. Jennifer's eyes were like glass daggers. That's when she realized that just because she couldn't think of what Jennifer could do to hurt them didn't mean Jennifer wasn't going to try.

The waiting room was small. Almost everyone around them didn't speak English, though Gail was aware that a number of the nurses were bilingual. A few were looking curiously at Hyde.

Selena didn't wait. She gave Jennifer her full attention. "Was there something you wanted to discuss?"

"Ever direct, it's one of the things I never really loved about you." Jennifer lounged into a chair, a sandal dangling off her toes. She took off her sunglasses and Gail had to tell herself not to react with awe to the perfect face. It was hard—that kind of beauty wasn't passive and Jennifer knew it. "So, how long has this been going on, really?" She indicated Gail.

"None of your business, but for old time's sake, there is no this."

Jennifer laughed. "Could have fooled me."

Gail decided there was no reason for her to be silent. "We're not boffing on the sly, not that it's your business." It was true in the present tense, at least, and there was no reason to admit that it was only true because Selena had been on the other side of the world for a lot of the time.

Selena shrugged. "You don't have to believe us."

"Okay," Jennifer said. "I actually do believe you. That's not my issue."

"So what is?"

Hyde's question brought Jennifer's gaze to him. "I'm not sure this concerns you."

"Oh, but I have a feeling it does. My agent is BeBe LaTour, and I think the two of you are peas in a pod."

"Oh really?" Jennifer was clearly offended.

"Sure. Gail acts circles around the rest of us. That's the bottom line. It's because she's so damned good that she's not stealing the scenes out from under us. She's being true to the writer's intent for the character. When it's Georgette's moment, Gail takes it. Otherwise, she lets everyone else shine. That alone, well, I'm guessing there'll be critics who notice. More press for her. That means less for the rest of us."

Selena almost nodded, and Gail realized that Lena had been worried about Jennifer's professional jealousy all along, and been hoping to protect her from it. She didn't really know what Hyde meant. Why would anyone be jealous of her?

Jennifer had colored slightly, but Gail couldn't tell if it was with anger or embarrassment.

Hyde went on, "That was bad enough, but now, not only is this incredible newcomer stealing some of your thunder, she's revealed as Selena Ryan's new girlfriend. The Selena Ryan. The one you dumped, but was still generous enough to give you a role in this not-so-sleepy little picture. In which, having seen all your films, my dear, you are doing some of the best work you've ever done."

Jennifer folded her arms. "Fine, sure, I resent the hell out of being upstaged. And I don't think you have a clue what that's like. You'll be sixty and still getting sexy leading man roles. When I'm sixty, I'll be hawking make-up in infomercials. If I'm *lucky*. I have perhaps five years left to establish myself as something more than a body or I'm going to have to marry some rich guy. So what's wrong with me wanting a legacy?"

He shrugged. "I know it sucks for women. We sell our movies on your bodies. Right now, movies are being sold on mine too. I'm here for the same reason you are, because I'm just another pretty face. Mine has a much longer shelf life than yours, but I want a legacy too."

"So you can see where I'm worried about getting upstaged?"

"Jennifer, I get why you're worried," Gail said. "I mean—I don't know about me being some kind of big talent. But I know what you mean about the ticking clock. I just don't know what you expect me to do."

"I do," Selena said. "And I won't."

Puzzled, Gail looked at Selena for an explanation. Hyde was chewing on his lower lip.

Selena explained, "There's a point when the producer of a film has to decide where to invest promotion, and that decision can weigh heavily on each performer's promotional arc."

Hyde added, "She means gigs on TV talk shows, invitations to speak, even what names surface in early buzz for voting on this award or that."

"I'm not cutting Gail out. It's not fair. It's not right."

Jennifer leaned back in her chair, her pose still in an attractive relaxed curve, but Gail nearly stepped back, thinking of an unleashed tiger. Jennifer gave Gail a long look, then Hyde. After a slow blink, she turned her gaze to Selena who stood calmly next to Gail. "Used to be Selena Ryan stood for always doing what was best for the picture, whatever the cost. Even when it makes her very unpopular with some people. When the director of the picture we made when we were together said a lot of my work was crap, it got edited out—and he was right. Selena Ryan took it out even though she knew the gossips would say it was retaliation because we'd broken up by then."

"Gossips you and your boyfriend supplied with a few helpful details," Selena said steadily.

Gail's breath caught. She hadn't know that Jennifer had indeed gone to the tabloids in the past. Lena had been protecting her from sharks she hadn't even seen in the water.

"Painful as it may be to you personally..." Jennifer slowly got to her feet. "It is undeniable that my full, eager participation in promoting this movie is going to help the bottom line more than a little bit of critical buzz about a newcomer. I don't think it's fair for me to work my ass off promoting the movie and then get edged out when it comes time for people handing out awards. I will make you and the investors more money. It's that simple. So, what is Selena Ryan going to do?"

Gail started to say that she hardly thought there was any chance of competing with Jennifer Lamont for awards, but Selena shushed her with a gesture.

"Are you giving me an ultimatum?"

"I'm just telling you the choices that I have." Jennifer paused to fiddle with her sunglasses. "I can be out there with a smile, or only mention this picture at gunpoint."

This time it was Hyde who shushed Selena. He didn't get up, but he did lean forward, elbows on knees. The laid-back country boy was nowhere in sight, though the drawl was more pronounced.

"You left one out, Jenny."

"I really do prefer Jennifer."

"Jennifer, then. You have one other choice. Think about those ball players who dreamed after years of busting up and down the court it was their turn, maybe, to be MVP. Then along comes Michael Jordan, who floats half the court to dunk. They're screwed. They know it. I admire all those guys who played with Jordan and even if it stuck in their throat, they said it was an honor to share the court with him. You can chose that, Jennifer. You can choose to be bigger."

Jennifer gave him a scathing look. "And that's supposed to comfort me when I'm sixty and can't get work?"

"It gives you a chance for something else. You can be sixty and hawking make-up because all anybody ever thought of you was how you looked. Or, you could be the stylish, classy lady everybody wants to do a guest turn on their hit TV show, because all the TV actors would be honored to share a set with you for a week or two. It doesn't have to be about your body. It can be about your character. Character lasts longer. I know it's hard for women—but you *do* have another choice. To ignore it is buying into the way the gossipmongers look at this business. It's proving them right that women are disposable and interchangeable."

Gail wanted to melt into the floor or disappear into the walls or something. She couldn't believe any of this was about her. Great, now that she was a Little Name Star, the Big Name Stars had power over her and were threatened by her. It was not what her ambition to be an actress was ever supposed to cause for other people.

Jennifer's lips had twisted into a bitter line. "So she gets Selena *and* the acclaim?"

"I'm only getting what I can earn," Gail said quietly.

Jennifer looked her up and down with an edge of disbelief. "I still can't believe they put the reincarnation of Hepburn in that body."

Gail had really had enough. "Is there a reason I shouldn't slap you for being rude?"

"If she doesn't, I will," Selena said. "Really, Jennifer—"

Jennifer held up one hand, then gave Hyde a sidelong look. "So what's the line I'm supposed to use? The one that will turn me into some sort of admirable figure?"

He came to his feet, grabbing her hands. "Lovely, lovely Jennifer, you and I are so proud to be mentors to the talented young actress, we wish her nothing but the brightest success, and it was an honor being in her first project, and we hope we get to work together again."

He swung her into a waltz as he spoke, clowning until she reluctantly laughed. "I should hate you. Villainy is my best skill. I'm really good at it."

Selena slipped her hand into Gail's and squeezed lightly. "No, Jennifer, I think that's the only part you thought you were allowed to play."

"Oh, okay." She let go of Hyde. "Maybe she'll be an utter flop."

"I'm standing right here," Gail protested. "And everybody could hate me, I know that. I'm Gawky Gail, after all. I really don't know what you're all so worked up about."

"And that's why it's delightful to work with you." Hyde snatched her from Lena's grasp, leading her in his insane waltz. The other people in the waiting area pulled their feet out of the way. "I promise when I am eighty and appropriately crotchety, you and I will open a little theater in my home town for a production of *On Golden Pond*. I'm booking myself now to be your co-star."

"Why not my home town?" Gail stopped dancing to spare everyone potential harm.

"We'll go there on *your* eightieth birthday."

Jennifer crossed her arms. "I can always change my mind, you know."

Gail didn't think she was kidding.

Selena laughed. "Jennifer, you'll still look young enough to play the daughter."

A nurse arrived to give them a very stern look, and they all meekly took seats.

"Well, I'm up for food. Join me?" Hyde patted his stomach and looked at Jennifer.

Jennifer gave Gail a slightly sour look.

"Yes, I'm staying," Gail said. She gazed at Lena, trying to say it all.

Selena nodded. "She's staying."

"C'mon." Hyde pulled Jennifer to her feet. "Let's go find some place where we'll be recognized. That's always good for my ego."

They departed, sunglasses off, Jennifer's arm linked with Hyde's and this time, heads were definitely turning.

"You don't suppose she'll try to hook him, do you?"

Gail shook her head. "He's already fallen for someone else. A dentist."

Selena burst into laughter, earning them another stern look. They giggled quietly together, and talked of their favorite movies and places they hoped to visit, hands lightly touching, until a nurse came to tell them Kim was awake.

"What are you thinking about?"

Selena pulled her gaze from the soft edges of Barcelona's skyline shimmering in the late afternoon sun. She was supremely conscious of the driver and their lack of privacy in the hired car, so she didn't want to express everything that was running through her mind. Gail's presence next to her in the back seat was both soothing and unnerving, and the mid-sized car both too large and too small, all at once.

"I was thinking that I'm so lucky to have Alan, and that I'm glad Kim's mom is on her way. I was thinking that Barcelona is beautiful, and the sea looks so inviting and I wish you could go out in the sun for a while." She didn't add that at least once every minute she relived the sensation of Gail's body on top of hers or the sheer power of Gail's arms, keeping her warm, safe and in one piece.

Gail smiled. "I've already taken on some color and been scolded for it, and I wasn't even trying. I can't be all tanned in the middle of the movie and back to my usual pale self at the end again."

"I know, the audience will figure out what order the movie was filmed in. Never good for them to be wondering about that instead of the movie. I was thinking about the murder-mystery I want to do, and that I like your cologne and that sometimes people are basically nice."

"That's a lot to think about all at once."

"I multi-task a lot." She loved that Gail's eyes were laughing at her.

"I was hoping you could be single-minded." Gail lightly rested one hand on Selena's thigh and the warmth spread out like the Spanish sun.

"I assure you, when the time is right, I am very focused." She

223

gave Gail a meaningful glance, which was returned and for a few moments their conversation was reassuring and silent.

Selena lazily traced a pattern on the back of Gail's hand. "What are you thinking about?"

"Privacy."

"Mm-hmm." Selena followed Gail's life line with her fingertip, then raised Gail's hand to press her own palm to it. "Your fingers are so much longer than mine."

Gail gently pulled her hand away, but not before Selena felt her shiver. She gave a meaningful glance at the driver and her accusing look seemed to say *Don't tease*.

She reached for Gail's hand again, this time to hold it easily, just to feel the security of Gail there.

At the villa, there were updates to give and more calls to be made. Gail stayed close for a while, but eventually she drifted toward the large common room.

Selena hung up from a call and went to find her, only to discover her fast asleep. She looked like a big kid, legs akimbo and curls mussed. When she huffled in her sleep and rolled over, her T-shirt twisted tightly around her torso.

She carefully perched on the arm of the sofa and looked her fill. The sharp line of Gail's jaw eased into a smooth column of throat she could imagine warm under her lips. She smiled to herself, thinking Gail had delicate ears. Her eyelashes were long enough to cast a shadow on her cheeks. The fire burning hot in her belly was undeniable, but she didn't think that she had ever looked at another woman with the indulgent tenderness she felt right now. Why hadn't she explored every inch of this woman when she'd had a chance? It all seemed like a foolish waste, especially after Jennifer's surprising capitulation. She would always, *always* speak kindly of Hyde Butler.

She knew, though, that Jennifer could change her mind. They weren't safe yet, and she ached, from places that had nothing to do with her body, to keep Gail safe from all the evils of this business. She felt protective, but not because Gail was weak or helpless. Maybe because she was rare. Rare and fine, a one-of-a-kind woman. Sweet-natured without being false. Earnest without being humorless. Sexy, God yes, sexy. Blood rushed in her ears remembering Gail's words: *The only power you have over me is what I give you.*

How could anyone earn a gift like that? Well there's your contradiction, she thought. It's a gift. If you have to earn something, it's not a gift. But once you have it, you have to keep it. That's where the work was. Not like in the movies. In real life, as she had proven to herself over and over, anything worth having took work to claim and keep, so love took work, more than she had ever done in her life, because she wanted to keep it forever.

The brush of something soft on her cheek at first only made her turn her head, then the image of the spider biting Kim hit her brain like a bolt of lightning. Gail jerked away, sat up, clonked her head against Lena's and collapsed again on the sofa.

"I was just kissing you!" Lena clapped both hands over her nose and plonked down on the heavy coffee table behind her.

Stars were dancing around her peripheral vision, just like in a cartoon. "I was asleep, how was I supposed to know?"

Lena, her eyes watering, peered anxiously at her hands. "Am I bleeding?"

"I don't think so."

She gingerly squeezed the bridge of her nose. "Do you know how to tell if someone has a broken nose?"

The room was gradually righting itself in Gail's vision. "No, but if you hum a few bars I can fake it."

"So much for a romantic wake-up."

"I'm sorry," Gail said. "I was just startled. Would you like to try again?" She immediately went limp and added a heartfelt snore.

Lena laughed. "No, wake up. We have to talk."

She opened one eye. "I don't like the sound of that. Maybe I should stay asleep."

Remaining where she was on the coffee table, Lena extended

a hand to Gail. When Gail sat up, their knees just touched. Lena took both hands and looked directly into Gail's eyes.

As far as Gail was concerned, time could have stopped right then. She wanted nothing more than to fall deep into the dark chocolate of Lena's eyes. "Did you know that your irises are ringed with purple?"

Lena shook her head. "I've been thinking how much I want to learn everything there is to know about you. And I've just realized that I want to learn more about me, through you. With you."

But she's looking like a funeral, Gail thought. How do we always end up like this? "Why do I hear a great big *but* coming?"

"It's not awful. It's just… All that's changed is that everybody knows we're interested in each other."

"Okay." Gail wasn't sure where this was leading, but as the astonishing conversation in the hospital waiting room had showed, her insights were not as subtle as those around her.

"We can't…" Lena gave a chagrined laugh. "I've just realized I'm being very presumptuous, but I was assuming you were interested in resuming…"

Well, that was something. So she didn't have a mind for the high-level twists and turns of the business yet, but the blush creeping up Lena's throat, combined with the suddenly shy look on her face reassured her that she did have some persuasive power. "Only in a more comfortable place."

Lena's blush intensified. "That's what I mean."

Gail leaned forward to whisper in Lena's ear, "I would very much like to explore every inch of you, for hours."

"Okay, yes, that's what I had in mind too. I mean me to you, not just, I mean…"

She kissed Lena, at first firmly, then with a lingering gentleness. "I'm glad we're clear on that."

Lena inclined toward her as if for another kiss, then rested back. "Well, that's the thing. Nobody's around right now. So we can get away with…flirting and this." She squeezed Gail's hands.

226

"But I don't want to be caught looking furtive and guilty. I don't want either of us to be seen sneaking in and out of our rooms. And it's not appropriate that we make anyone else uncomfortable by being open either."

"But if Hyde's girlfriend was here—"

"Different rules. If you had a girlfriend here that would be different too. As long as you didn't disrupt anyone else, it would be fine. But this is really about *me*. It's not appropriate for *me* to be distracted by having an affair with one of the other people on the set. If you and I disappear for thirty minutes during lunch it'll cause talk."

"And this is about gossip?"

"It wouldn't be gossip. It'll be fact. Selena Ryan took up with an actress during a film shoot. Anyone could tell that story and it would stick, because it was true."

Gail wanted to be grown-up about this, but it just didn't make sense to her, and the longer she sat this close to Lena, the less maturely her brain functioned. "So you're saying even though Jennifer isn't going to make some stink we shouldn't act like we mean anything to each other until…?"

"Until the shoot is done. And we can act like something, but we have to leave out the physical part. For now. We can't disappear during lunch and have everyone thinking we spent it having sex. We have crew members who'll find that intrusive, and not because we're two women. I actually don't want to know if anyone is having a quickie during lunch either."

Reluctantly, Gail admitted to herself that Lena had a point. She studied Lena's eyes, and had the sudden thought that there was something else, something Lena wasn't admitting. She let her gaze drop to their joined hands, then lifted Lena's palm to her lips. She wanted to pull Lena's hand to her swollen breast, and her brain ran a movie from there, on the coffee table, the sofa, the floor, sweaty, needy *Body Heat* sorts of scenes.

She felt Lena shudder and tried to focus her eyes. There were goose bumps on Lena's arms, and the flush on her chest and throat wasn't embarrassment. Her breath came in sharp gasps, her mouth was begging to be kissed, but there was fear in her eyes.

"Have mercy on me, Gail. This isn't easy."

She immediately let go of Lena's hands. "I'm sorry."

"I tried not to feel." Lena leaned close but Gail still had trouble hearing her. "I'm not just afraid for my professional reputation, or for yours. The honest truth is that we'd never have a quickie at lunch. We'd never get out of bed. I want to disappear with you. I want to *drown* in you."

Gail rested her cheek against Lena's for a moment before sliding back on the sofa, breaking all contact. "We probably shouldn't be alone then, because I want to ravish you, in every possible sense of the word."

Lena's smile was grateful and resigned all at once. "Understood."

"And Lena?"

She had risen and partially turned back to her papers. She gave Gail a crimson velvet look that took Gail's breath away.

"Okay, first, you can't look at me like that," she said. Keeping her voice low, she added, "And after I ravish you I want to sleep in your arms. And I want to wake up and plan our next date."

Lena took a deep breath, briefly closing her eyes. "Thank you for that. I do want that too."

"Then all we have to do is wait just a little bit longer." As least it's not any easier for her than me, Gail thought.

It helped. Not a lot, but it helped. Still, there was that worry that wouldn't go away, that after the shoot there would be another reason why the timing wasn't right, and then another and another.

The final week of filming was a whirlwind, culminating in a series of difficult shots where a Steadicam operator already in a wired harness circled a tableau, then was lifted slowly off the ground by a helicopter. Gail spoiled the first take by watching the cameraman—she couldn't help herself. There'd been a delay when the prevailing landward wind had inexplicably died for two hours, making the helicopter's overhead wind effect too obvious.

The take had to be on the last day because she and Hyde would spent most of it standing in the sun, likely to get skin-reddened even if they didn't outright sunburn.

When Eddie called, "Cut! That's a wrap," she was so hot and tired and dirty that she sat down right where she was standing.

Hyde rolled onto his side. "Could someone get this knife out of my back?"

Jimmy, who was only in the scene briefly, pulled off the prop. "You're going to have major tape issues."

Selena, as dusty as the rest of them, announced, "There will be champagne poolside back at the house. While I have you all, I just got a text from Kim. She's back in the office as of today, and will cuss us out if we have a wrap party without her."

Hyde helped Gail to her feet and they made their weary way to the shuttles. He didn't mind when she fell asleep on his shoulder, either.

A shower and a dip in the pool later, she felt much better, and the champagne and snacks made her feel almost whole.

"I can't wait to get home. Every day I miss my little girl." Jimmy relaxed on the lounger next to hers. "Some of us were going to see about booking a harbor cruise for dinner. Interested?"

She glanced over at where Selena was deep in discussion with Eddie. The actors' work was done, for now. For Selena, there would be weeks more effort as film and sound editors went to work under Eddie's eagle eye. Tomorrow they all started scattering. Hyde was flying directly to Miami where his lady love was picking him up at the airport. Jennifer, who had thawed but never warmed to Gail over the last few days, was going directly to a round of talk shows in London to support the release of her prior movie's DVD in the UK. Most of the rest of them were taking a charter to Atlanta, where Gail would then make her own way to Iowa.

"Sure," she said. "It was on my list of things to do while I was here."

She saw Selena give her a guarded but thankful smile. She'd been subsisting on similar small looks, a fleeting touch of hands here and there. Yet for the last several days her small worries had magnified, even though there was nothing to make her think Lena's intentions had changed. It was just hard to be near her and unable to ease the pulse of her own desire with a hug or goodnight smooch. Right, as if that would ease anything, she thought. Who was she kidding? A hug outside a bedroom meant they'd be inside the bedroom door moments later. As far as she could tell, none of the cast and crew had attached any special interest to them. The make-up artist had stopped flirting with her, which was fine. But conversations didn't stop when she came into a room and no one gave her sly looks. As far as she could tell, everybody still liked her.

It was all too soon that they were transferring from a shuttle to a sleek jet identical to the one that had brought them there. Her phone's memory was full of photos she couldn't wait to show Aunt Charlie. She was both sad and glad to be leaving. She'd not seen anything like enough of the country, but just wasn't adventurous enough to stay on her own.

It was after four local time when they left Barcelona behind, but flying toward the west, Gail would be arriving in Iowa when it was still early evening. Sleep was the best thing, but she only achieved a light doze. She could hear Selena talking to Eddie, still, about a mix-up on studio time. Apparently the new location didn't have the kind of digital equipment their sound editor wanted.

They were about an hour out of Atlanta when Selena passed her seat on her way to the galley in the rear of the plane. She heard Selena tell the steward not to get up, she knew how to pour a cup of coffee, so when she joined her, they were alone.

She felt lame for saying only, "Hi."

"Hi."

"You look exhausted."

"Complications." Lena stirred a yellow packet of sweetener into her coffee. "There are always complications."

That's what concerned her. "I'm sorry I'm going to Iowa."

"Don't be." Lena briefly touched her arm. "You need to go."

"I'm afraid there will always be complications and…other things needing us." There—she had found a way to put her nerves into words. "This past week, I don't want it to be what life is like. Together but not. You pulled one way, me another. Not talking. Letting things be more important than us."

Selena sipped her coffee before she answered. "You know what I thought, when Hyde said that about you both being old and you'd do *On Golden Pond* together? I thought, good lord, I so want to be there. I so want to watch you work, for all the years in between. I want to be in your life, every minute."

"I believe you, Lena, I do."

"But?"

"How can we try to find a life if we can't seem to get started?"

She hadn't meant to cry, and she quickly averted her eyes. She didn't need to make Lena feel any worse, but the past week had been such extremes. Part wonderful and part simply awful.

It was a shocking pleasure to feel those warm arms go around her. "I know. Sometimes I hate being the boss."

If she didn't find a way to laugh, she'd go on crying, or she'd try to unzip Selena's pants or unhook her bra or something equally crass, all of two feet away from the cabin steward. Some big shot movie star with a debauched Hollywood lifestyle—no Mile High Club for her.

She finally managed, "You're not the boss of me."

She was gratified that Lena did laugh. "When you get back to L.A. I promise to meet you at the airport. I promise."

"You don't even know when it is."

"You're a high priority calendar event." Lena smiled, but it dimmed when Gail couldn't find it in her to laugh. "Sweetie, I'll be there even if I have to insert Pradas up backsides for real."

"Okay." Gail felt as if huge strips of her skin were tearing off when she stepped away from the shelter of Lena's arms. It just plain hurt. "That's Friday."

She ought to have felt better, but she didn't.

They all had to exit the charter and go through customs, then onward through the domestic security lines, and she was never far from Lena in the process. When the point came to turn toward her airline she couldn't help herself. She gave everyone else quick hugs and kisses, promising she'd see them at the official wrap party, but she left Lena for last. That kiss was not quick and when she tried to pull away, Lena held on to her, the kiss deepening until Gail felt incandescent, burning bright and hot.

When Lena let go of her she said in a funny, breathy voice, "See ya."

Gail felt as dizzy as Lena looked. She answered, "Bye." And walked away.

Buzztastic # #

The girl gets around! Oodles of pics of the delectable Jennifer Lamont arriving in London. The Brits are wild for her! Love the dress, J.L., wish all the girls knew how to keep a waistline. Half the hometown babes look preggers this summer, and they're not! Check out the parade of porkers at the trough at last night's awards show after-party.

Word has it that eligible bachelor Hyde Butler is taking himself off the dating carousel! Sorry girls! He was spotted at the Miami airport with a velvet box and down on one knee! Nobody got pictures! Let's find out who the lucky lady is!

Viv-About-Town is sporting an engagement ring courtesy of the linoleum mogul Chas. Meller! She'll look great in the commercials and we're told Chas. doesn't mind if she continues her acting career. Here's hoping Mrs. Meller graduates from shower scenes to bath tubs, all with the best in 100% synthetic flooring.

Chapter 13

The jet lag was already bad and Selena couldn't believe she was only halfway home. Her legs were like lead and her carry-on seemed to hit every bump in the floor as she pulled it behind her. It seemed like miles to their gate. The remaining Los Angeles-bound cast and crew had outdistanced her.

Her phone buzzed and she was cheered to hear Kim's voice, steady and strong. "Your flight's on time, but you already knew that."

"I did. I'm not looking forward to two hours of waiting, though. I feel like crap."

"Uh huh. Is there anything you didn't tell me about the time I missed there?"

Selena felt herself flush. "Like what?"

"I just had the most informative conversation with Jennifer Lamont. She thinks her primary make-up kit got mixed up with the production supplies and wants it back. But she also asked how we'd all be adapting to your new love life."

The silence was long and accusatory.

After a sigh, Selena said, "Well, there is no new love life. Yet. Not while we were shooting." She was glad Kim was far, far away and couldn't see that Selena was leaving out the more interesting parts of the story.

"How come Gail's going to Iowa?"

"She's a little worried about her aunt, and she made the plans before we…clarified things."

"Uh huh."

"Kim, I'm so tired, I feel like I can hardly walk. I'll tell you all about it when I get home."

"Have you considered that maybe the problem is you're walking in the wrong direction?"

Selena stopped dead. "I have to come home."

"Uh huh."

"Don't I?" There were dozens of meetings, deadlines, schedules to be drafted, whining agents, important decisions she'd put off for her arrival back at her desk…

She could hear Kim's fingers on her keyboard. "You're going to have to move fast. Make that run."

First class was nice. Gail knew she could get used to it. It looked like a lot of people flying to Iowa couldn't afford it, because she was practically by herself. She'd sleep, hopefully, and maybe she wouldn't look like the world was ending. It was only five more days, after all. She really shouldn't have guilted Lena like that—it was hardly Lena's fault.

She declined the offer of a soda while they were waiting for the last pre-flight checks. They'd close the door any minute and she hoped taxiing was soothing enough that she could doze off. She reclined her seat and closed her eyes, shutting out the world until she felt someone drop into the seat next to her.

Annoyed that one of the empty rows hadn't been chosen, she debated whether to open her eyes and possibly get stuck chatting with someone all the way to Iowa or keeping them closed and enjoying just a little more peace. When something touched her cheek she snapped her head around to glare—at Lena, flushed and grinning.

"Didn't clonk my head that time," Lena said. "That's progress, isn't it?"

She closed her eyes and opened them again. Lena was still there. "How did—I thought—what about—"

Lena pressed her fingers over Gail's mouth. "You're more important than any of that. That's my lesson for today. The film is in the can, and there's no reason for me to put anything above *us*. You are always my critical high priority appointment, whenever I can make it so. Sometimes what I owe other people may make my choices very hard."

"I can live with that. I understand that. And if I get lucky there will be times when I can't think about anything but a part, or I have to go someplace far away. No one will force me to go, of course, but—"

"You'll do it because it's your dream. I'm not getting in the way of your dreams."

"Well, I don't want to sleep my way into anything but a life with you."

"Know what?"

Gail shook her head.

"I don't want to talk about it anymore."

Gail didn't care if they scandalized the stewardesses. She didn't care that a few more passengers walked by them as they kissed. Maybe a picture of them would show up in the blogosphere with captions like *Sapphic Mile-High Make Out* or *Selena Snogs with Starlet* and she didn't care about that either. There had to be times when none of that mattered.

She smiled against Lena's lips.

"What?"

"I was thinking that it's supposed to be so sad when an actor is 'between projects.' I don't think I'm going to care."

"So this is the house where you grew up?" Selena peered out of the taxi window as they pulled up to the small, picture-perfect one-story Midwestern house, complete with picket fence and a screened-in porch. It was so solid and ordinary compared to the variety of places she'd lived growing up.

"Not entirely. I moved in here with Aunt Charlie my last year in high school, after my folks died. She was closest to my school, so I didn't have to change. I lived with her all through college, too. I don't think her daughter can bring herself to sell it, even though I don't think Aunt Charlie's ever going to live here again."

"She seems happy where she is. And obviously, she needs the care."

"I hope they can kick her cough before winter, though."

Selena paid the cab driver after he unloaded their bags while Gail dug for the key Aunt Charlie's daughter had brought with her to the rest home. She'd liked the old woman, quite a lot, and hoped she would someday be able to visit them in Los Angeles, as they'd happily discussed in their brief visit. Aunt Charlie hadn't batted an eye at Selena's introduction as Gail's girlfriend, though clearly the daughter had been taken aback, if only briefly.

Their cases dragged inside, Gail locked the front door behind them and switched on a light. Selena had a brief impression of décor caught in a 1980s time warp, then allowed Gail to pull her up a very narrow set of stairs.

"My room is in the attic."

She hardly took in the pile of old college textbooks, a thick winter coat still hanging on a peg when Gail pulled her close for a demanding kiss.

"You can look around later."

Her body was seething for Gail, and the effort to keep it banked had been enormous. But now, when she had no reason to still Gail's hands on her body, she did so, not sure what was wrong.

Gail looked at her, obviously puzzled.

She's going to get angry, Selena thought. She's going to think I don't want her, that I've been playing a game all along.

"What is it?"

She could only shake her head. She felt as if she were wet to her knees, that her clothes were literally melting off her body. She wanted Gail desperately, so much she knew she wasn't thinking, not at all.

"Oh honey," Gail said softly. "I won't hurt you. Not now, not ever."

She shuddered, her breath a ragged gasp. How could Gail know what she didn't? She was scared to her very soul. "I feel like I'm going to break. I've been so foolish, we could have—"

Gail's tender kiss silenced her.

She let Gail move them to the narrow bed, and they kicked off their sandals before curling up. The soft, light kisses continued and Selena let them wash over her, like the tide coming in. The relaxing, soothing warmth was first at her toes, then rushing over her legs. There would come a time when she would have to decide if she'd let the tide take her or if she'd move up the shore to safety.

She held Gail still for a moment, needing to look into her face. Her not-quite-green eyes were feverish with desire, her lips bruised from their kisses. She could feel the heat rising off them both, but why did she have to ask herself whether any of this was an act? Because Jennifer had looked like she loved her too?

You're going to have to let it go, she told herself. *Let it go now or carry it around forever. Take one more chance. You know you feel it. Not saying it makes no difference.*

"I love you," she whispered. "Please love me back. I don't think I'll survive if you don't."

Gail let out a breathless half laugh. "I was afraid to say it. Afraid you'd think I was just acting because—"

This time Selena stopped the words with a kiss. This time she didn't stop her hands. The tide rushed up and rolled them both over. Straddling Gail, she eagerly pulled up her shirt, helping

Gail get her bra off. The pleasure of Gail's tongue on her nipples sent waves down her back. She fumbled at the zipper to Gail's shorts.

"No," Gail whispered. "You. I want you."

Her arms became liquid as she poured onto the bed, eagerly helpless, utterly abandoned, but not afraid, not this time. Open, and open, until there was no place left untouched by the love Gail brought to her, no remote pain where dark could linger.

Open, and open, until she cried out, lost the time, lost her name and none of it mattered. She was stretched to her limits by Gail's mouth and yet safe in the circle of her arms.

She stirred once in the night, felt Gail move.

"I'm sorry the bed is so small."

"It's just right," she whispered. She reached behind her for Gail's hip and her lazy stroking seemed to earn a shiver.

"You should finish what you started."

"Is that a request?"

"Please."

Not a tidal wave this time. The quiet dark held them close, a few more whispers, then a different kind of silence. Selena loved the soft sounds that Gail made, equally as welcome as the powerful beat of Gail's heart that lulled her back to sleep.

Buzztastic # #

Wherever you are, keep refreshing the page! Today's the day! Non-stop photos behind the scenes as the stars come out to see who gets to take home the little man! We're still stunned that Cannes' best actor got stiffed by the Academy for a nod, but wedded bliss might ease Hyde Butler's bruised ego. Lovely Jennifer Lamont is rumored to be wearing Alexander McQueen, right off the stage from last week's Paris runway walk. We're all hoping she gets the statue, but when one of the other nominees is dead, the competition is stiff, get it? Bookmakers are also picking J.L.'s discovery, supporting actress Gail Welles—lucky girl getting the best in the business to show her the ropes. Some folks are saying it'll finally be the Grand Dame, but sorry, eighth time is probably not going to be the charm, even though it could be the last time unless the Botox starts working.

Epilogue

"We have to get dressed."

Selena wrapped her arms tight around Gail's waist. "Not yet."

Gail gave a pleased sigh when Selena's fingertips finally found what she was looking for. "Goodness, woman, you're going to be the death of me."

"I'm trying. Making up for last week."

"I'm really glad the roofers finished."

"Is that all you're thinking about? The remodeling being done?" Selena applied a little more pressure and was gratified that Gail's entire body quivered. Little circles, a light squeeze... another wonderful shudder that drew a gasp.

"Don't tease."

"Okay."

Lazy, Sunday morning kisses. Gail was right, they had to get dressed. But not this very moment. She shimmied down so she could listen to the thudding of Gail's heart. She'd been in Seattle and Gail in Atlanta until last night, and right now, this was all she cared about.

Gail made that little noise, the one she loved, and Lena pushed her fingers deep, aroused by Gail's immediate response. She shifted to straddle Gail's thigh, nodding yes when Gail's hand slipped between them. They moved together and it felt new and familiar all at once. And it felt really, really good.

"We have to get dressed," Gail said again, some time later. "The hairdressers and seamstresses will be at the house in fifteen minutes. Shower…"

Selena laughed. "We can shower together, saves time."

"Not the way you do it."

Shampoo in her hair, Gail swatted her hand away the first time, but not the second. Their hair was still dripping when they left the new master suite added to the pool house over the winter. They paused briefly to gobble down handfuls of nuts to ease their shaky legs and went hand-in-hand to the main house.

After the tyranny of curling irons, eyebrow tweezing and squeezing into a braless dress that had to be stitched closed, Selena tried not to be grumpy. Gail was hugely nervous, with good reason. They both knew she really didn't have a chance of winning, not for a first picture. The nomination was a gesture of encouragement from her peers. *Barcelona* was in the running for original screenplay, and she was very pleased for Delilah too. Tonight she would not think about the film's bottom line in the DVD market and how much it would improve if any of their nominees won. She was not a producer tonight. Tonight, she was a best supporting actress nominee's wife.

When the dressers had done their best and they stood side-by-side, she did like their reflection in the mirror. Her own gown was in keeping with her usual understated style, though rhinestones along the sleeves and collar would probably keep anyone from noting she was dowdy. She didn't want anyone to notice her tonight. "You look perfect, darling. Aunt Charlie will be proud."

Gail pulled at the waist of her velvet sheath, head to toe pure 1930s vintage, right out of a madcap comedy where the spunky heroine wins the heart of her true love. "Do you think so? I feel weird."

"You're going to feel weird all night."

She made Gail turn, plumped up the brocade ruffles on the cap sleeves of the gown, and couldn't help but kiss her.

"Ladies! You can't do that," the make-up artist protested. "Now you're smudged. You have an hour to the red carpet, and you can't smudge!"

"I can't feel my lips anyway," Gail said.

"Okay, no more kissing."

She turned back to the mirror and Gail stepped behind her, wrapping her arms around her and resting her chin on Selena's shoulder.

"Can I take a picture," the hairdresser asked. "For my portfolio?"

"I don't care what you do with it," Selena answered. "As long as we get a copy."

Gail startled at the flash. Selena patted her arm.

"You'll get used to it, darling."

"Stay close and I'll be okay."

There was a crunch of slow-moving tires on the drive outside. "I promise," she said. She touched Gail's face. "The limo's here."

The End

About the Author

Karin Kallmaker's nearly thirty romances and fantasy-science fiction novels include the award-winning *The Kiss That Counted*, *Just Like That*, *Maybe Next Time* and *Sugar* along with the bestselling *Substitute for Love* and the perennial classic *Painted Moon*. Short stories have appeared in anthologies from publishers like Alyson, Bold Strokes, Circlet and Haworth, as well as novellas and short stories with Bella Books. She began her writing career with the venerable Naiad Press and continues with Bella.

She and her partner are the mothers of two and live in the San Francisco Bay Area. She is descended from Lady Godiva, a fact which she'll share with anyone who will listen. She likes her Internet fast, her iPod loud and her chocolate real.

All of Karin's work can now be found at Bella Books. Details and background about her novels, and her other pen name, Laura Adams, can be found at www.kallmaker.com.

WARMING TREND by Karin Kallmaker. Everybody was convinced she had committed a shocking academic theft, so Anidyr Bycall ran a long, long way. Going back to her beloved Alaskan home, and the coldness in Eve Cambra's eyes isn't going to be easy. $14.95

WRONG TURNS by Jackie Calhoun. Callie Callahan's latest wrong turn turns out well. She meets Vicki Brownwell. Sparks would fly if only Meg Klein would leave them alone! $14.95

SMALL PACKAGES by KG MacGregor. With Lily away from home, Anna Kaklis is alone with her worst nightmare: a toddler. Book Three of the Shaken Series. $14.95

FAMILY AFFAIR by Saxon Bennett. An oops at the gynecologist has Chase Banter finally trying to grow up. She has nine whole months to pull it off. $14.95

DELUSIONAL by Terri Breneman. In her search for a killer, Toni Barston discovers that sometimes everything is exactly the way it seems, and then it gets worse. $14.95

COMFORTABLE DISTANCE by Kenna White. Summer on Puget Sound ought to be relaxing for Dana Robbins, but Dr. Jamie Hughes is far too close for comfort. $14.95

ROOT OF PASSION by Ann Roberts. Grace Owens knows a fake when she sees it, and the potion her best friend promises will fix her love life is a fake. But what if she wishes it weren't? $14.95

KEILE'S CHANCE by Dillon Watson. A routine day in the park turns into the chance of a lifetime, if Keile Griffen can find the courage to risk it all for a pair of big brown eyes. $14.95

SEA LEGS by KG MacGregor. Kelly is happy to help Natalie make Didi jealous, sure, it's all pretend. Maybe. Even the captain doesn't know where this comic cruse will end. $14.95

TOASTED by Josie Gordon. Mayhem erupts when a culinary road show stops in tiny Middelburg, and for some reason everyone thinks Lonnie Squires ought to fix it. Follow-up to Lammy mystery winner Whacked. $14.95

NO RULES OF ENGAGEMENT by Tracey Richardson. A war zone attraction is of no use to Major Logan Sharp. She can't wait for Jillian Knight to go back to the other side of the world. $14.95

A SMALL SACRIFICE by Ellen Hart. A harmless reunion of friends is anything but, and Cordelia Thorn calls friend Jane Lawless with a desperate plea for help. Lammy winner for Best Mystery. #5 in this award-winning series. $14.95

FAINT PRAISE by Ellen Hart. When a famous TV personality leaps to his death, Jane Lawless agrees to help a friend with inquiries, drawing the attention of a ruthless killer. #6 in this award-winning series. $14.95

STEPPING STONE by Karin Kallmaker. Selena Ryan's heart was shredded by an actress, and she swears she will never, ever be involved with one again. $14.95

THE SCORPION by Gerri Hill. Cold cases are what make reporter Marty Edwards tick. When her latest proves to be far from cold, she still doesn't want Detective Kristen Bailey babysitting her, not even when she has to run for her life. $14.95

YOURS FOR THE ASKING by Kenna White. Lauren Roberts is tired of being the steady, reliable one. When Gaylin Hart blows into her life, she decides to act, only to find once again that her younger sister wants the same woman. $14.95

SONGS WITHOUT WORDS by Robbi McCoy. Harper Sheridan runaway niece turns up in the one place least expected and Harper confronts the woman from the summer that has shaped her entire life since. $14.95

PHOTOGRAPHS OF CLAUDIA by KG MacGregor. To photographer Leo Wescott models are light and shadow realized on film. Until Claudia. $14.95

MILES TO GO by Amy Dawson Robertson. Rennie Vogel has finally earned a spot at CT3. All too soon she finds herself abandoned behind enemy lines, miles from safety and forced to do the one thing she never has before: trust another woman. $14.95

TWO WEEKS IN AUGUST by Nat Burns. Her return to Chincoteague Island is a delight to Nina Christie until she gets her dose of Hazy Duncan's renown ill-humor. She's not going to let it bother her, thoug $14.95